THE COLDNESS
OF OBJECTS

PANAYOTIS CACOYANNIS

Cover Design by Keith Voles

Acknowledgments

With thanks to my editor Oliver James of Blue Pencil Agency for his tenacity and brilliant suggestions, to Keith Voles for the excellent website and cover design, to Michael Duerden for his patience and technical wizardry, and with unbounded gratitude to my beloved mother Phaedra, whose absence I shall always feel profoundly, for helping shape the character of Malcolm and making this novel so special to me.

Τι μέλλει γενέσθαι;

What does the future hold?

For my Mother,
Who will always be 'here'

ONE

Monkeys

Undaunted by any fear of flatulence or heartburn, Mr Rubens was thoroughly enjoying his mid-morning coffee.

"There is a time and a place for everything," he was fond of saying, and as a matter of ritual, not routine – an obvious distinction – this was certainly true of the orderly way in which he chose to live his life.

Always served in the same gold-rimmed porcelain cup, never more than half-full, carried through from the kitchen at the centre of a massive silver tray whose handles formed the antlers of ivory stags (making up with grandeur for the necessary rationing of caffeine that prevented more unfortunate mishaps), midmorning coffee was had in the sitting room at ten forty-five. And at six minutes to five in the afternoon, a small part of the Meissen tea service would be extracted from the curved wood Scandinavian sideboard, piece-by-bone-china-piece, and the necessary number of its hand-painted menagerie of monkeys – the teapot's three chimpanzees, two macaques on a cup and two more on its saucer, a pair of spider monkeys sprawled across the milk jug, and a spectacular orangutan wrapped around the sugar bowl - would be transported on the same silver tray to the kitchen, and carefully arrayed across the kitchen table as though ready for a whirligig spin in a circus parade.

Mr Rubens was already sixty-eight when he took the decision that he must forsake sugar, his *very* sweet tooth notwithstanding. But he was too fond of the orangutan to keep him locked away with the side plates' baboons and the cake platter's gorilla, and so the empty sugar bowl invariably made an appearance. After warming the teapot, Mr Rubens would fill it with a scoop of the finest India tealeaves and just enough hot water for two cups. At five o'clock exactly, he would pour a dash of milk into his first.

Before, after, and in-between mid-morning coffee and afternoon tea, Mr Rubens liked things to unfold in as regular a fashion as possible. This was not to say that even now, at a little over seventy, his life lacked excitement, or that he was afraid of taking risks; not at all. If that were the case, for example, he would have long ago given up coffee. No, it was rather that he liked to plan his excitement, just as he liked to plan everything else.

In the exquisite comfort of his favourite armchair – an original, and signed, 1960s *Amoeba* – Mr Rubens contemplated his surroundings with pleasure. He was a man of impeccable taste, if he said so himself: a real connoisseur. One leg crossed over the other, rather sprawled in the vastness of this singular piece of design, he basked in the warm, affectionate light of the fibreglass lamp that loomed overhead, suspended from the ceiling by invisible threads. Mr Rubens held his cup in mid-air in a satisfied reverie as if to savour the moment for longer, though precisely what moment he savoured, and why, Mr Rubens would have found it hard to describe.

Please ring the bell

Tap. Tap-tap.

If on that unseasonably warm October day he had been in any other room in the house, or if it had been colder and the thick velvet drapes that kept out the draught from the hallway had had to be drawn, he would almost certainly have missed the perfunctory knock on the front door.

Tap-tap.

Insipid like a limp handshake, he thought to himself, getting up from the *Amoeba* and straightening his back before making his way in small and careful steps to see who it was.

"All these rugs… They'll be the death of you one day, mark my words," he remembered his sister, Eunice Guernica Rubens, warning him on more than one occasion as she stomped around his sitting room pointing with disdain at the ever-growing multitude of crinkles, creases and turned-up corners. "I mean, look at the state of them, Pablo, they're shabby and mangy like run-over carcasses riddled with lice. Get rid of them, for God's sake, before it's too late."

"I'll have you know that two of them are rare Persian pieces. *Extremely* rare!" Mr Rubens had always riposted, to Eunice's theatrical gesticulations and dismissive rude noises. But although he had not heeded her advice and the rugs were all still there, crinkled and creased, corners turned up, if nothing else as a mark of respect for his sister he now always manoeuvred around them as though traversing the most dangerous minefield.

Tap-tap. Tap-tap.

Insipid or not, as far as Mr Rubens was concerned impatience was rarely not impertinence and was always impolite. While he muttered to himself words of elderly indignation before opening the door, high above the frames of his strong varifocals his pair of unkempt eyebrows, too predominantly black for his age, rose and fell, folding into crinkles like his rugs.

"Yes?" Uniforms had always made him nervous, and as he tried to smooth his face, he worried he had sounded too testy.

"Special Delivery for Anthony Pablo Rubens," the postman answered in a monotone.

"That's me," Mr Rubens confirmed with a hesitant smile.

"Special Delivery," the postman repeated, handing Mr Rubens a large brown envelope.

His voice might be dull, but his uniform was clean, his tie well knotted, and his pencil moustache perfectly groomed. There *had* been some improvements, not even Eunice could have argued with that. Mr Rubens may have never been particularly partial to moustaches, but this was a presentable young man who took pride in his appearance, and for that he deserved to be commended. Not *explicitly*, perhaps. Any compliment might come across to him as lewd insinuation; he distinctly gave the impression of being *very* strait-laced. No doubt drummed into him at school as part of the more general indoctrination at the heart of the modern curriculum, it was apparently a quality demanded of all public servants. Mr Rubens found it too militaristic. He couldn't help hoping that when he was off-duty the postman was more natural and able to relax and have fun, as all young people should. But in the world of New Britain in 2030, sadly the reality was likely to be different.

Poor kid, thought Mr Rubens, *even though he's barely out of his teens he's probably been married off to a Government Party fanatic who's borne him two children already.*

All the same he was very good-looking. There was something very crisp about the symmetry of his features, all so understated but accentuated by his cheekbones and somehow enhanced by the boy's total lack of expression...

Yes, it was his boyishness Mr Rubens found attractive more than anything else. Wooden like a still life of a young man at odds with his good looks, he reminded Mr Rubens of himself in the early 1980s, almost half a century ago.

While Mr Rubens looked him up and down - from the tip of his cap, to the pistol in the visible holster round his waist, all the way down to the lustre of his polished black shoes - the young postman clung to his impassiveness tenaciously, staring straight ahead, at nothing in particular as far as Mr Rubens could tell, and certainly not looking Mr Rubens up and down.

Tall and trim, no heavier now than he had been in his thirties, and still able to maintain an erect, upright posture in spite of his age, Mr Rubens towered over the postman by several inches, the young man's indifference barely grazing his shoulder as it flitted into several directions at once, magnified by Mr Rubens' varifocals.

Bowing his head just a trifle to the right, Mr Rubens cleared his throat before pointing with a finger at the prominent sign that invited every caller to 'Please ring the bell.' It annoyed him that since he had put the sign up, and his own sister had wired practically every room in the house with a separate buzzer, *no one* rang the bell any more.

The postman looked vaguely at the sign before turning back to face Mr Rubens' varifocals with a squint.

He's got two rolling eyes and doesn't seem able to focus, thought Mr Rubens, now regretting he had made such an issue of the sign for the bell.

But the postman seemed unfazed. Handing Mr Rubens a clipboard and pen, and this time a little bit louder, supposing perhaps that Mr Rubens was deaf, he continued to look hither and thither as he spoke once again in a gruelling monotone:

"Number 5. Print name and sign in the box."

After signing for the letter and returning the clipboard and pen, whereupon the postman had saluted him unsmilingly by touching the tip of his cap, Mr Rubens watched him disappear down the grey deserted street with the clank of perfectly regular strides as if marching to the drumbeat of a military band, on parade after returning from the front, tired but triumphant.

Mr Rubens lived alone in a two-storey house at the end of a long cul-de-sac, one of several in the periphery of Highgate Village, astride one of its peaks that boasted greener green and an inevitability of subsidence that Mr Rubens had soon learned to live with. Lining both sides of his street, the gnarled London plane trees had shed all their leaves, exposing their tangle of emaciated limbs as though proud to have been stricken with arthritis. This ancient guard of honour's quaver contrasted with the unquestioning purposefulness of the uniformed youth cutting through it. As had always been the way of the world, something old was giving way to something new. The sheer strength of this impression stung Mr Rubens with the pangs of an almost forgotten regret. Almost forgotten? Even if the past had contained it, he was uncertain whether or not he had felt it before. Perhaps the past had kept it well hidden, or perhaps – and Mr Rubens considered this more likely – it, too, was something new.

But really, he should ask for an appointment at Moorfields and see an ophthalmologist.

Unless...

Snapping out of his melancholy brooding on the uncertainty of the past, and pushing out preposterous thoughts, with long deep breaths Mr Rubens filled himself with the invigorating chill that suddenly he had become aware of, its sharp metallic tang the harbinger of swiftly changing weather. That was something he *knew* the past had contained. Ever since he could remember, even as a young boy he had been a more reliable forecaster of the weather than his father's Swiss barometer or that blur of meteorologists' voices making their predictions on the wireless, all of them affecting excitement as though they were broadcasting a reading of tealeaves.

Air

Mr Rubens could claim no known scientific basis for his 'gift'. But he did know it had something to do with how the air would slowly seep into his consciousness once he had taken it deeply inside him, and a spontaneous weighing-up of both its odour and its taste had occurred. As a matter of fact, his 'gift' was not confined to forecasting the weather, or indeed to air he had inhaled outdoors. On his first train journey as a child, no sooner had he settled down beside his sister than he gulped with three big breaths the accumulated smell of passing crowds, inbreathing air filled with lives that each at different times had marked the drab interior with the momentary essence of a story. The air's musty staleness, as though dispersing vital particles of sadnesses and joys, had contained an embodiment of human endeavour, its cumulative instances permeating every surface, surviving the strongest detergents.

"I can smell all your secrets," he had once said to Eunice, leaning over her to take in her breath.

"No you can't."

At first she was laughing at him, but as she rolled him around onto his back and climbed on top of him, getting ready to pinch his nose shut, the waft of her laughter betrayed her.

"Yes I can, and if you hurt me I'm going to tell."

"Tell what, you little liar? You've got nothing to tell."

He was flapping like a fish, trying to keep his nose out of her grip. "Get off me or I'll tell everyone about George Harrison and you'll be sorry."

His sister would have known exactly which George Harrison he was referring to: the older boy giving her French kissing lessons, *not* the Beatle.

"Whatever anyone's been saying, it's a *lie*, you hear?" Spitting rage filled with more of the truth in his face, she was pushing down his shoulders so hard that little Anthony Pablo hadn't dared to contradict her.

"I believe you, I believe you, now get off me!"

He must have been eleven or twelve. She was three years older, and strong.

"Not before you tell me who it was. Who told you this *lie*?"

"Ow! You're hurting me."

"Tell, tell, tell, or I'm going to hurt you more!"

My nose, he had wanted to say. But that would have been only half true. His nose had told him what she had been up to, but it hadn't told him who she had been up to it with. He had seen George Harrison winking at her at the fish and chip shop round the corner from school but had thought nothing of it at the time. Only after getting a sniff of her breath had he put two and two together.

"No one told me, I *swear*! I saw him winking at you and I guessed."

"Well, you guessed wrong. Now say it!"

"I guessed wrong, I guessed wrong!"

From then on, he had kept his nose *well* out of Eunice's trysts first with George Harrison and then with the rapid succession of boys with whom she would later be free – *increasingly* free – with her favours. He had kept his sister's secrets to himself by keeping his own under wraps.

Things

After turning slightly colder tomorrow, the temperature would plummet to zero at the weekend. Then it would rain non-stop for eight to ten days.

Before going back inside, Mr Rubens reached for the doorbell. As the sound of Eunice's favourite symphony roared in the hallway, it occurred to him that he had no way of knowing if all the separate buzzers were in good working order. They had never been tested. It had taken Eunice an entire afternoon and a good part of the evening to install them, and in the end she had fallen asleep in the *Amoeba*. That was the last Mr Rubens had seen of his sister, more than two years ago now. She had stolen away in the middle of the night while he soundly slept upstairs in his bed, and one month later she was dead, killed in the terrible fire that had burnt down her house in Belsize Park. Remembering his sister with fondness, Mr Rubens did his best to console himself: the matter of the buzzers was hardly of importance. The bell, after all, never rang.

Unless...

An earlier fleeting thought was forcing its way back. No, he could not have been mistaken. For five to ten minutes, while they stood no further than inches apart the young postman had exuded no scent – no whiff of anything at all had reached Mr Rubens.

How strange, he thought.

Unless...

Unless the postman had been not a boy but a machine; yes, a machine - *only* a machine could have eluded his 'gift' absolutely. The weather was a natural phenomenon; the air a vital sign that contained its foretelling. People, too, carried with them always their own unmistakeable odour, in constant flux as it absorbed changing moods and emotions, telltale signs of all their secrets. Machines, on the other hand, were *things*, made up of dead substances and wires brought to life by pinprick microchips and electrical currents.

Emboldened by the strong taste of anticipated rain that lingered at the back of his throat, and energised by the resurgence of memories and feelings for too long suppressed, Mr Rubens had immersed himself in bold suppositions that perhaps were not so bold after all. His sister had needed no gift, nor a visit by an odourless postman, to predict them years before as the inevitable way of the future: a secret army of human simulacra, programmed by the State to do its bidding.

As he closed the front door behind him, after shifting the envelope from one hand to the other Mr Rubens scrutinised it through his varifocals while he held it at arm's length. It was not particularly bulky or heavy, but unusually it didn't bear a stamp.

TWO

Museum Service

Anthony Pablo Rubens had been selected for Museum Service. Unless an application for exemption was made to the Museums Ministry within five working days, a Ministry official would be contacting him to arrange a convenient time for an Evaluation Panel to visit his home. Mr Rubens liked museums. Naturally, he had never before been an exhibit himself, nor had he ever visited a People's Museum. The prospect nevertheless filled him with immense excitement. The People's Museums had been conceived *expressly* as a way for the State to honour and celebrate its citizens by putting them on public display for a day, and he, Anthony Pablo Rubens, was being summoned to be honoured and celebrated. The letter could not have been clearer. 'Dear Mr Rubens,' it began. 'You have been selected,' etcetera. Did 'selected' not imply recognition? Moreover, he had been selected for service at the National People's Museum, and as far as he knew the National People's Museum was the showpiece of all the People's Museums.

The laws setting up the Museums Ministry and introducing compulsory Museum Service and the People's Museums had been passed quite some time ago now, along with a swathe of new legislation introduced by the Government Party after its sweeping electoral victory. As the Government Party fulfilled one by one its far-reaching electoral promises, ranging from the abolition of trial by a jury of one's peers to wholesale new restrictions on the flow of information, and culminating in the internment, and eventual deportation, of that section of the population stripped of its citizens' rights, one institution after another that had long been regarded elitist had been closed and then converted to a variety of alternative uses.

Mr Rubens had shared the gist if not the vehemence of his sister's indignation at many of the Government Party's reforms, including the closure of so many institutions that had once been the pride of the nation. But to be fair to the Government Party, the people *had* been consulted. Telephone polls had been conducted on an unprecedented scale, in what the Government Party was still fond of describing as 'the largest exercise in direct democracy in the history of mankind', and millions of people had spoken.

As part of this mammoth programme of cultural restructuring, the capital's International Museum of Modern Art, which Mr Rubens had visited on countless occasions, had closed and reopened as the country's National People's Museum. Naturally the ideal would have been if the two could have stood side by side; Mr Rubens readily acknowledged that, but that was democracy. Resources were limited, and priorities had to be set. And the contents of IMMA – and of the other museums and galleries that had had to make way for the local People's Museums – had not been destroyed. They had been carefully packed and stored away for safekeeping, in case the people one day changed their minds.

It was true that most probably it had not been possible to salvage everything. One imagined that some of IMMA's more precarious exhibits, such as the butterfly and chocolate fountain that had stood in the Atrium, or the huge ongoing installation made up of all manner of debris painstakingly collected from places laid waste to by war – which had been poignantly hailed by the critics as 'the twenty-first century's *Guernica*' – might indeed have been lost, and naturally Mr Rubens regarded this a matter of the most profound regret. But life had made him stoical.

"At least we've still got cinema."

"We've still got cinema to watch their propaganda."

"It's not *all* propaganda, at the Curzon they're still showing Almodóvar."

"Because apparently our New Leader is a fan."

"There's music at the New Albert Hall, kids have pop... And no one's burning books any more, I honestly think that things are getting better all the time."

"Pablo, listen to yourself. A mealy-mouthed apologist, that's what you're beginning to sound like."

"I'm no one's apologist, Eunice. But this was what the people decided – no opera, no theatre, no art. It's what we used to call 'democracy', remember?"

"Democracy, my arse! Can't you see? These are all just clever ways to distract what's left of everyone's conscience – to make people forget what these thugs have done in their name, and your name and mine, Pablo, don't let's forget that."

"They did what they promised to do, and they wouldn't have been able to do it if they hadn't won the election."

"That doesn't stop them being thugs. And as long as they're in power, things are *not* getting better."

Victory

In a climate of fear and suspicion, the Government Party had won by a landslide. It had been a bitter victory, secured by angry votes. The 2020 virus pandemic had exhausted the world, but it had not united peoples or nations, and its aftermath of grief had proved a fertile ground for terror.

Soon the helplessness against disease had given way to outrage, and a craving for the certainties of overreaction.

In 2023, an inconclusive early general election had led to a government of national unity that had failed either to govern or to unite. The newly formed Government Party's appeal was the comfort food of easy, and deadly, solutions. Openly inciting racial hatred, its leaders orchestrated violent riots in support of its outrageous demands, and in an effort to blunt its propaganda by exposing its presumed lack of widespread support, the government dissolved itself and called another early election in 2024, in which its various ineffectual parts once again campaigned against each other, practically refusing to acknowledge that the Government Party existed, let alone represented a credible threat.

On the night of the election on Thursday, September 11, Eunice was with Mr Rubens in Highgate, watching an Election Special on the one remaining channel of the BBC while waiting for the exit poll results to be announced at 10 pm.

"What flavour are those crisps?" Eunice asked.

"Salt and vinegar," answered Mr Rubens, leaning forward in the *Amoeba* as though to double check. For this special occasion bowls of savoury snacks and assorted crudités had been wheeled in from the kitchen on the stainless-steel shelves of a trolley that had served in the Second World War as a battlefield repository for surgical equipment.

Eunice scooped up a handful of the crisps, and Mr Rubens watched as she crunched on them loudly.

"What's wrong?" she said, when already she had dipped into the mix of Spanish olives, without making use of a toothpick.

"Nothing," said Mr Rubens.

"Are you sure? You've been looking at me sheepishly all evening. You haven't voted Tory, have you?"

"I voted Green, like I always do."

Eunice gave a sigh as she washed down the olives with an even bigger handful of crisps.

"They're *all* bloody useless," she said.

"That's more or less the Government Party's motto," said Mr Rubens, resisting the temptation to fetch the mini vacuum for her crumbs.

"Filthy racist scum! At least they'll finally be trounced into oblivion tonight, whoever comes on top."

"I wouldn't be so sure," said Mr Rubens, taking off his glasses so he couldn't see the crumbs.

The latest opinion polls had given the Conservatives the slenderest lead, with Government Party support in single digits.

"People aren't entirely stupid," said Eunice.

"Let's hope you're right," said Mr Rubens.

"Turn the sound up, Pablo, it must be nearly ten."

Mr Rubens gave his eyes a rub before putting his glasses back on to look at his watch. "Five to," he said. "Let's see if they're more accurate this time." In the previous election, the national exit poll had wrongly predicted an absolute majority for Labour. In the end, no single party had won overall control, hence the year of ineffectual coalition.

"The talk around Westminster is of a late surge in support for the Government Party, with some reports even suggesting they're on course to hold the balance of power." The BBC correspondent cleared his throat. "But with both main parties ruling out the possibility of sharing power with the Government Party, most pundits are predicting another grand coalition of national unity."

"'Grand', my arse!" Eunice yelled at the TV.

The camera cut to Big Ben.

"The polls are now closed, and we join Martin Kingsley for the exit poll result."

The screen went momentarily black. Then the numbers appeared, and the mournful voice of Martin Kingsley read out the projected result: an outright win by the Government Party, with an absolute majority of between 90 and 110 seats.

When the camera cut back to them, for a few seconds the BBC presenter and his guests seemed as stupefied as Eunice – and almost as pale.

"I told you so," Mr Rubens felt like saying to his open-mouthed sister, but at the sight not so much of her teeth as of her colour – an off-white shade of off – he desisted.

"Eunice, are you all right?"

"That's bollocks, those numbers are wrong," she answered drily. "People obviously lied, just to give the other parties a shock. Wait and see. Once the actual results are in, they'll be lucky to end up with more than a dozen MPs."

"They're projected to have won almost four hundred," said Mr Rubens. "A dozen sounds a bit like wishful thinking."

"Oh, Pablo. As if you've ever understood politics or people."

"You're right, I haven't," said Mr Rubens, "but I do have a degree in Mathematics."

"There are unconfirmed reports of sporadic acts of violence, and of rival crowds gathering in Parliament Square," announced the BBC presenter. "We'll bring you more information as soon as we have it. In the meantime, Martin Kingsley is with a spokesman of the Government Party."

"Mr Avery, if the exit polls are accurate–"

"'If' is not in our vocabulary, 'if' is for losers. No 'ifs', no 'buts', no more excuses. Our country is in crisis, Mr Kingsley, and today all the *true* British people have voted for the party that was brave enough to offer them the only true solution."

"No 'ifs' no 'buts', my arse," said Eunice.

Martin Kingsley adjusted his earpiece. "Reports are coming in of unprovoked attacks by armed Government Party supporters against members of religious and ethnic minorities, perhaps you'd like to take this opportunity—"

"I'd like to take this opportunity to *thank* our supporters, for putting their trust in the Government Party and for giving us a glorious victory against all the odds - a victory they've every right to celebrate."

"Pfft, talk about them counting their chickens!" Eunice snatched the remote from the arm of the *Amoeba* and switched the TV off. "Come on, let's go."

"Go where?"

"We'll take a minicab. But no, we should catch the bus to Archway and then get the tube. The roads might be blocked."

"What roads?"

Eunice had stood up and was pacing up and down.

"And I doubt we'd find a minicab driver willing to take us," she said.

"Take us where?"

"To join the protests, where do you think? We'll get off in Charing Cross and then we'll walk."

"But what exactly are we protesting? If you're right and the exit polls are wrong—"

"*Of course* I'm right. But I wouldn't put it past those Nazi bastards to claim that they've been cheated. If there's one thing they're good at, it's coaxing people into actually believing their lies."

"I thought you said people weren't stupid."

"Being brainwashed isn't the same as being stupid."

When Mr Rubens reluctantly agreed to join his sister and whoever wasn't brainwashed or stupid in a protest, the first *real* results had not yet been declared, allowing Eunice to cling onto hope. His neighbours on the other hand appeared to be taking no chances. Mr Rubens' long cul-de-sac was deserted, and although it was not yet eleven all the houses were dark. In the gentle breeze, the leaves of the plane trees gave the murmur of a muffled tambourine, and the domes of dusty light that cascaded from the streetlamps dotted the pavement with a curving line of shimmering halos. Even on the high street there was hardly any traffic; everywhere the night was eerily still, the lights of the city giving in to the moon and the stars – *so many of them tonight*, thought Mr Rubens. It was as if to make up for the half of the moon that was missing, a million new stars had been born, to form a blanket of subdued illumination that lay softly over the city like a shroud. But then a silent flash of colourless fireworks tore into every part of the sky, and the moon and the stars disappeared.

Light had travelled faster than sound.

Eunice was checking her phone to see when the next bus was coming when the road became the swell of a mob, surging, bulging, rolling as it swarmed its way downhill. Its barbarous chants and the sound of smashing glass shook the night, and hair-raising screams that were *not* those of fanatics rose above the mayhem to mark the beginning of darkness.

Without either of them daring to speak, Mr Rubens took his sister by the arm and led her away from the bus stop back in the direction of the house. In the air the stench of burning rubber mixed with ugly human smells, filling Mr

Rubens with an overwhelming sadness that caused him to break into sobs.

By morning the exit poll result had been confirmed, catastrophically: if people had lied, they had lied to *conceal* their support for the Government Party, not to make it up. When all the votes had been counted, their victory was even greater than predicted: a whopping overall majority of 149 seats. All the other parties had been routed.

Pablo

Given their family history, Mr Rubens had always suspected that his sister might well have belonged to one of the few ineffectual underground movements that occasionally managed to daub anti-government slogans on government buildings - "Don't ask!" she would say, perhaps just to tease him, or more likely than not to protect him.

Although unlike Eunice, and precisely because of their family history, Mr Rubens had never become an overtly political person, this had not prevented him from having opinions, or from privately expressing his strong reservations about some of the Government Party's more unorthodox policies.

"Extreme, Pablo! Let's call a bloody spade a spade, these people are murderers!"

Was it possible for two contradictory truths to exist side by side? There was no getting away from the fact that today, long after the worst of the visible cruelties had stopped and the blackest hours had passed, the people seemed more than content with the new status quo. Almost everyone who had been ordered out of the country had found somewhere to go, and most of the camps had been dismantled. There was no longer much appetite for conflict and controversy, some kind of consensus had at last been achieved.

For all Mr Rubens' regret at any injustices – and there must have been many – was it not, as he had rather convincingly once said to his sister, *some* vindication of its radical programme that within just a few years of its coming to power all the old parties had either disbanded or merged with the Government Party? Abroad, too, hadn't increasing numbers of countries, across every continent, followed the Government Party's example? Was this not proof that the Government Party's solution, if not a perfect solution, was the only solution there was? Had his sister forgotten that for years one outrage had followed another, causing discord with carnage and huge devastation until finally people had snapped?

Eunice had offered no arguments. Instead she had embraced him and called him a fool.

"Ah, Pablo, Pablo..."

She had always insisted on calling him Pablo, more often than not, Mr Rubens suspected, as a means of rousing what little she thought might have been left of *his* conscience.

For himself, Mr Rubens couldn't help thinking that Pablo and Guernica were names that Ernest had given his children to honour their grandfather's cruel, irresponsible folly. Harry Rubens had travelled to Spain, to fight in a country that wasn't his own, because of a painting. Without a second thought, he had left his pregnant wife alone in a country that wasn't *her* own.

"It wasn't because of a painting," Eunice had always protested. "He went to fight for the cause that had brought them together."

"It wasn't his war."

"It was everyone's war. Remember what actually happened in Guernica, Pablo. Guernica wasn't a painting. It was a town bombed by the Nazis in a slaughter of innocent people. Marta Beatriz was glad that he went."

"How do you know that? Did she say that she was? Did anyone ask her?" Mr Rubens very much doubted if anyone had. He was certain that his grandmother, whose country had taken already the lives of her parents and both of her brothers, would have rather her husband had stayed where he was. "Men are selfish. They always do what they want. And it's always the women who pick up the pieces. *They* are the heroes. What good did it do that he went?"

"He went to join the fight against Franco and fascism."

"And was ambushed unarmed at the border, killed before firing a shot, buried who knows where. Can you imagine how Marta Beatriz must have felt? Because *I* can."

"No, Pablo, you can't. And instead of being so ready to judge them, maybe you should try and be more like the *brave* men you accuse of being selfish."

Whatever the cause - and Mr Rubens would not have denied Eunice's claim that the cause had been just – their grandfather's actions had blighted the lives of the people he loved without ever touching the lives of the people he had wanted to fight for.

Who *had* he wanted to fight for? Enemies were easier to pinpoint than trustworthy comrades. His sister might have thought him naïve and self-centred, perhaps even a coward, and he had never made the slightest attempt to discourage (if anything, he had *encouraged*) judgments he himself had allowed to become so entrenched, but the reality, he liked to think, was rather different. He was not as uninformed as Eunice had always assumed. It was just that he had never been as able as his sister to imagine a world so stark and clear-cut in its contrasts.

The pencil moustache

With his mother gone and his father a distant figure, as a child Mr Rubens had withdrawn into himself, close only to Marta Beatriz and his sister. But discovering and then embracing his sexuality had made him social.

The young man with the pencil moustache who had irritated him by not ringing the bell had not been a robot. What had duped Mr Rubens' senses was not any inorganic composition, but on the contrary the postman's striking resemblance not to Mr Rubens himself, as had been his initial impression, but to another young man with a pencil moustache, to whom he owed the solitary love of his life.

"Joel. But you can call me Joe."

The postman had reminded Mr Rubens of the moment when he realised he had fallen in love.

THREE

Malcolm

It was the early 1980s. With a degree in Mathematics and a dull job in the civil service devising methods of manipulating numbers – in other words compiling statistics for a government he loathed - Anthony took every opportunity of waxing his thick head of hair into a quiff and joining Malcolm (who worked in the same department) in his room in Kings Cross, from where they walked together to *The Bell*. It was an almost nightly pilgrimage, and it lasted through the war in the Falklands and a second election win for Margaret Thatcher, right up until the summer of 1984, when for Anthony and Malcolm it ended.

"*Where will it end, where will it end?*" Joy Division asked night after night, long after Ian Curtis had decided on an answer.

"*When you're in love, you know you're in love...*" Phil Oakey and The Human League were right about that. And wrong about it, too.

When you're in love, *sooner or later* you know you're in love...

"I'm in love!" In the years before he moved out of the house he and Eunice had grown up in, to a studio flat in Vauxhall with views of the derelict Battersea Power Station, Anthony had lost count of just how often Eunice had come home in the morning after sleeping with whoever she had met the night before, to utter those same words with a passion no amount of repetition had been able to diminish. Long gone were the days when only through his nose would Anthony uncover the secrets of Eunice's nocturnal assignations. "I'm in love!" his sister had exclaimed time after time, year after year, often in a twirl around the objects in his finely furnished room – every weekend, come rain or shine, Anthony would get out of bed, run water through the ramshackle ruins of his quiff, and begin his expedition to the markets: Camden Lock for 50s kitsch and the odd piece of mid-century furniture, Portobello and Camden Passage for art deco, and Brick Lane for bric-a-brac, humble precursors to the heights of his rarefied taste in interior design.

In the end, while leaning back in a rickety Charles Eames to contemplate a chipped Clarice Cliff, Anthony had formed the firm belief that 'I'm in love!' was just a shell of empty words serving as a euphemism for a life of promiscuity and wild abandon. And if it suited his sister, mightn't it also suit him?

It didn't. Soaking up the atmosphere of camaraderie and general licentiousness filled him with a sense of freedom he had never felt at home, but it had failed to stop him feeling an apartness that increasingly he imagined as his destiny. Every awkward attempt to break away from it had gone awry, every casual encounter cut short. Not once had he been tempted, even insincerely, to utter the words 'I'm in love!'

The 'alternative' gay scene was small and incestuous in those days, and almost everyone Anthony knew had slept with someone who had slept with almost everyone else. That 'someone' just so happened to be Malcolm. The life of the party and the soul of indiscretion, he knew Anthony's secrets long before his best friend had confided them to him.

On the evening of July 15, a Sunday in the summer of 1984, Anthony was failing to get comfortable as he lay across the sofa in Malcolm's room watching Malcolm getting ready, swinging this way and that, striking playful poses while staring at himself in a tall piece of mirror that was propped against the wall.

Buzz and vibe

Roughly eighteen hours earlier, Anthony and Malcolm had parted on the dance floor to The Gang of Four's disjointed *Damaged Goods*. They had met again in the morning, too early after a late night that for both of them had started but not ended at *The Bell*.

At eight o'clock sharp, while clutching a watery takeaway tea Anthony was waiting for Malcolm on the opposite side of the High Street outside Camden Town Station.

At eight fifteen, he took one last sip and disposed of the Styrofoam cup while it was still half full. Less than five minutes later, wearing jeans and a surplus sailor's T-shirt (white and navy blue) Malcolm spilled out of the station in a glut of new arrivals – teenage punks sporting colourful Mohicans, gangly students carrying instruments for busking, white-robed Evangelicals heading for church.

Malcolm stood out in a crowd even from a distance, his physical presence taking possession of space and defining it entirely as he cut his way through it, displacing air while at the same time somehow filling it with an intangible translucence: whereas Anthony's 'gift' seemed to always cast life in a shadow, Malcolm's was to inundate its mysteries with light.

Already under his spell, which had nothing to do with sexual attraction, Anthony caught Malcolm's eye and crossed the road to greet him.

"You're late again," he said. "You're *always* late."

Malcolm crushed him in a bear hug. "*Don't*, I've got a headache," he said. Pulling back, he wiggled his long fingers as he dug them into Anthony's hair, running them through it as though stroking a tune along a piano keyboard. "Your hair looks as bad as I'm feeling."

In the company of his friend, Anthony's experience of the world was suffused with a sense of belonging that it otherwise lacked. He loved Malcolm's ease and the naturalness and affection of his touch, as unselfconscious in a Camden crowd of strangers as it was while they were dancing in the friendly semi-darkness of *The Bell*. Malcolm by his side served as an appendage to himself, like a beacon that eclipsed his own shortcomings.

"If you're feeling even *half* as bad as that, you should still be in bed."

"What, and miss our date?" Retrieving his fingers, Malcolm pinched Anthony's cheek, "No part of you could ever look *that* bad," he said, breaking up his laughter with a cough. And keeping an arm over Anthony's shoulder while looking around at the swell of youthful colour, "I like it here, I'm glad you asked me to come."

"Really?"

Camden Lock was a sprawl of market stalls, some clustered outdoors in makeshift rows of tables with roofs of tarpaulin, others crammed in various conversions by Regent's Canal or inside and outside the old stable buildings that led towards Chalk Farm. While the force of the crowd carried them in that direction, Malcolm swivelled on his plimsolls and marked the air around them with a sweep of his hand.

"I love it, I do, and not *just* because I'm with you. The place has a buzz and a vibe that I'd never have imagined possible so early in the morning on a Sunday."

He used his other arm to pull Anthony's face closer to his, so close that the breath of his words caressed Anthony's cheeks in gentle waves.

"It's like a melting pot of allsorts that you can't help feeling part of, a multi-coloured anarchy of oddballs and misfits and freaks, every one of us the same and yet all of us so gorgeously different. Now I understand why you come here every week."

Anthony had only ever been able to experience Camden's multi-coloured anarchy as a nuisance.

"I just come here for the antiques," he said.

Again Malcolm's laughter seemed to catch in his throat, and he rapped at his chest with a fist.

"Malcolm, are you okay?"

"Just catching my breath," Malcolm answered gruffly with a nod of reassurance, his fist breaking up into fingers that spread around the side of his neck. "That's what comes of overdoing grabbing life by the balls," he said, and his laughter now was uninterrupted, as though browbeaten by the threat of strangulation. Then in a whisper, almost sadly, "I'll soon be having balls coming out of my ears, if I'm not careful. I feel so bloody *tired*."

"I'm sorry," Anthony said.

Malcolm shaded his eyes from the sun as he swung around again to fix Anthony with knitted brows. "Why?" he asked, but gave Anthony no time to answer. "As a penance you can buy us both a hat." He hooked his naval T-shirt by the neck, and pulling it away from his body he blew air down his chest. "Will you miss all the bargains if you take me somewhere first for a sandwich and a coffee?"

"Before or after buying us both a hat?"

"And a cheap pair of shades," Malcolm said. "I *hate* the sun."

"Before," Anthony decided. "But we don't have to stay if you're tired."

"I didn't mean it literally," Malcolm said. "Now come on, I'm *starving*."

Malcolm was so thin, and mentioned food so rarely, that not for all the bargains in the world was Anthony about to miss the opportunity to feed him.

"There's an Italian café in Parkway."

"Yum!" Malcolm said.

Fighting buzz and vibe, they walked back in the direction of the station and turned right into Parkway. They would order cappuccinos and two full English breakfasts – Anthony's with extra bacon instead of sausage, Malcolm's with double of everything, if Anthony could have his way.

Signed and numbered

Save for an excellent breakfast, two pairs of shades and a couple of second-hand panama hats, their expedition so far had proved a dangerous fiasco. The day had got hotter and hotter, and for all his good-natured bravado, there had been moments when Malcolm had given Anthony the impression of being on the verge of collapse, even as he feigned newfound interest in 50s geometric bric-a-brac. After two solid hours in and out of the sun, meandering without complaint past table after table brimming with twopenny-halfpenny kitsch, his whiteness had been blotted by the heat with the yellowish purple of bruises. But resisting every attempt to cut their visit short, he had insisted on a systematic tour of every nook and cranny of the market, accusing Anthony of vicarious hypochondria while improbably insisting he felt perfectly fine. Confronted with the blotchy evidence of Malcolm's face, Anthony had not been convinced.

Relieved when at last they had reached the tail end of the market, and were inside the stable buildings where the air was relatively cool, he had just picked up a Fornasetti plate – decorated with the face of a woman set within the image of a light bulb (circa 1960, *very* expensive) - and while he was inspecting it for hidden cracks and chips, he noticed Malcolm drifting into one of the furniture stalls.

"Oh, I quite like this." Barely audible to anyone else, the flat exclamation, which even he would not have heard if the wall that divided him from Malcolm reached beyond its short six feet all the way to the roof, was to Anthony's honed ear a rarity pregnant with the spur to please his friend: whatever it was that Malcolm had 'quite liked' so spontaneously, he would buy it for him. It was the least he could do after giving him heatstroke, and putting down the light-bulb Fornasetti – much too roughly, judging by the dealer's dirty look - he bounded through the entrance of the *20TH CENTURY FURNITURE* enclosure that had once been the home of a horse.

Ensconced within an armchair's overlapping leaves, like a luminous pearl set against mutations of black leather emanating from the abstraction of a cardinal cell, with one leg over the other and his arms over the armrests like butterfly wings, Malcolm radiated bliss.

"I don't believe it," Anthony said.

"A rather magical sight, I agree," someone said, forcing Anthony to turn around. A portly, middle-aged man dressed for cocktails in a mystery by Agatha Christie grinned at him lasciviously. "It's only very rarely that I make an exception at all, and more rarely still that I make it so wholeheartedly." With an extravagant movement, he handed Anthony a piece of card that instructed calligraphically: *Please don't sit on me!* "And now not one but *two* boys of beauty patronising my establishment at once, it's all rather too much for one's delicate and fragile constitution." His rounded jowls wobbled as he spoke, drooping over his elaborately knotted cravat.

"You should definitely buy it," Malcolm said to Anthony.

"I don't believe it," Anthony said again, as his gaze ping-ponged back from the cravat to the mutations.

"Like Zeus reigning over mortals from his throne on Mount Olympus," said the dealer.

"It's an *Amoeba*," Anthony gasped.

"Two *sophisticated* boys of beauty, I don't think I can bear it!"

"Only one, I'm afraid," Malcolm said. "I can't say I'd ever heard of an *Amoeba* before."

"It's a classic piece of 1960s design," Anthony said.

"What you're sitting in is a *museum* piece," said the dealer. His plumpness was bloating his eyelids, his eyes like hungry slits as they fixed themselves on Malcolm's anatomy. "But how marvellous that you were drawn to it *naturally*, as one is drawn to one's first love. Alas, we all become so *jaded* after that."

"I've honestly never sat in anything more comfy," Malcolm said unsentimentally, stretching out his arms before bending them to tie his hands around the back of his head, striking Anthony as more delicate and fragile even than the dealer's constitution. *Like a stigma to the Amoeba's ovary,* he thought, as he conjured up the image of a lily.

"*Comfy?* My dear boy, that hardly even *begins–*"

"It's beautiful," said Anthony, as though still hypnotised by the entanglement of the entire composition.

"And it's signed," the dealer bent forward to whisper in his ear.

"I believe they all were," said Anthony.

"Signed and numbered," the dealer conceded, and with a nod towards the *Amoeba*, "Rather aptly, No. 69 would you believe!"

"There's certainly the room for it," said Malcolm, while the dealer chuckled sleazily. His hair, straight and thin and lustrously amber, was parted so extremely to one side that an arc of it flopped across his forehead lopsidedly, serving as a curtain of effete insinuation...

The lurid imagery of his stereotyping prejudice made Anthony cringe, and to escape it he forced his gaze back to the oyster of the *Amoeba* and its pearl.

"I'm going to buy it for you," he said to Malcolm.

"Ah, young love," said the dealer.

"Don't be ridiculous," Malcolm said, and after an ambiguous silent space: "There's no room to swing a cat in my room, if you like it you should buy it for yourself." Then with a flutter of his eyelids he turned directly to the dealer, with the look of a boy in a portrait by Egon Schiele. "Is it *very* expensive?"

"As it happens, you're in luck," said the dealer, his tone now deep and businesslike. "Take it off my hands today and you can have it for *half* the asking price, a bargain if ever I saw one."

"That would rather depend on the asking price," said Anthony, just as easily slipping into bargaining mode. He caught Malcolm giving him a sulking frown, as though accusing him of spoiling his fun.

"The price is on the card in your hand," said the dealer.

"*Please don't sit on me!* is on the card in my hand," Anthony said, reading out the instruction without emphasis.

"The other side," said the dealer.

Anthony flipped the card around and read out the price:

"£499."

Below the figure's elongated curves was another calligraphic scribble: 'T49', which meant the maximum discount for trade was £49. In other words, the dealer would probably be willing to drop his price all the way down to £400. And half of £400 was £200, expensive but probably worth it. Anthony had brought with him £300. He would start by offering £175, and stretch to £225 if absolutely necessary, perhaps even to £250. An *Amoeba* in mint condition was a rare find indeed. He might never come across one again in his life.

"We can only afford a hundred," said Malcolm. Spreading out his arms over the armrests and using one foot as a pivot, he caused the *Amoeba* to lurch from side to side.

"Malcolm, stop!" Anthony said.

"Too much? Then how about seventy-five? Cash."

The dealer smiled insouciantly. "The double act," he said. "I should have known."

"Please excuse my friend, he gets carried away," Anthony said.

"Fifty then, and we'll be doing you a favour," said Malcolm, now flattening himself across the *Amoeba* as though hanging in a hammock from a tree. "I mean, let's face it, it may be a 69 and a stunning example of 60s design but it's a *whale* of a thing, which would explain why you've been stuck with it for *God* knows how long, dead wood taking up all this valuable space. And that can't be good for business, can it?"

"We'll give you half the asking price," Anthony almost said, but the dealer spoke first.

"Give me a hundred and get out of my sight. Go on, before I change my mind."

Anthony took out the cash from his pocket, and was counting each note as it landed on the dealer's open palm. "Fifty, sixty, seventy–"

"And you'll deliver it to Vauxhall, of course," Malcolm said.

"Don't push your luck," said the dealer.

"Eighty, ninety, one hundred."

"All yours!" The dealer clenched his fist around the money like a conjuror.

"I'm not carrying that to Vauxhall," said Malcolm, springing out of the *Amoeba* like a jack-in-the-box. "And it's never going to fit in a cab."

"It's got an aluminium frame," Anthony said. "It shouldn't be too heavy. And we don't have to take it to Vauxhall. We can carry it to my grandmother's for now."

'For now' was to prove a rash prediction.

All queens are equal

"I can't believe we managed to get an *Amoeba* for a measly hundred pounds," Anthony said. "And it was all thanks to you, I'd have gladly paid the asking price."

"And then some, I'm sure," Malcolm said.

"One flutter of your eyelids and he was eating off the palm of your hand."

"He was hungry," Malcolm said. "And you were hungry too, for the *Amoeba*."

"But only one of us got what they wanted. 'Rather aptly, No. 69 would you believe!'" Anthony parroted the dealer's words in a high-pitched effeminate voice. Had they not been carrying the *Amoeba*, probably he would have also bent his wrist. "Jesus," he said. "What a queen!"

"We're *all* bloody queens," Malcolm answered softly, "and no queens are more equal than others, just because they call themselves 'alternative' and traipse every night to *The Bell*. His name is Charles, by the way, and he's just let us fleece him, so the least we can do is be grateful."

"You're right, I'm sorry."

"We all say things without thinking," Malcolm said. "I'm sure you meant no harm."

Just as Anthony had thought, the *Amoeba* was not very heavy, and he and Malcolm had managed to manoeuvre it successfully, cutting through the two opposing currents of students and skinheads and punks (all of whom seemed to have lost their earlier buzz even for Malcolm) to at last reach the tranquillity of the street.

"But now I need a drink," Malcolm said, and when he lowered his side of the Amoeba to the ground, Anthony was forced to do the same.

Back outside when the sun was at its most intense, Malcolm's face, so fetchingly insubstantial in the greyness of the badly lit stables, when subjected to exertion and an excess of light had again become ghostly. The boy in a portrait by Egon Schiele had become a dead young soldier in a lithograph by Otto Dix. A drink was the last thing he needed.

"I've exhausted you," Anthony said, and as if that were his cue Malcolm slumped into the *Amoeba*. His rapid breaths sounded empty, like a drip of liquid metal that failed to fill his lungs.

"I just need a minute," he said, smiling with what seemed like an enormous effort as he pressed down on his chest with both his fists, still gasping as he spoke, but a little less urgently now. "There, I'm feeling better already." And with his next deep breath, his chest rose with his fists as it filled with all the air he had swallowed.

Anthony looked northwards, in the direction of Chalk Farm and beyond. The heat made the pale asphalt shimmer as it crawled its way uphill, where it merged with the sky in a blur. All the movement was behind them, the crowd at the busy three-way crossing below the railway bridge almost frozen by the speed of its steady and constant flux, its noise like the din of a playground, barely muffled by the rattle of a train as it passed overhead. Looking northwards again, the road was almost empty, the glint of its apex broken only by the occasional car, the light at its edges blanching the small group of newcomers who were inching their approach like the smudge of a dozen-legged bug moving in slow motion. Even without taking into account Malcolm's frailty, in this suffocating heat, unbearable in spite of their second-hand panama hats, there was no way they could carry the *Amoeba* all the way to his grandmother's house, which was *not* so close after all. In the excitement of the moment, by comparing the relative proximity of Belsize Park to the sheer impossibility of Vauxhall, he and Malcolm had miscalculated badly.

"Eunice!"

Cheered by Malcolm's burst of energy, Anthony was mystified as to its meaning.

"Eunice!" Malcolm said again with equal gusto.

"Yes," Anthony said, "I heard you the first time. What about her?"

"She has a van, is what about her."

This was true, but it was sadly not a van for transportation. All three sides at the back had been fitted with shelves filled with handyman tools, leaving hardly any standing room for Eunice herself, let alone the space for an *Amoeba*.

"I'll call her," Anthony said. The van was not a viable option, but his sister had a practical mind, far more practical than his, and might come up with an alternative idea. "But first we need to get you out of the sun."

"And some water," Malcolm said, taking off his shades to look up at him.

There was nothing to be done to save the *Amoeba*. To save Malcolm, it had to be dumped, abandoned by the roadside ignominiously. Anthony would fetch some water, then he would hail down a cab, or call Eunice, if he could find a phone box nearby, and get Malcolm home as soon as possible. But no, first he needed to get Malcolm in the shade. No shade anywhere, no cabs, where was there a shop to get some water? There was a pub across the road. Shade, water, somewhere to sit, and hopefully a phone to call Eunice from...

"Behold how the angel has fallen!"

"Charles, thank God!" Malcolm said.

Charles clicked his tongue. "Never mind God," he said, "it's me you should be thanking."

"What for?" Anthony snapped.

Charles raised an eyebrow. "For being the fool who is about to give you a lift."

"Oh, thank God," Malcolm said again.

"I'm assuming your grandmother lives somewhere not too far?"

"Just after Belsize Park," Anthony said.

"That's acceptable," said Charles. "But only on one condition. You get your hundred pounds back and the *Amoeba* stays with me."

"Over my dead body," Malcolm said flirtily.

"Hmm... I shouldn't have to wait too long, judging by your sorry state." And turning to Anthony: "What *were* you thinking, exposing your young friend to this heat?"

"Malcolm is the same age as me," Anthony answered dumbly.

Charles rolled his eyes and clicked his tongue a second time. "Honestly, just look at his complexion, he's as pale as Judy Garland."

"Is Judy Garland pale?" Malcolm asked.

"I thought she was dead," Anthony said.

But Charles didn't seem to have heard them. "He's practically melting in this heat," he went on, "and I shouldn't be surprised if he's running a fever. At least stand over him and keep him shaded while I go and get the van."

"We're not giving back the *Amoeba*," said Malcolm.

"As if I'd have the heart to deprive my Cinderella of her slipper," said Charles.

Anthony took five pounds out of his pocket. "Could you please get some water for Malcolm? And I know we should have thought to bring some with us, you don't have to say it."

"Put your money away," said Charles.

FOUR

A May Day demonstration in Paris

Once the *Amoeba* was inside the back of the van, and Anthony had sandwiched himself between Malcolm and Charles so that Malcolm could sit by the window, the journey shouldn't have taken more than twenty minutes. But a burst water main between Chalk Farm and Belsize Park had caused a half-mile tailback. Workmen in luminous vests were installing temporary traffic lights, and in the meantime, traffic wasn't moving at all.

"Anthony's grandmother is Spanish," said Malcolm, when Anthony had given Charles the address. "Marta Beatriz."

"I *love* Spanish names," said Charles.

"Then you'll *love* Anthony's middle name," said Malcolm. "Pablo, and Eunice's is Guernica. Eunice is Anthony's sister."

"Guernica," Charles repeated uncertainly.

"It's a city in Spain. The Nazis bombed it for Franco, and then Picasso painted it."

"He didn't actually paint the city," said Anthony.

"I know the painting well," said Charles. "It's terribly dramatic."

"Anthony's seen it in the flesh," Malcolm said.

"I've only ever seen reproductions," said Charles. "It must have been magnificent seeing the actual painting."

"It was," Anthony said, his mind already drifting back to 1982 and the hot May Day afternoon in Madrid, seventeen difficult years after their mother had left, when their father had taken them – not his two grown-up children who had come to Spain from abroad, but very much Guernica and Pablo on that special day – to see in the flesh the painting that had marked three Rubens generations in such an indelible way. It had finally returned to the country to which it had always belonged.

The three of them had walked hand in hand all the way to the museum from their hotel, Ernest in a loose linen suit, the beret he always wore on demonstrations, and a tightly knotted tie that matched the blood-red rose on his lapel, Pablo in baggy blue trousers and a long-sleeved white shirt whose stiff collar had to stay buttoned up, his sister, wearing lipstick for the first time, in a simple cotton dress wrapped inside the flowers of their grandmother's mantilla.

Anthony would never forget the sparkle in Eunice Guernica's eyes. Transfixed by its power and the horror of its beauty, she had stood in front of the painting unable to speak. And he remembered how that same sparkle had shone in their father's eyes also, as he came to recognise himself in his daughter. Anthony also remembered the sharp twinge of jealousy young Pablo had felt on that day at the Reina Sofia, and how almost at that very same instant he had set himself free by forgiving his father at last for having never loved him or his mother enough.

"Anthony's grandfather was actually a hero," said Malcolm.

"He was a selfish, irresponsible fool," Anthony said.

"Don't let your sister hear you say that," said Malcolm. And to Charles, "Harry Rubens, from a very wealthy family in London. He and Marta Beatriz met in Paris, just after Guernica was bombed."

Anthony had heard the story a thousand times. After losing her father and both of her brothers to the war against Franco, and shortly afterwards her mother to grief, Marta Beatriz had sought refuge in Paris. Harry was visiting the city on a business trip. United by outrage at Guernica's plight, they had joined thousands of other protesters on the largest May Day demonstration the French capital had ever seen.

Strangers among strangers marching side by side, the swell of the crowd had pushed them so close to each other that the red flags they were waving became tangled up. As their eyes met, they both smiled, simultaneously dissolving into blushes that were redder than the red of their flags.

"Bonjour," yelled Harry above angry slogans in Spanish and French.

"Bonjour," yelled Marta Beatriz.

"Parlez-vous anglais?" yelled Harry above united cries of "*¡NO PASARAN!*"

"Ach, just a little."

For hours they continued to yell back and forth. By the end of the day they had fallen in love, and had woken up together the next morning. A month later, a notice had been published in *The Times* announcing their engagement, a visa had been issued to Marta Beatriz, and the couple were in London making the arrangements for their wedding. By August they were married, and for their honeymoon they travelled back to France, to visit the Spanish Pavilion at the Paris Exposition.

"And when Harry saw Picasso's painting, he decided he had no other choice," Malcolm went on. "He *had* to join the fight against Franco, even though by then Anthony's grandmother was pregnant."

A few visits to *Los Hijos*, a small Spanish émigré bar in the Marais, had been all it had taken to make the arrangements. Led by Narcís, a handsome twenty-six-year-old Catalan boy who spoke fluent English and French, a group of volunteers – no more than a dozen - would cross the border somewhere near Figueres, where Republican fighters would be waiting to receive them.

After kissing her husband goodbye at the door of their hotel room, reassured by the secrecy that had prevented her from saying goodbye to him anywhere else, Marta Beatriz had refused to leave Paris until Narcís was back with news that everything had gone according to plan, and the men in his charge had arrived in Spain safely. After that, she had reconciled herself to no more news; only the knowledge that from that moment on, her husband's life would constantly hang on a knife-edge.

When two weeks had passed, she returned to *Los Hijos*. Narcís was not there, but the atmosphere was calm; it was not yet time to be worried. Night after night she would go back, and many nights would pass before the night that would be different, its hush so much louder than the loudness of the voices that on every other night had drowned each other out. A woman she did not know embraced her, to whisper terrible words in her ear.

The men had failed to make their rendezvous. The following day their bodies had been found in fields less than one mile away. With makeshift military honours, the fighters who found them buried them where they had fallen.

Was Narcís among the dead?

Narcís was missing.

Was he the betrayer?

The men and women in *Los Hijos* who had known him refused to believe so; they were certain he must have been captured. Marta Beatriz wondered how much young Narcís had been a man of discretion and how much a young Narcissus, eager to be liked, too eager to brag. It was possible that one of his defenders was the traitor.

If not Narcís, then who?

Silence.

When Marta Beatriz walked out of *Los Hijos*, she left the unanswered question behind her. Her beloved Harry had laid down his life for a cause that was just, and was a hero whether or not he had fired a shot. *What difference did anything else make?*

"What a terribly sad story," said Charles. "But somehow with a happy ending, no?"

"Somehow how?" Anthony asked.

"Well, your grandmother survived and obviously so did her child, who honoured Harry's memory with you and your sister's names."

"That's a *very* happy ending," Malcolm said, poking Anthony's ribs with his elbow."

"It might have been a happy ending if my father hadn't driven my mother away and himself to an early grave."

"I'm sorry," said Charles, "I hadn't realised your father had died."

"Two years ago, just days after our trip. He hadn't even turned forty-five."

It was as if Ernest had foretold his own death, and had wished by the family visit to Madrid, if not to make amends, then at least to bring to life before his children the moment more than forty years before that had not so much inspired as *compelled* his own father to travel to Spain in order to fight for a cause. Consumed by that pivotal moment in Paris, whose almost certain consequence had been an impulsive young life lost entirely in vain, and unable to accept that Harry had abandoned his wife and unborn son on a whim that had lacked any purpose, Ernest had devoted every moment of *his* life, not to his own family, which he had started while still in his teens, but to looking for proof that his father had *not* died entirely in vain. It had been a Sisyphean task, condemned to a continual failure that Ernest had at every stage refused to accept as conclusive.

Anthony's mother had left when he was five, and had made a new life across the Atlantic with the man she had met during one of Ernest's many absences. She had never written, much less made any attempt to claim her children back. Anthony could not remember her and never spoke her name, but felt no trace of bitterness against the woman whose black and white photograph he always carried in his pocket.

"I thought you said you'd forgiven him," Malcolm said to Anthony.

"I have, but it's complicated," Anthony said, and as he felt Malcolm's arm slip in behind him to give him a squeeze, he was filled with the warmth of their friendship.

"It's life," Charles said. "Where would we all be without our stories?"

Before Anthony could say that Malcolm's story was more interesting than his, which Malcolm would have probably disputed, the temporary traffic lights turned green and they were moving. With his head leaning back, taking care not to press too hard against Malcolm's softness, in the silence everyone observed while Charles was driving, Anthony surveyed the shifting architecture.

Most of London was ugly, but not in a way that he found unattractive. There was something reassuring about the blandness of its terraces; about the labyrinthine interlocking of its streets; about the close proximity of different browns of bricks to the white of Georgian facades and the concrete of post-war social housing. London wore its history openly; its inequalities were plain for all to see. The seedy dereliction of Kings Cross lay but half a mile away from Chancery Lane and the splendour of the Inns of Court. The steel and glass buildings of St Mary Axe in the City shared the same skyline as the poverty of the East End's high-rise blocks. Fashion rebels travelled from their squats south of the river to cruise the King's Road in opulent Chelsea every Saturday afternoon.

Chalk Farm, which they were driving through now at a snail's pace, ranked high among Anthony's favourite neighbourhoods. It had about it an illusory grandeur, with imposing big houses that, if you looked closely, were mostly in a bad state of repair, as though all their owners had fallen on hard times and couldn't keep them up. When Anthony decided he was moving to a place of his own, he had thought about living here, but the idea of being within walking distance from his sister and grandmother had put him off, tipping the balance in favour of Vauxhall.

In Belsize Park the feel was more suburban. Many side streets to the east were close to or even bordered the Heath, aspiring more convincingly to the affluent air of Hampstead Village further north. Driving past the Screen on the Hill - where not long ago he and Malcolm had been stunned by Ingmar Bergman's *Fanny and Alexander* - was like crossing an invisible line that filled you with fresh air but completely cut you off from the throbbing heartbeat of the city.

FIVE

In flagrante

The white Transit van, bearing three equal queens in the front and an *Amoeba* wrapped in blankets in the back, was pulling over in the leafy street, outside Anthony's grandmother's house.

"There's Eunice," said Malcolm.

"She looks menacing," said Charles.

She did. Arms akimbo, she must have spotted the alien van approaching, and her demeanour as she poked into the air with her nose, as though to sniff out the Transit's intentions, was not that of a welcoming party.

"You can't park here," she yelled, now wagging a forbidding finger at Charles. "Shoo, I said, are you deaf? Parking is for residents only."

"That's not true, don't take any notice," Anthony said.

Malcolm stuck his head out of the window. "Eunice, it's us," he shouted at the top of his voice.

Eunice jerked her head in the direction of his voice. "Malcolm? Is that you?" Her angry face broadened as it smoothed into a smile of recognition. "What on earth are you doing in a van?"

"Good afternoon, young lady," said Charles, after turning off the engine.

"Who are you?" she asked him suspiciously.

Charles gave a bow of his head without leaving his seat. "Charles Willoughby, purveyor of only the *finest* mid-century furniture, at your service."

"Eunice Guernica Rubens, general dogsbody, owner of similar van," Eunice answered brusquely, pointing at a van across the road, pale blue with *NO JOB TOO SMALL* and a telephone number painted across it in black.

"Ah, delighted," said Charles, giving her a proletarian thumbs-up.

"You're far too old for Malcolm," she told him.

"Eunice!" said Anthony loudly, craning his neck so she could see him. "Have you told her you're gay?" he whispered to Malcolm.

"Your sister's not stupid," Malcolm whispered back.

"I should have known," said Eunice in a distant voice. Then returning to Charles, "Are you a Tory?" And before he could answer, "You're a Tory, I can tell."

Malcolm had already jumped out of the van and was storming at her with an open embrace. Charles and Anthony joined them on the pavement.

"What's my brother been up to now?" Eunice asked, fixing Anthony with a mistrustful look over Malcolm's shoulder. As usual she was dressed like a boy, in blue jeans and a short-sleeved 50s shirt whose elaborate pattern was in Anthony's opinion better suited to a curtain.

"Labour through and through, as it happens," said Charles. "If it were up to the Tories, I'd be chemically castrated and locked up to rot in the closet whence I only very recently escaped."

"But you're old," Eunice said to Charles while holding on to Malcolm.

"Eunice, you're being rude," Anthony said.

"It's quite alright," said Charles, laughing. "I *mis*spent my youth in marriage, I'm afraid, to a rather dreadful Tory, as a matter of fact - a Lady, no less, although she couldn't have been less of a lady if she tried, which I assure you she did, constantly. Our little charade ended quite abruptly when she caught me *in flagrante* with the chauffeur. Thankfully we had no babies."

"With the chauffeur?"

"Your sister is a hoot," Charles said to Anthony. "So anyway, to bring my story happily to a close, the chauffeur is my partner now, in business as well as in bed. Terrific chap, and *very* well endowed. Nearly killed me when I told him I'd let go of the *Amoeba*."

"What on earth is an *Amoeba*? Have you all been drinking? Is that why Malcolm's looking so poorly?"

"How many inches?"

"Malcolm!" said Anthony loudly.

"I was just wondering what '*very* well endowed' actually meant," Malcolm replied nonchalantly. And turning to Eunice, "Do I really look so bad?"

"Nine," said Charles.

"Fuck!" said Malcolm. "And we thought you were hungry…"

"Oh, I'm *ravenous*," said Charles.

"I never said you looked bad," Eunice said to Malcolm.

"He could *never* look bad," said Charles.

"Apparently the heat doesn't agree with my complexion," said Malcolm.

"The heat, the pollution… Modern life is a death trap," said Charles.

Malcolm's short burst of laughter rattled in his throat, and he coughed a little as he tried to catch his breath.

"It's all my fault," said Anthony.

"Nothing's anyone's fault," said Malcolm.

"He just needs to cool down," said Charles.

"Would you like some cold lemonade?" Eunice asked.

"Later," said Anthony.

"I was asking Malcolm."

"The *Amoeba*," said Charles.

"Yes!" Anthony agreed, eager to unload the *Amoeba* and get rid of Charles as soon as possible.

"An *Amoeba* is a signed and numbered chair," Malcolm explained to Eunice.

She made a scrunched-up grimace, as if to say: *Who cares?* "We should get you inside as soon as possible," she said.

"We should," said Anthony.

"The boys are really quite extraordinary at negotiations," Charles said to Eunice while unlocking the back of his van.

"And you're equally extraordinary at being generous," said Malcolm.

"Never underestimate your powers of persuasion," said Charles.

I wish he'd keep his mouth shut, Anthony thought.

And sure enough, ten minutes later Charles had driven off, and with his second-hand panama hat in his lap Malcolm was lounging half asleep in the *Amoeba*, in the house where Anthony and Eunice had grown up.

"Do you like it?" Anthony whispered to his sister.

"You must have paid a fortune for it," Eunice whispered back, still clutching the glass of icy lemonade she had prepared for Malcolm.

"Only a hundred pounds."

"*Only* a hundred pounds?"

"I almost paid double that," said Anthony.

"*Two* hundred pounds for a stupid *Amoeba*, throwing your money around in front of Malcolm, knowing that he grew up in poverty?"

"*One* hundred pounds," Anthony answered non-negotiably. "And Malcolm really liked it, I was going to buy it for him."

"Oh, so why didn't you?"

"He said it was too big for his room."

"His *room*, exactly," said Eunice.

"It was Malcolm who insisted I should buy it."

"I assume you're going to give it to him when he's moved to a bigger place?"

"Of course I will," said Anthony.

"You'll do no such thing," Malcolm said, yawning as he bounced all the way to the front of the gigantic *Amoeba*. Then softly to Eunice, "Antiques are Anthony's passion, the buzz he gets from finding them is part of who he is, and I *like* who he is, he's always looking out for me and this morning he bought me a cappuccino and a full English breakfast, as well as this wonderful panama hat; he didn't *just* give me heatstroke. I'd hate you to think that growing up in poverty has made me begrudging."

"I never said I thought you were begrudging," Eunice said, her eyes on fire as her cheekbones coloured up. "And the *Amoeba* isn't really an antique."

"I'll have you know it's an important piece of 60s design," Malcolm told her, giving Anthony a surreptitious wink. "A *museum* piece, no less. *And* it's bloody comfy, one more reason I should visit you more often. But now I should go. Tonight, your selfish brother will be dragging me out yet again, so I need to go home and have a rest."

"Maybe we should give tonight a miss," said Anthony.

"Come to mine around seven," Malcolm answered categorically. "That should give me enough time to rest, make a few phone calls *and* have a shower. I might even do some writing."

"Grandma will be sorry to have missed you," said Eunice.

"Oh, she'll be much too excited by the *Amoeba* to be thinking of me."

"Here, I made you some lemonade," said Eunice.

Cruising ground

"Ach, what in heaven's name is *that*?" said Marta Beatriz. She had just arrived back from the baker's with a couple of baguettes and a box of éclairs, and was standing in front of the *Amoeba* open-mouthed.

Anthony and Eunice had been drinking lemonade in the kitchen, but had raced each other to the sitting room as soon as they heard the front door.

"It's an *Amoeba*," said Eunice.

"It's hardly microscopic," said Marta Beatriz.

"Apparently it's a museum piece," said Eunice.

"It's a chair," said Anthony. "If you don't like it, I'll take it to Vauxhall."

"I don't like it," said Marta Beatriz. "I *love* it. Even though it makes everything else in this room look insipid."

It didn't. Anthony's grandmother's taste was functional, unfussy and frugal, which suited the *Amoeba* to a tee. Among the simple lines and lack of clutter, it complemented the room grandiosely. Rising up in the midst of a forest of wood — parquet floor, slimline dining furniture, a small rosewood bookcase — and keeping its distance from an unassuming three-piece-suite at the opposite end of the room, its modernity did not feel out of place; while bringing out the elegance of its modest competitors, it imposed its extravagant supremacy absolutely.

"But at the same time, it somehow fits in," said Marta Beatriz. "It's almost like it's *always* been here. I'm trying to imagine how the room would look without it and I can't."

"Or how the *Amoeba* would look without the room," said Anthony.

"Oh, for God's sake," said Eunice.

"No, your brother's right. It's a magnificent piece, and we've found the perfect spot for it!"

"It's also very comfortable," Anthony said.

"Let me see," said Marta Beatriz, and after handing Eunice the baguettes and the box of éclairs, she fell into the *Amoeba* in a swirl.

It was remarkable how youthful she looked for her age. When Anthony had once complimented her, he remembered her laughter abruptly becoming a sigh; she had then answered him sombrely that she had been too busy to grow old. Looking at her now, spread out across the *Amoeba* in her loose scarlet dress, the beauty of the girl he had seen in old photographs was still plainly visible. Like those of a Master, the brushstrokes of age had if anything made it sublime. Anthony found it curiously befitting that she reminded him so much of a Picasso painting – an early twentieth century portrait of Gertrude Stein. Her features were attractive without being ostentatious: a large forehead and prominent nose that brought out the expression in her eyes by giving them more depth, light pink lips, short hair that gave the outline of her face the austerity of a sharper definition.

In the Che Guevara T-shirt and denim shorts she had changed into, Eunice, too, looked much younger than her twenty-seven years. Anthony's sister was windswept without being weatherworn, as though roughened but not blighted by the family misfortunes she took pride in.

"Now I understand why it's called an *Amoeba*," said Marta Beatriz, lying back in its embrace with her eyes lightly shut. "Sitting in it is like floating in air... or rather in something more liquid than air... One feels so strangely weightless..."

"You shouldn't get too used to it," Eunice said.

"I shouldn't?"

"Anthony bought it for Malcolm. We're only keeping it until he's moved to a bigger place."

"Ach, but it's not so very easy to get out of…" Marta Beatriz reached out for Anthony's hand, and he helped her stand up. "Now come on, you two, it's glorious outside, I think we should all go for a walk. It's a long time since the three of us did something together."

While his grandmother was gently massaging his fingers, Anthony watched silently as the older woman used her eyes to plead with the young one. He was happy he had always been the easy one; the one Marta Beatriz could rely on without argument or fuss; the one she almost took for granted.

Eunice let the side of her face rest on her grandmother's shoulder. "A walk would be nice," she said.

It was early afternoon. "It's too hot," Anthony decided, after just a single breath of air.

"You and the bloody weather," Eunice said.

"An hour ago I was to blame for giving Malcolm heatstroke."

"Malcolm's too fair for the sun," Eunice said.

Letting go of Anthony's fingers, with a rapid movement Marta Beatriz brought her hands together in a thunderclap. "We'll take a cab to Spaniards Inn and walk among the trees of my favourite part of the Heath, where it's never too hot."

"I like it there too," Eunice said.

"I'm not sure," Anthony said.

"He's worried about me," said Marta Beatriz. "He thinks I'm too old to go out when it's hot."

"It's too hot for all of us," said Anthony.

"Then we'll all wear a hat and drink lots of water," said Marta Beatriz, steadfast as she leaned against the back of the *Amoeba*. In the flow of her redness, she looked like a cardinal plotting to topple the pope.

And when Anthony had shrugged his shoulders in half-hearted acquiescence, "According to Malcolm, your favourite part of the Heath also happens to be Europe's most famous cruising ground," Eunice said to Marta Beatriz.

"What's a cruising ground?" asked Marta Beatriz.

Eunice rolled her eyes. "It's where gay men go to look for anonymous sex."

"You mean with strangers?" asked Marta Beatriz.

Eunice rolled her eyes again. "In the bushes."

"Surely not in broad daylight," said Marta Beatriz.

"I'm not really an expert," said Eunice. And turning to Anthony, "Does it go on in the daytime as well, or only at night?"

"I've really no idea," Anthony answered sharply.

"Oh my God, you didn't know Malcolm was gay!" Eunice was taunting him, egging him on to come out. Her face had lit up like a flare that had gone up to expose him.

"Of course I knew Malcolm was gay," said Marta Beatriz, as though deliberately cutting in before Anthony could think how to answer. "He's a delightful young man, I like him very much." And then sweetening her voice as she retook her grandson's hands into hers, "Is he your boyfriend?"

When Eunice burst out laughing, Anthony did too. "You, you're out of order," he said, pointing a finger at her. And then turning to Marta Beatriz, "Did you really know, or were you just pretending?"

Marta Beatriz shook her head, as though not understanding his question.

"Pretending that you already knew I was gay," Anthony said.

"Finally!" said Eunice.

Anthony was taking it all in his stride now. "But no, Malcolm's my best friend, not my boyfriend."

"Shame," said Marta Beatriz. "And is there someone else?"

"Not at the moment, no."

"And do you and Malcolm visit these cruising grounds together? Or shouldn't I be asking?"

No, she really shouldn't be, but Anthony had no choice but to answer. Eunice would make mincemeat of the slightest hesitation. "I've been with Malcolm once, to have a look."

"In the *daytime*?" Marta Beatriz seemed more fascinated than appalled.

"At night," Anthony told her.

"And did you *just* have a look?" Eunice asked.

"Hardly even that," Anthony said. "It just wasn't my thing."

"Was it Malcolm's?" asked Marta Beatriz.

"We both stayed on the path for five minutes, and then we left. I think what put Malcolm off was that hardly anyone spoke. 'Too much cloak and dagger,' he said. 'Where's the fun if you can't have a conversation?'"

"So Malcolm likes to talk during sex? Your grandfather, he used to like to whistle while we–"

"No, Grandma, don't!" Eunice used a finger to cover each ear. "Bah, bah, bah," she said, like she used to as a child when she wanted to shut Anthony up.

As though lost in reminiscence, Marta Beatriz gave out a big sigh. "Yes, he was really quite amazing with his tongue, my sweet, sweet Harry!"

"I think Malcolm meant before and after, rather than during," Anthony said. "Now can we please change the subject?"

"Yes, of course," said Marta Beatriz, still holding on to his hand. And as she squeezed it one more time, "But how amazing that such places exist, and just a stone's throw away from where we live!"

"I should've told you earlier, I know," Anthony said. "That I'm gay, I mean, not about the cruising ground. But maybe it's for the best that I didn't tell Daddy."

"It's your father who told me," said Marta Beatriz.

"Don't look at me," Eunice said. "I didn't even know Daddy knew."

"Oh, your father knew everything," said Marta Beatriz. "And he was proud of you both for being yourselves. 'Pablo's taken after you,' he used to say, 'and Guernica after my father. What more could anyone have wished for their children?'"

Spain is here

"Ach, one feels so *small* here, and at the same time so *young*!" Without straying from the well-trodden path, where brief, unobtrusive encounters led to hidden assignations in the bushes, Marta Beatriz had Anthony and Eunice by the hand, punctuating eager strides with exclamations. "These trees!" And now three pairs of eyes and four entangled hands were pointed at the sky. "So tall and so *ancient*, their movement so graceful, the music of their susurrus so utterly majestic!"

Anthony let out a whoop of delight.

"You're making fun of me," said Marta Beatriz, her voice suddenly musical, almost singing the words.

"As if I'd ever do that," Anthony sang back in his baritone voice.

"Laugh all you like," answered Marta Beatriz.

Two middle-aged men walking in front of them turned around to give them a cursory glance before veering off the path, heading for a cluster of seemingly impassable green.

"There they go," Eunice said, as they nimbly disappeared into the thicket. "Gay men are so *brazen*!" Was her intonation one of envy or of reproach? Anthony decided it was one of admiration.

"Just look at them!" With a sharp tug, Marta Beatriz had brought them to a halt, and was gazing not towards the invisible men but skywards again at the trees, her face a variegated composition of shadow and sunlight – a strong, solid, three-dimensional face very much worthy of Picasso, Anthony thought. "One can't fail but feel a part of something bigger," his grandmother went on, filling him and the air with her awe.

Anthony thought of the two men vanishing among the trees his grandmother had marvelled at so evocatively, and he imagined them convulsed by the same contortions of pleasure and pain he had seen in the faces of men having sex, sometimes mingled with the unnecessary shame of being different. And as the vastness of creation that Marta Beatriz had evoked was transformed into a mirror that he held in his hand, he saw in his reflection the face of a man having sex with a man without feeling shame. The sight confronted him for barely an instant before it disappeared, and with it the mirror in his hand that was once again the vastness that contained him.

"I'm not surprised that men come here for sex," said Marta Beatriz. "Just breathing in the air must fill them with absolute freedom. And at night... under the stars, while the leaves rustle gently..."

They were walking again, still hand in hand with Marta Beatriz in the middle dictating their pace, so much more leisurely now.

"When Daddy took us to Madrid to see *Guernica*, you didn't come with us," Eunice said.

"No," said Marta Beatriz.

"It was probably the happiest day of his life," Eunice said.

"And he had both of you with him."

"But don't you ever miss Spain?" On the other side of Marta Beatriz, Eunice was hidden from view, but from the tension in her voice it had not been difficult for Anthony to imagine her face – strident, but only reluctantly hard - as she countered her grandmother's awe by trying to bring them back to a world in which they should all still be mourning her father.

"Spain is here with me, in Europe's most famous cruising ground," answered Marta Beatriz with a voice that remained unrepentantly cheerful. "And *here*, where my Harry and your father are, too," she went on, bringing four hands together to press against her breast. "It may sound like a cliché but it's true."

When Eunice gave an almost inaudible gasp, the air remained fresh.

SIX

New Brighton

Contrary to his demeanour, Malcolm's history was bleak, and Anthony would listen to it with the feeling that Malcolm as a little boy would have told it very differently, if able while still living it to tell it at all. The only child of Catholic parents who had lapsed into miserable lives of abuse and alcoholism perpetuated by the ritual of weekly confession and cheap absolution, he had grown up faithless and poor in New Brighton, a deprived Merseyside town with ideas above its station thwarted by Northern industrial decline. Defying the defeatist expectations of an unambitious school accustomed to failing its students, after more than fulfilling the terms of his conditional offer from UCL, on his last day at home he had worn a borrowed kilt and ridiculous make-up and had swingingly come out to his parents. Purely as an act of revenge, and mooning them as a finale, he had left them thunderstruck in the ruins of their lives in New Brighton.

For three years he had lived within the means of his maintenance grant, had graduated with a First, and eschewing many lucrative offers from the City he had literally romped through the exams for the civil service, and revelled in the free time afforded by a job he could do with his eyes shut.

He spent almost all his money on books and going out. But he had not chosen his room only because it was cheap, or because it was so close to *The Bell*. He had chosen it because the barefaced display of its seediness made Kings Cross authentic, its air full of the menace of real life. And it was real life; Anthony himself could have attested to that, even as he witnessed with distant unease, unable to share it, Malcolm's effortless familiarity with the troubled men and women they frequently encountered in the street, almost all of them reciprocating with a down-to-earth humanity that anyone but Malcolm would have thought beyond their means.

"That could have been me," Malcolm would say gravely, after sharing a few words with a man down on his luck, or buying a working girl a cup of tea.

Without words, Anthony would put his arm around his friend and pull his slender body close to his, a spontaneous act of friendship that served also as an admission of coming up short. This alien world was too overwhelming for him; if he allowed in all its secrets, he knew they would choke him.

"You're such a big girl's blouse," Malcolm would tease him. "Hey, lighten up, at least you're not pretending to be something you're not." And for a few precious moments, all his warmth would be Anthony's alone.

This quality of Malcolm's was innate, as innate as Anthony's capacity to sense and separate the many-layered essences that constituted life. Whereas his own 'gift' he increasingly was coming to regard as a curse, Malcolm's was as though tailor-made, bound to serve him well: the young man from New Brighton *knew* he would be a writer one day, published and acclaimed, and judging from the few scraps he had read out to Anthony, Malcolm's confidence seemed hardly misplaced. The economy of his writing served as cover for a quality of sheer originality. Its audacity jumped out at you, from *behind* the lines of practically every sentence. Each scene read like a cleverly laid ambush, a salvo of fresh surprises that never felt contrived: the bizarre, the surreal, what in Malcolm's hands became the quintessentially *queer*, once the sense of violent shock had been absorbed, would in retrospect appear entirely natural.

It was visceral writing. Anthony's impression was of a wolf in sheep's clothing going on the rampage, ravaging the senses.

"A wolf in sheep's clothing... Yes, I think I'll take that."

"It won't be to everyone's taste, some people might not like being led astray. Most people, probably."

Malcolm shrugged his shoulders.

"I'm just trying to find out who I am," he said. And while pressing on his temple with two fingers as though he were holding a gun to his head, "What goes on in there when I'm *not* in control of my thoughts, when I'm dreaming or imagining or thinking with my cock, all of which I'm doing rather a lot of. But you, you're different, it's like you're always *too much* in control."

It smells of sex in here

At a few minutes before seven o'clock, Anthony had plopped himself down on the sofa in Malcolm's room, which after lounging in the *Amoeba* for part of the afternoon felt like the equivalent of being subjected to an English café's cup of coffee after one of the Italian's cappuccinos.

"Marta Beatriz fell in love with the *Amoeba* the minute she saw it, and when she sat in it she went into raptures, she was literally screaming."

"Uh-huh," Malcolm said, slowly moving his chin up and down.

"Then I told her I was gay, which she said she already knew."

"Uh-huh."

"Have you heard a word I said?"

"Uh-huh," Malcolm said, slowly turning his head from side to side. His attachment to the bare piece of mirror which Anthony had helped him carry over from the street one late night after *The Bell*, up two flights of stairs to his room in the small terraced house divided into bedsits, signified not vanity, as one might have imagined, but rather a degree of affectation, which in Anthony's opinion he had cultivated as a means of playing his part with greater conviction. It was unclear what that part was, as unclear to Malcolm, Anthony suspected, as it was to Anthony and everyone else. Malcolm was an open book, but a complex one, with pages that seemed non-sequential, their disorderly narrative a composite of blatant discrepancies that fitted together exactly on a plane that fell beyond interpretation.

The mirror was a prop. Thin and pale, with oddly recalcitrant features that somehow came together inextricably, Malcolm could not have been more comfortable in his skin. Anthony was certain getting ready to go out was a ritual they indulged in as a substitute for actually caring about how they looked. The two of them might as well have been twins. In summer they always wore jeans and a T-shirt, white socks and canvas shoes. In winter they wore jeans and Doc Marten's boots, and a T-shirt with a jumper on top. Malcolm never arrived at *The Bell* with a coat, saving the cost of the coat-check, whereas even in warm weather Anthony would never leave home without a jacket, more than happy to part with a pound for the sake of an excuse for a chat with the boy who always took his money with a smile.

"Not bad, huh?" Malcolm said, taking one step back and standing still, as though surrendering to Anthony the final word. A customary scene was being re-enacted, whose very needlessness gave revived expression to an intimacy otherwise unspoken. And how could Anthony have answered? Smiling wanly as he faced him from across a shiny surface, Malcolm represented not an object of desire but something altogether more precious. In his oversized T-shirt, he looked thinner than he usually did, breakable almost, but the buzz of energy that constantly ran through him gave him an invincible veneer.

"You should eat more," Anthony said. "And you should stay out of the sun."

"I like this look," said Malcolm. The reflection of his eyes, wells of almost orange luminescence deeply set into the paleness of an angular face, had broken into a spirited dance, momentarily abandoning the surface of his image to search for his friend's.

Absently Anthony gave him a nod. "Are you sure you're okay? We don't have to go out if you're still feeling unwell."

"Honestly, I've never felt better."

"Did you manage to rest?"

Malcolm nodded vaguely. "I rested while I wrote."

Taking air in, Anthony winced as he let out a sigh, letting go of one unsettling impression only to be filled with another.

"It smells of sex in here," he said.

"You *always* say that," said Malcolm, narrowing his eyes as he patted down his eyebrows in one final sizing up.

"Because it's true."

Malcolm turned around to face him, beaming with amused irritation.

"How can it be true when I've *never* had sex in this room, like I've told you a hundred times."

Anthony already knew that, because what he could smell was an old smell, of sex that had had to be endured and had not been enjoyed. It had taken possession of the room like a ghost, and he felt it like a dull twinge of sadness every time he breathed in too deeply the air in Malcolm's room. He had wished a hundred times that Malcolm might be able to dispel it, and had known a hundred times that nothing Malcolm said ever would, which a hundred times had failed to stop him from indulging in the same conversation again. If Malcolm ever moved, Anthony was terrified the sadness would go with him, as though Malcolm had by now become its host.

"So how come you decided to come out to your grandmother today?"

"Oh," Anthony said.

"I'm *always* listening," said Malcolm.

"Eunice was goading me," Anthony said. "But apparently I'd been outed by my father already."

"Oh," Malcolm said.

"And he actually told Grandma he was proud of me. He was also proud of Eunice, of course."

"And so he should have been," said Malcolm.

Invisible Man

"Tweet, tweet, guess what a little bird told me."

Malcolm dwelled on nothing for too long; it was one of his traits that Anthony liked most. Life was a succession of moments, every one of them cherished but impatient.

"About what?"

"About last night."

"Last night?"

"Last night, the night before... Every night you break another heart."

"I hardly think so," Anthony said.

Malcolm rolled his eyes.

"You *are* aware how *hot* you are, aren't you? All men are created equal, what a load of bollocks!"

"Now you're talking nonsense."

"Oh, really? Those eyes *alone* are to die for, and my God, that *body*! Young Adonis, eat your heart out."

"Please, Malcolm, stop!"

"And as if total gorgeousness wasn't enough, I'm told you've also got the perfect cock – in length, girth, shape, I've heard it even *tastes* divine, and *everyone* who's had a peek of it is telling everyone who hasn't. You know what that means, of course, don't you? No, not that I'm dying to give you a blowjob... What it means is you're a nightmare to go out with."

"I'm not going out with anyone."

"And therein lies the rub: being single makes *all* the boys imagine you're available, and that every night might be the night when they might be the one. So there I am, standing next to you on the dance floor, wildly shaking to the DJ's doom and gloom and feeling like the Invisible Man, all eyes on Your Majesty giving you the come-on, and all that's *ever* left for me are the crumbs of your cast-offs. Then lo and behold, last night I hear you've copped off, and stupidly I think, hallelujah, he's met someone *nice*, and finally the rest of us might get a look-in. But same old, same old, by morning you've already come and gone. So tonight, I'm again the resistible pauper escorting the irresistible prince to the ball, and ending up in bed with another of his frogs. And I know I'm being a slut while I'm looking for love, but at least I have the decency to make myself wake up with the frog I went to bed with. Unlike you, I *never* do a runner after sex. If I'm invited to stay, I stay and that's that. It's the proper thing to do, and in case you didn't know, by all accounts poor Barry was really quite upset."

"Sorry, you've lost me. Poor Barry who?"

"My God, you're so *evil*, perfect bloody cock or not. Poor Barry that you *didn't* wake up next to this morning, remember?"

"And he minded?"

"Now you sound surprised, like you don't even *realise* you're evil. Of course he bloody minded, he invited you to stay and you said no!"

"Does that make him nice?"

"I'm *telling* you he's nice. Which you might've found out for yourself if you'd let him cook you one of his specials for breakfast."

"So you had this 'poor Barry' before he was one of my 'cast-offs'."

"It was a long time ago, and you're missing the point."

"You're right. I wish I were like you but I'm not. I'm cold, I like to keep my distance, and I'm grateful to be blessed with a cock that *doesn't* have a mind of its own – a *stupid* cock, happy to do as it's told. All this time I've been going through the motions; that's probably the point I've been missing. So I've made a decision. I don't *want* to be a slut and I'm giving up sex."

Malcolm rolled his eyes again.

"Ooh, *drama*, keep your hands off Mr Precious, he's just *not* that kind of boy!"

"I'm being serious."

"Well, I suppose we'll soon find out. But no, my dearest Anthony, you're neither cold nor distant, and I'm sure that your delicious perfect cock isn't stupid at all, I bet you it has a *very* high IQ. Now come on, let's get going or we'll miss all the fun."

"And if I *had* stayed for breakfast with Barry, I'd have definitely been too full to have breakfast in Camden with you."

"And if your grandmother had balls, she'd be your grandfather," said Malcolm.

"Ach, and if she had balls coming out of her ears, she'd be you."

SEVEN

Movements

Sunday at *The Bell* was *Movements*, their favourite night of the weekend, even though it ended earlier, at midnight. Malcolm took the road almost in leaps, but the spring in his step had a thrust that seemed more practical than eager, as if not hurrying *to* but *away from*. In spite of longer legs, Anthony was struggling to keep up.

It was a melancholy evening, with the sun brightly brushing the dirty shop windows with the orange aftertaste of daylight. Above them other windows were open, hoping to let air in that didn't exist. As though the heat had broken into folds, the few cars on the road seemed to jerk their way forward like flies. *The Bell* might not be cool, but at least it would be dark, and everyone would move to the music.

At the end of Cromer Street, they had turned left onto Gray's Inn Road, crossed over to the other side, and were walking past the *Scala* when Malcolm leaned over to draw in his breath as he whispered in Anthony's ear:

"You really are *not* cold and distant."

Anthony stopped dead in his tracks, as though a heavy finger were pressing at his chest and another at his back, holding him immobile in mid-stride.

Malcolm did a double take and swung around to face him.

"Something's wrong again, you're wheezing," Anthony said.

"What's wrong is that it's Monday tomorrow, and it's almost nine o'clock."

"Malcolm, your breathing's not right, I mean look at you, your chest's racing up and down and you're panting."

"Maybe I'm just unfit. But no, I *shouldn't* be, not with all the acrobatic wild sex I've been having. No wonder I'm feeling exhausted."

"You're feeling exhausted?"

"My God, what's *wrong* with you tonight? You're driving me up the wall!"

"What's wrong with me tonight is that after what happened this morning in Camden, I can't help feeling worried."

"This morning in Camden we bought an *Amoeba*."

"This morning in Camden you nearly collapsed, and everyone thought it was *my* fault."

Malcolm nodded, and when he spoke again, he spoke slowly, with a gentle, unaffected smile and his natural voice.

"Anthony, my love, I promise you I'm fine."

"Are you sure?"

"Yes, I'm sure, cross my heart and hope to die. See? I'm not even wheezing any more."

He wasn't, and Anthony felt reassured. He arrived at *The Bell* feeling free – from worry and the obligation to have sex.

That was how that night had begun. How it would end was something else. And nearly fifty years later, it would fall to a postman to bring it all back.

Joe

Anthony was paying for a pint of Guinness at the bar, only vaguely aware of the body that had brashly burrowed through to squeeze in right beside him.

"Joel. But you can call me Joe."

The voice was firm and deep, its timbre self-contained in an almost three-dimensional way.

In an almost three-dimensional way...

"Joel. But you can call me Joe."

As the echo of the words resonated through the hollow in his chest, from the intensity of the heat that was burning his face, Anthony knew he was blushing. In the reddish dimness of the line of shaded light bulbs that lit up the edge of the bar, *I must look like the devil*, he thought, and he answered without turning his head:

"Anthony. But you can't call me Tony."

"Rubens, right?"

Who *was* this impertinent stranger, who had just pronounced his surname in prolonged ringing tones as though he had been rolling it around in his mouth for some time? Unable to contain his curiosity any longer...

A god!

"Change," the barman had been calling from behind the narrow counter at the bar.

A god who knows my name!

"I'll have one too if you don't mind," God said to the devil.

"So? Another pint of Guinness?" the barman asked impatiently.

"Yes. Yes, please." *Another pint of Guinness for God*, Anthony had stopped himself from saying, and his hand was already in his pocket looking for the extra money he would need for another pint of Guinness *for God*, but the coins seemed to be slipping through his fingers. The whole length of Joe's arm, bare from the shoulder, was rubbing up and down against his, so gently and systematically that it was rolling up the sleeve of his T-shirt, wet and malleable like clay with the melding of two people's sweat.

"Another pint of Guinness," said the barman, causing some of it to spill as he slammed down God's drink with an irreverent gesture. "Anything else?"

"Top it up!" God instructed three-dimensionally, clutching at the devil's hand before it could let go of its coins.

Sheepishly, wordlessly, the barman obeyed the word of God.

Enough of that now, he's just a cute guy and that's all. Around the same age as Malcolm and him – twenty-four, maybe twenty-five - with arms carved of stone, cropped hair like a skinhead's and a pencil moustache, eyes that brimmed like an eagle's and lips shaped like petals at the heart of a man-eating orchid, the cute guy was a *very* cute guy.

"We both like black, that's not a bad start," said the very cute guy, holding firmly on to Anthony's hand after leading him across flashing bodies to a corner off the far end of the dance floor.

"Black?"

"Guinness."

"Ah, the black stuff."

"What did you think I meant?"

"Black guys?"

"You like black guys?"

"I didn't say that."

"So you *don't* like black guys?"

"I didn't say that either," Anthony said. And then, with a shrug, "I like guys I like."

Joe gave a slow backward nod, as though Anthony's multiple answer had not entirely pleased him.

"You like *this* guy," he said.

Was it a question? It sounded more like a command, which even as it mildly riled him made Anthony hard.

"How did you know my name?" he asked meekly, grateful for the dark.

"Oh, *everyone* knows it."

"I don't think so," Anthony said.

Forbiddingly, Joe raised the tightened palm of one hand. A passing light painted it blue.

"But that's all in the past now, right? No more black guys, or liking guys you like." The wild look in his eye was irresistible.

"*Love, love will tear us apart, again...*"

Already dizzied by a jumble of emotions, his hardness even harder than before, *painfully* hard, Anthony was also being distracted by Malcolm. Over Joe's left shoulder, as the entirety of their bodies pressed against each other and he felt the warmth of Joe's join the tingle in his as though in a shiver, through the blur of seduction that had numbed all his senses he stared at the gesticulating figure of his friend, whose apparently satirical attempts at sign language seemed to also signify the movements of a war dance.

A whirl of blinking lights slowed everything down. The haze of cigarette smoke made the stillness atmospheric.

"*Love, love will tear us apart, again...*"

And now Malcolm had spread out his arms as though in a desperate plea whose meaning could not be deciphered – even as he kept his eyes fixed in Anthony's direction, his face had no expression.

"*Love, love will tear us apart, again...*"

All the lights were suddenly out, and for a matter of seconds the dance floor was a swell of seething shadow, a mass of Joy Division adulation. They came back on in fitful waves, more frantic than before, thin rays of whiteness and ribbons of colour that made Malcolm's crucifixion psychedelic.

As Anthony's chest rose and fell to the rhythm of Joe's unsteady breathing, the quiver of a cool drift of sweetness made him blink. When he opened his eyes, Malcolm was gone, and he shut them again as the sweetness made its way into his mouth. In his bodily commotion, the thrill of that sweetness was the only taste of Joe he was able at that moment to make out.

"*Run away, turn away, run away, turn away, run away...*"

Jimmy Somerville had filled Malcolm's absence on the dance floor, and was eyeing up the area all around him to the beat of his own voice.

If only the night wouldn't end; then Anthony would not have to confront its dilemmas. In the mayhem of its bliss, by leaving its seconds uncounted he may have lost the measure of their passage, but no amount of make-believe or wishful pretence could have caused them to be lost in a time warp. Midnight had arrived in a bright fluorescent flash, yielding to the babel of a crowd abruptly at a loss in the absence of music.

From the perch of a stool that someone had dragged over from the bar, crisp and cool even in his wetness, Joe laughed loudly as he observed at close quarters the spectacle of Anthony's frenetic rearrangements – of an upright stiffness too clearly defined as it pressed against the inside of his jeans, of the creases in his T-shirt pasted together by sweat, of whatever had remained of his quiff.

Of whatever had remained of his pride.

"I have a jacket in the coat-check," Anthony said.

"I'll wait for you outside."

Anthony gave him a nod, uncertain of what he was agreeing to.

Maybe more than best mates

"Malcolm said to say good night," the smiling boy told him, while riffling through the hangers for the ticket with his number. "He didn't want to bother you, he said."

"Bother me?"

"Silly bugger forgot his inhaler."

"His inhaler?"

"For his asthma. Had a bit of a wheezing attack earlier on. Just a dizzy spell, really. Didn't last more than five minutes. Looked scarier than it was, I'm sure. Probably brought on by all the smoke, it was *choking* tonight. So the landlord had him drink a pint of water, and then a couple of the lads took him outside for a breather. Felt much better straight away after that. Good night's rest was all he needed, he said, and he'll see you at work tomorrow."

"Did someone go with him?"

"Couldn't really say for sure, but I don't think so," said the boy. "Here we are, number forty-three, down on your knees, and I should be so lucky!" And handing Anthony his jacket, "Hey, I know you two are best mates, maybe *more* than best mates, and I'm telling you don't worry, I'm sure he'll be just fine."

The night outside was hot and oppressively heavy with moisture, hardly the place for a breather. No sooner had Anthony stepped into it than its hours broke up into fragments, overcrowding him with images of Malcolm — exhausted in Camden, full of mischievous words in his room, holding back his wheezing in the street, silent as he stretched out his arms on the dance floor. But there, when a cold drift of sweetness had caused him to blink, Anthony's memory ended, and as one after another the images he hadn't witnessed rapidly began to take form, he felt choked by the weight of his absence.

A posse of boys in black broke their semi-circle.

"You took your time," said Joe, striding through them to stand in his way.

"Something's happened," Anthony said matter-of-factly.

Joe threw a side-glance at the lingering posse. "I know *all* about Malcolm," he said, the timbre of his voice three-dimensionally smug. "So he saw you getting off with someone else and faked a fainting fit to get your attention, what's the big deal? You're looking at me strangely... Oh dear, oh dear, oh dear, please don't tell me you're the last one to know!"

"To know what?"

"To know that Malcolm's completely besotted with you."

"Maybe *more* than best mates," the smiling boy in the coat-check had said.

"Don't look so glum, he'll get over it sooner or later. I mean he'll have to now, won't he?"

"I hope you're right," Anthony said.

"Course I am," said Joe. "Now come on, let's get you back to mine for some *proper* cheering up. We'll catch a cab in Euston Road."

"No," Anthony said.

"No?"

"No."

"Meaning what, exactly?"

"I hope you're right about Malcolm. That he was faking feeling sick to get my attention."

"Course he was, I told you."

"And that he did it because he's besotted with me."

"Which should've been as obvious to you as to everyone else."

"I hope you're right, because you've just made me realise that I'm also besotted."

"Course you are," said Joe. "Erections speak louder than words, as they say, eh, Mr Horny?"

"I meant with Malcolm."

"You're kidding me, right?"

"I've never been more serious in my life," Anthony said.

The posse of boys in black united in another semi-circle to make scandalised noises.

"Let me get this right," said Joe, his face shrivelled into an ugliness spitting with fire. "You're about to blow me off because suddenly you've realised you want Malcolm instead?"

"That's only one of the reasons," Anthony said. He spoke loudly, so that the posse of boys in black could hear.

As though at the snap of invisible fingers, Joe took back control of his face. One by one all the furrows were gone, and the squashed-up pucker of his brows was stretched out by the breadth of a smile that made Anthony squirm.

Joe's pencil moustache, so animate around angry words, now rippled only gently, like a hazy horizon. "Joe Devin," he said. "Remember the name." And with that he walked away, quickly followed by the posse of boys in black. Soon the air was filled with the roar of their laughter, first Joe's and then his fawning entourage's.

EIGHT

Emotional recluses

Pacing back and forth, and making his carpets more threadbare, as he read and then reread the 'Explanatory Notes' that had arrived with his summons, Mr Rubens couldn't help but feel his excitement steadily give way, first to confusion, and then to a growing apprehension. Repeated deep breaths detected nothing in the air of the empty envelope, and no meaningful odour in the papers themselves, but Mr Rubens, rather than allowing this absence to allay vague suspicions, on the contrary regarded it almost as definitive proof that a deliberate attempt had been made to deceive him – to put him off the scent, so to speak.

But how would anyone have known either that they needed to *or* how to do that? First the postman was a robot, now this: one absurdity leading to another, as so often absurdities did. The mere coincidence of an unfortunate resemblance was causing Mr Rubens to indulge himself with wild extrapolations. The idea that the ruthless machinery of the State would have gone to the trouble of devising an elaborate plan that by dint of some mysterious and convoluted bureaucratic ruse was directed personally against him, was the biggest, most ridiculous absurdity of all. Really, he was being too egocentric.

All the same, the so-called 'Explanatory Notes' had failed to answer *any* of his questions. He had been 'selected', but on what grounds? How *did* the Ministry make its selection? There was nowhere a mention of selection criteria, of the process – some kind of process must surely exist – by which people were chosen to serve.

When Museum Service was first introduced, had it not been presented as part of the Government Party's plan to update and democratise the country's discredited system of honours? Might it not be the case, then, that someone had nominated him – an old colleague, perhaps, from the Department where he had worked as a diligent servant for more than four decades, until it was finally abolished and he opted for early retirement; or someone who believed that his consummate passion for interior design deserved recognition? But if that had been the case, would it not have been explicitly mentioned? Perhaps the selection was made on the basis of details collated in the annual census. Or perhaps it was totally random. Then what on earth was the point of the People's Museums?

"Just another bloody gimmick," Eunice had called them. "Fifteen minutes of fame for the masses."

Mr Rubens remembered that clear September day in 2026 as though it were yesterday. In a domino effect, the recollection of Eunice's words had brought its moments back one by one in a faithful photographic reconstruction.

The loss of a man – a different man - had made both of them emotional recluses, but they had not shut out each other with the rest of the world. Their incessant quarrels had never come between them, and it helped lighten their grief that without dwelling on it they were able to share it with someone they loved. In a ritual of remembrance, the names of the two men were often brought up, though rarely in the same conversation, their memory being kept alive in a way that rebuffed any need to move on. Neither Mr Rubens nor his sister ever questioned one another's self-denial, knowing from their own experience how thick and hard the shell they had wrapped around themselves had become, thicker and harder with every year that passed, not a burden they regretted but an easier way of life, negating any future obligation to forget.

I knew my sister inside out, and she knew me, thought Mr Rubens. *We always understood each other's feelings, even when they hadn't been expressed.*

Losing Eunice had been a devastating blow. Suddenly not only could remembering no longer be shared, but the single-minded effort it required had doubled. And it occurred to Mr Rubens just now how, even before it had doubled, the pressure of this effort had decimated other memories and kept them cast aside in the shadows. But the postman, and the contents of the envelope he had delivered, had set in motion trains of thought that were converging as though purposely to shine a torch into these hideouts of the past, and resurrect forgotten ghosts.

Frippery and fluff

Mr Rubens had been dozing in the *Amoeba*.

"Pablo?"

The loud crack of Eunice's voice made him jump. "You'll give me a heart attack one of these days."

"Your doorbell isn't working, so I let myself in."

"Yes, I can see." Mr Rubens stretched out without getting up.

"I've brought cake," Eunice said.

"Mmm, carrot?"

"Banana."

"It's not quite teatime yet," said Mr Rubens after looking at his watch.

"Really, Pablo!"

"What?"

"You've become a prisoner of habit; you don't dare *fart* without checking with your watch first."

Mr Rubens lifted the side of his bottom and let out a protracted, hiccupping fart. "There," he said. "Happy now?"

"Oof, what *have* you had for lunch, rotten eggs? I'll put the cake in the kitchen then, shall I? Since apparently it would kill you if you had a slice now."

"Yes, dear, you do that."

They both simultaneously sighed, like they often did, ever since they were children.

"One day I'm coming over to fit a new doorbell for you," Eunice said, as she strode back from the kitchen empty-handed, surveying the space around and above her, turning as she poked a finger first in this direction, then in that. "With buzzers in the hallway… in here, behind the sideboard… and also in the kitchen… one upstairs on the landing… and another in your bedroom, of course."

"Of course," said Mr Rubens. "Now sit down, please, you're making me nervous."

Eunice kicked her shoes off and sat over her legs on the leather two-seater. "I'm *knackered*," she said. "I had a nightmare of a plumbing job south of the river this morning, trying to rescue a parrot called Elvis who'd got himself trapped in the drains. And I did, I got him out alive and in one piece, eventually. Poor thing looked like poo, and smelled like it, too, but he seemed ever so cheerful, squeaking '*love me tender, love me tender, love me tender,*' non-stop."

"I'd have throttled him," said Mr Rubens.

"And on the way back, I had to drive past the old IMMA. It's so depressing; the place looks like a prison now. I mean, honestly, Pablo! Just when you imagine these thugs can no longer surprise you, they come up with a ridiculous idea like the People's Museums."

"A ridiculous idea that people voted for," said Mr Rubens.

"Because people like gimmicks. And that's exactly what this is, just another bloody gimmick. Fifteen minutes of fame for the masses. Museum Service, my arse!"

"You're a snob and a cynic. Why shouldn't the State celebrate its citizens?"

"Oh, Pablo, is that really what you think this is about? First they stole our country, then they stole our art to pay for their crimes, and now they're filling up the empty museums with gullible people who've been flattered into thinking it's an honour. They're just trying to distract people's memories with frippery and fluff."

"I thought it was our consciences they wanted to distract."

"The best way to ease a conscience is to make it forget. They're murderers, Pablo, and we *mustn't* forget."

"I know they've done some terrible things in the past, but does it automatically follow that everything they're doing now must also be bad?"

"Yes, Pablo, it does, because they *are* bad, and everything they do is propaganda. Would you say that so flippantly about Hitler - that he did 'some bad things', but that not everything he did was necessarily bad? *Of course* it was bad. Evil always acts indivisibly. This is hardly Nazi Germany, you'll say. Well, it's hardly Nazi Germany *for you* – you're still here and in one piece."

"Like the parrot you rescued this morning."

"You're still here and in one piece but hundreds of thousands are not, and that's shamefully the reason why these hoodlums are so popular still, after two years that have felt like forever. By feeding and then pandering to prejudice, they've managed to perform a collective lobotomy, which means we're living in a nightmare worse than *1984*, a hideous world where people don't *need* to be watched by Big Brother."

"People were exhausted, first by the virus and then by the bombs. Can you blame them for wanting some peace?"

"Peace at any price is no peace at all."

"It is for the people who are able to enjoy it," said Mr Rubens. "And you can't say that science is evil. How many breakthroughs have there been since the Government Party came to power?"

"It was scientists who made them, not the Government Party."

"Biodegradable plastics made out of weeds, clean biofuel–"

"They've cleaned up the air and instead they've polluted our minds. Personally, I wouldn't call that progress."

"Vaccines for the virus and all its mutations, *and* for HIV–"

"Yippee, ruled by criminals we're living in a world of healthier zombies! People aren't entirely stupid, my arse!"

Eeny, Meeny, Miny, Mo

Even though it was not yet time for tea, Mr Rubens got up from the *Amoeba* to make it, and with his customary aplomb served it with slices of Eunice's cake. Already he was cutting down on sugar, but could never find the willpower to resist his sister's baking, and in any case was glad of the opportunity to bring out the Meissen gorilla: Eunice might think of it as hoity-toity, but today they would have tea with the monkeys. They were familiar creatures even to her, and collectively had fascinated Malcolm; a Rubens family heirloom confined to a dusty arrangement on the shelves of an old dresser, they had moved from Belsize Park with Mr Rubens to the relative freedom of Highgate.

The sitting room was still bright with sunshine, oblong shapes of it that fell across the floor before dispersing. There was a pleasant draught of air from two open windows, and Mr Rubens' old TV shimmered on its stand at one corner of the triangle it formed with the *Amoeba* and the unsung Bauhaus glory of the leather two-seater. In the prevalent barbarianism of the times, Mr Rubens felt like an anachronism in a mausoleum, idly waiting to be swept under a threadbare Persian carpet.

Some things hadn't changed. Looking at his sister was *too much* like looking at himself, as it had been throughout their lives. Their features had shared a striking handsomeness in youth, and had aged not dissimilarly in old age. Eunice's good looks had always been manly, as had her agile and snake-hipped physique. She was slightly scrawnier than him now, and her face more shrunken, in a not so cruel foretelling of his own deterioration. Their hair short and thick and similarly fashioned, its black unevenly peppered with white and naturally curling upwards in the front, they resembled an old and an older Samuel Beckett, whose deeply chiselled face had seemed somehow to repudiate age. Mr Rubens had always found it fiercely imposing, in a way that was the opposite of statuesque.

The only thing my sister never had and I did was a perfect cock, thought Mr Rubens. Impulsively he looked down at his crotch, where the erstwhile perfect cock used to make quite a bulge. He sighed again, this time alone. *Oh well, my leaking, sagging, invisible friend, I never made much use of you even when everyone said you were pretty.* He gave a muted chuckle, amused that as a consequence of shrinkage he and his sister were more similar than ever before.

"The place is spick and span," Eunice said, settling in the leather two-seater after washing down a sliver of banana cake with a second cup of tea – taken with no sugar and just a dash of milk. Thankfully, she hadn't made an issue of the monkeys.

"It's Wednesday," said Mr Rubens, happy to avert his gaze from the absence of a bulge.

"Gloria," said Eunice.

Mr Rubens nodded. "She's really quite thorough," he said.

Gloria was another anachronism – a Brazilian who had overstayed her visa long before the mass expulsions, but had been allowed to stay after marrying an elderly stalwart of the Government Party who had since divorced her, rendering her paperless again. While waiting in detention at Heathrow, almost ready to be bundled into a plane bound for Rio, she had been allowed to take the pregnancy test that she always used to carry in her handbag. For some reason Mr Rubens had never quite been able to fathom, the positive result had won her a reprieve even though a child had never materialised. "I think is better we say nothing, Mr Rubens. I just tell you I rather die than go back to Brazil."

"I'm sure she's a spy," Eunice said. "And she wants you *to know* she's a spy. Why else would she have volunteered such a cock and bull story?"

"Wuthering prose," said Mr Rubens.

"I'd hardly call it that."

"Remember Samuel Beckett?"

"Ah, *Happy Days*," Eunice said.

"*Waiting for Godot*," said Mr Rubens, even though his favourite had always been *Molloy*.

"She's not really a spy," Eunice said. "She's actually quite a remarkable woman. And every word of her story is true."

"You've changed your tune," said Mr Rubens.

"Think about it, Pablo. We've known her now for over ten years, since *long* before the country went mad."

"It's not me who decided she was probably a spy."

But something had diverted Eunice's attention to the shimmer of the silent TV.

"What is it? You look like you've seen a ghost, you're as white as a sheet."

"I've seen *an evil cunt*, is what I've seen!"

"Eunice, really!"

"Turn the volume up," Eunice commanded. "Now!"

"I don't have the remote. Gloria must've tidied it up."

"Oh, for God's sake, how is hiding something tidying it up?"

"She may be a remarkable woman, but she can never remember where anything goes."

While Mr Rubens wandered aimlessly around the room, Eunice shot out of the Bauhaus two-seater and kneeled down on the floor right in front of the TV. Among its shifting pixels, a group of white men made grotesque faces, rapt in soundless applause.

"I found it," said Mr Rubens, and suddenly the applause was no longer soundless.

"And there's the evil cunt *again*."

"**We are all servants of the people!**" exclaimed the New Leader, tall behind a lectern like a latter-day Messiah, his voice rebounding off the walls of Mr Rubens' sitting room like a sonic boom, quickly followed by the thunder of a standing ovation.

"Servants of the people, my arse!" Eunice howled at the TV.

Cutting back to the auditorium, while the New Leader kept an ominous silence the camera zoomed in to survey in painful close-up all the goggle eyes and Cheshire cat grins who had risen to their feet in the front row, as though scanning every one of them in turn for signs of ideological pollution.

September was 'conference season'. Since all other parties had ceased to exist, it was the time of year when the Government Party's apparatchiks gathered for a week in a British seaside town to enumerate and then congratulate themselves for the Government Party's most recent achievements. The last day, however, was devoted to 'blood sports': an orchestrated cataloguing of the areas in which Ministries had fallen short took up all the hours of the morning, and was followed by the interminable terror of the New Leader's speech in the afternoon, in which admonishing strictures, conditional reprieves and even deadly denunciations were dispensed, while body-builder henchmen waited eagerly in the wings. The Government Party always proudly conducted its purges in public, in the naked glare of television lights.

The Great Yarmouth Hall of the People was hushed. Taking on a grave expression, the New Leader slowly moved his head from left to right. He lifted an arm, extended a finger, and with short violent jerks pointed it along the line of Cheshire cats. *Eeny, Meeny, Miny, Mo,* Mr Rubens couldn't help thinking, when with one final thrust the pointing finger stopped.

"And another one bites the dust," Eunice sang melodiously.

"**Minister Devin!**"

And now the camera was face to face with the lean, steady figure of a distinguished-looking man who sported a pencil moustache.

Mr Rubens gasped. "Jesus Christ, that's Joe," he said, leaning so far forward in the *Amoeba* that he almost toppled over.

"You *know* this man?"

"To betray the people is a capital offence!"

"Fuck you, George!" Joe Devin yelled at the New Leader, dissolving his raised fist to give him the finger in a condemned man's last act of defiance.

"Take him away!"

The Hall was again on its feet, bursting out in yet more tumultuous applause, and no more words or gestures by Minister Devin were either heard or seen.

"Never must we equivocate–"

Mr Rubens pointed the remote at the TV and switched it off. "Jesus Christ," he said again.

"Don't you ever watch the news? That's the Minister of Information," said Eunice. "Or rather *was*," she corrected herself. "How on earth did you know him?"

Proust

Someone should warn the young postman that his pencil moustache risked causing a dangerous misunderstanding. If someone were so minded, they might read into it an act of seditious provocation, and implicit support for the man who had told the New Leader to fuck off. But that was not Mr Rubens' concern.

More than anything else, what the memory of that day had brought back was not the shock of Joe Devin's position at the top of the Government Party, nor his more dramatic fall from grace, nor the coincidence of watching it after discussing with Eunice the People's Museums, but the pleasure of eating a slice of her cake. Really it had been delicious. Its taste had travelled through time to make his mouth water, and had brought with it and filled him with the love he had felt for his sister. *Finally I understand Proust's madeleine*, he thought. *Oh dear, does that make me pretentious?* Mr Rubens shrugged, not caring if it did or it didn't.

Drawing in and then exhaling a lungful of air, as though to give his love tangible form and fill the room with Eunice, Mr Rubens turned again to the 'Explanatory Notes': 'Under 16, over 80, gravely ill, or suffering from a serious mental disorder.' The list of exemptions was forbiddingly short. And the penalties for failure to attend were severe: a maximum of five years' imprisonment and/or an unlimited fine. Museum Service was clearly regarded as a duty, not a privilege. Mr Rubens reflected that perhaps on this matter even Eunice might have been too naïve. Perhaps Museum Service and the People's Museums had been conceived as sinister instruments in the hands of a sinister State - a day at the People's Museum as a laughing stock. As he bent over the papers in despair, the air around him thickened, and when he felt the weight of kindness settle on his shoulder, he turned his head slowly.

"Hello," said Malcolm.

Bouncing off the *Amoeba*, Mr Rubens leaped to his feet.

"I told you I would never leave you," said Malcolm.

NINE

A convenient appointment

"Is that Mr Rubens? Mr Anthony Pablo Rubens?"

Eight long, anxious days after Mr Rubens had received his summons, a Museums Ministry official was calling to arrange 'a convenient appointment'.

"Please allow for the Evaluation Panel's visit to last three to four hours, Mr Rubens. And there may well need to be further visits."

She was polite but brisk, most likely speaking from a script, Mr Rubens suspected. Her tone of voice was even and flat, not unlike the postman's, but the lack of a physical presence made it more eerie.

Feeling Malcolm's presence and hearing his voice had been neither unusual nor eerie. For more than a week now Mr Rubens had carried on his shoulder the weight of Malcolm's hand, just as he still carried the sensation of the last time Malcolm held him in his arms, or of all the times they kissed. These were not phantom sensations, like the imaginary pins and needles in the limbs of amputees. Rather their reality - which although it was not constant could be summoned at will - was contained in the infinity of the air Mr Rubens inhaled in a sigh, or in the breath-stopping gulps of a sob. It had all to do with keeping intact a thread that was a gateway to the past, with all the love it had contained not lost and remembered but always alive. Life was labyrinthine, but ultimately all its tangles were united.

What exactly was the purpose of these visits, Mr Rubens asked the official politely.

"That is something Mr Anderson and Mr Evans will certainly be able to explain," she replied in a spiritless drone, from which it was impossible to make any deductions: she could be young or middle aged, happy or unhappy with her job, with or without joy in her private life.

"Who are Mr Anderson and Mr Evans?" Mr Rubens asked.

"They are the gentlemen coming to see you."

Was she being stupid, indifferent, downright rude and deliberately abstruse, or was she acting on specific instructions to be as unhelpful as possible? Perhaps it was official policy that the State's bureaucratic machine should aspire in its entirety to be Kafkaesque.

"But who are they? What's their position?" Mr Rubens insisted.

"Mr Rubens," the official answered curtly, "as you know, you have been selected for Museum Service at the National People's Museum. You have made no application for exemption, as specified in the 'Explanatory Notes' you received with your summons. Mr Anderson and Mr Evans are members of the Evaluation Panel assigned to your case."

"My case?"

"That is correct, sir, yes."

"Am I on trial?"

"No, sir, not as far as I'm aware. Have you committed an offence?"

"No, of course I've not committed an offence. I'm just trying to understand who these people are and why they are coming to see me."

"As I was saying, sir, Mr Anderson and Mr Evans are members of the Evaluation Panel assigned to your case, and they are coming to see you next Thursday, October 24, at

10 am. You have agreed to this appointment, have you not?"

"Yes, I suppose so," said Mr Rubens.

"Mr Anderson and Mr Evans will explain everything then. You will be able to put all your questions directly to them when they visit."

Mr Rubens stood his ground. Could the official please explain the procedure by which he had come to be chosen for service? And could she please try and explain in a little more detail the function of the Evaluation Panel? What was it, precisely, that they wished to evaluate?

The lady from the Ministry said she was sorry, but she was simply unable to answer his questions.

"So you can't give me any more information."

"No, sir. I don't have any more information."

"And is there no one else I can speak to? I mean apart from Mr Anderson and Mr Evans. Is there no other official I can speak to today, on the telephone, now?"

"No, sir. The purpose of this call is to arrange an appointment—"

"And naturally you are the only official in charge of arranging appointments."

"Yes, sir, that is correct."

"In that case, would it be possible to speak to Mr Anderson or Mr Evans before the day of the visit? Do you have a telephone number for Mr Anderson or Mr Evans?"

"No, Mr Rubens, I don't have that information."

Mr Rubens hung up. It seemed pointless to insist any longer, the official's evasion had been unrelenting. Plainly she would have resisted all further questioning. Mr Rubens had no other choice but to wait for the visit. Today was Friday. He had another six days, almost a week, to think carefully about the questions he wanted to ask.

An imaginary obituary

That night would be almost sleepless, and what little sleep he managed was riven by nightmares. In one, Mr Rubens had been tied onto a chair barefoot and blindfolded, in a room filled with the odours of death, and was waiting to the sound of his heartbeat – *boom-boom*, *thump-thump* - for his turn to have his toenails extracted by a dentist. He woke up too frightened to go back to sleep, although that too might have been part of his dream. In another he had been on stage at an ancient amphitheatre, dancing to Ravel's *Bolero* in a tutu. A posse of boys in black shuffled in a semi-circle to one side, humming like the chorus in a tragedy by Aeschylus. When the music ended abruptly, a middle-aged Joe Devin appeared as though by dint of a *deus ex machina*, and was yelling in the young postman's voice: *Fuck* you, Pablo, *Fuck* you, Pablo, *Fuck* you, Pablo...

Unshowered, Mr Rubens had dragged himself downstairs to the kitchen at six in the morning (one full hour earlier than on any other day), and had forced himself to eat his usual breakfast – cereal, fresh fruit (banana and blueberries) - but on this exceptional occasion served with a carelessly strong cup of coffee. In every other respect, it had been the same for the last forty years, except for a short period at the height of the country's isolation, when there had been a severe shortage of bananas (curiously, there had never been any shortage of blueberries or coffee), and during that time Mr Rubens had settled for apples instead.

Even while sanctions had been in place, somehow ways must have been found around them. For the new 'elite', probably nothing had changed, but even for most ordinary people, at least in terms of everyday living, what small changes there had been had been short-lived.

"And you know why, don't you? Well, who do you think's been funding the Government Party?"

"The New CIA?"

For years, Eunice had been blaming 'the New CIA' for practically everything, even for the atrocities that had precipitated the Government Party's success at the polls, so the answer she demanded hadn't been too difficult to guess.

"They had to start the ball rolling somewhere; see how things panned out in someone else's backyard. And if all went to plan, which unfortunately it did, all they had to do was sit back on their backsides, waiting for the cancer to spread and become yet another 'new normal'. Sanctions, my arse!"

Events had proved her right, and for the first time Mr Rubens felt a heavy pang of shame at how easy he had found it to adjust to 'another new normal'. He had chosen to withdraw from the world even before it had been turned upside down, first by an insidious pandemic and then by the Government Party. Had it not been for Eunice, and the temporary shortage of bananas, probably the new world's rancid stench would have entirely passed him by. By clinging on to grief so implacably, he had made himself impervious to life.

Sitting at the kitchen table, Mr Rubens stared abjectly at the wall in front of him. Like the rest of the kitchen, it had been papered with original 1960s wallpaper, its colourful op-art design treated with a modern preservative, to seal it and stop it from fading. As if lost in a trance induced by the spatial confusion of the wallpaper's repetitive pattern – "It's better than drugs!" Eunice had teased him – he felt a numb indifference to all the beautiful things he had so eagerly collected over many years, from which once he had derived such enormous satisfaction.

I've been summoned to make an exhibition of myself. Why? Who am I? My life has been a shallow skirting over – a denial. Everything good belongs to a long-ago past that I've stubbornly refused to move on from.

Mr Rubens imagined his death. Then he tried to imagine that a serious and erudite obituarist, rather than a gossip or scandal enthusiast, had been commissioned to pen his obituary, for publication in one of the national newspapers. Mr Rubens knew very well that if he really were dead, no one would be writing his obituary, and even if by chance someone did, perhaps out of a morbid fascination with his family's history, no newspaper would want to publish it. Back in the days of quality broadsheets, when the press was relatively free, something *might* have been written - unlikely, but perhaps not impossible. Today's newspapers, however, were unconcerned with the lives of people like him; their readers would not find them interesting. Why should they? Mr Rubens was old. He had sought, and achieved, neither fame nor notoriety. His career in the civil service had been dull. His interests were esoteric. His life had been memorable only to him. Unlike his sister, he had not been blessed with their grandfather's passion. But say, for argument's sake, that for some unknown reason an obituary had to be written, reducing his life to, at most, a few hundred words. How would it describe him? How would he be judged? Who might he be compared to? And most importantly of all, what would Mr Rubens himself make of this imaginary obituary?

TEN

As one with the stars

The melancholy evening had become an urgent night, its stillness broken by the hiss of passing cars, its blackness made more violent by the criss-crossing of headlights on the surface of the road with the shimmer of reflections from signs above the shop fronts and the yellow that cascaded from the lampposts overhead.

Anthony walked briskly, taking in the air in short, shallow breaths, afraid of the enormity of what it might contain, not wanting it inside him polluting the only pure and unequivocal sensation of his life.

I'm in love. I'm in love. I'm in love. Tonight, the words belonged to him, and the strength of the possessiveness he felt towards them was proof not only of the certainty of their truth, but also of their transcendence: they were words that went far beyond words, precisely *because* they were words. Or perhaps he was filling his head with the absurdity of ridiculous thoughts, because how else could he shut out... *I'm in love. I'm in love. I'm in love.* Filled with these repeated words, he would not make room for anything else, not until he was with Malcolm and Malcolm was safe, not until three words could be spoken to Malcolm directly – *I love you! I love you! I love you!* Not until he and Malcolm were filled with each other instead.

At the corner with Cromer Street the night seemed to take on a different dimension in which all it encompassed was united at last, the trickle of light from inadequate light bulbs becoming as one with the stars. Anthony felt himself enveloped by a cloak of tender darkness, its caress propelling him forward as though wishing to deliver him safely to where he belonged. And suddenly he was in front of Malcolm's bell, his finger pressing down on 2B with the unnecessary force of his frustration at not hearing any sound - even though he knew all the separate bells had been muffled. But now footsteps were approaching and the door was about to be opened.

"Malcolm's been taken to hospital, mate." That had been Anthony's fear. He would ring Malcolm's bell, someone else would open the door...

As his eyes adjusted, to scrutinise the figure of the boy who had opened the door in shorts and a loose-fitting T-shirt, Anthony's finger stayed fixed on the doorbell.

"I'm here now, you can stop ringing the bell," Malcolm said softly.

"It's you," Anthony said.

"Were you expecting someone else?"

But instead of returning the most beautiful smile he had seen in his life, all Anthony could do was shake his head this way and that very slowly, before breaking into mute uncontrollable sobs.

"Hey," Malcolm said, when already he had Anthony in his arms, weeping over his shoulder. "Hey, what's the matter? Has that awful Joe Devin upset you?"

"It's you, it's you." He wanted to say more, so much more, but his voice was too broken, thwarted by the double effort of speaking and catching his breath.

"Shh," Malcolm said. "Come on, let's take you upstairs. Tonight, you're staying with me."

Anthony's nodding was more violent than his sobs, and Malcolm must have felt his chin digging deep into his shoulder, again and again. The thought he might be hurting him made Anthony stop.

"Yes, thank you," he said, his chest forcing out in a garble three wrong, inarticulate words.

Now Malcolm had one arm around Anthony's waist, supporting his weight, and together they had shuffled to the bottom of the stairs. With a foot on the first step, and with Malcolm about to bear the brunt of manoeuvring two bodies up the zigzag of flights that led to his room, Anthony faltered for a moment as he struggled with deep breaths, one, two, three, four, only with the fifth managing at last to shed his body's limpness in a long exhalation. Then he used all his strength to draw out all the longing that had sunk to his furthermost depths, and cupping Malcolm's head with the palm of one hand he gently pushed him back towards the wall. And after another deep breath, this time he spoke clearly and he spoke the right words:

"I love you. I've always loved you, even if I didn't know it."

Malcolm answered not with words but by pressing backwards into Anthony's hand to give his head a tilt that aligned their lips exactly. With his eyes tightly closed, as though to shut out any threat that he might or might not have imagined, Anthony moved forward by the breadth of no more than a thread. Without even the pressure of a touch, the taste of Malcolm burst inside his mouth into innumerable pieces, pins and needles of love that instantly filled him entirely.

Breaking up their kiss, "You forgot your inhaler," Anthony said, his eyes now wide open. "What was that all about?"

Malcolm brought an upright finger to his mouth and leaned on it until it touched both their lips.

"I've always loved you too," he said. "But can we please go upstairs now?"

Broken mirror

Together they had taken the stairs in movements that to Anthony had felt almost weightless, effortless coordinated steps that had led to Malcolm's room.

"I had a small accident earlier, so be careful," Malcolm said.

"An accident?"

They both hesitated at the open door.

"The mirror's broken, and I've not had time to pick up all the pieces."

"It looks like you haven't picked up any," Anthony said.

In the harsh fluorescent light, the thousand shiny fragments that were scattered on the floor shimmered like the ingredients of a curse – fish scales, tails of lizard, witch's toenails, dragon's teeth, all remembered from the fairy tales that Eunice had told him in the years after their mother had left.

Shiny and sharp and a curse to careless feet...

"We can't leave them like this. Have you got an old newspaper?"

Malcolm fetched a broom, and methodically swept all the pieces into a heap, out of the way.

"I'll get rid of them tomorrow, I promise."

"What happened?"

"At *The Bell*?"

"To the mirror," Anthony said. "It looks like you laid into it with a hammer."

"Come and sit with me on the bed."

"Yes." Anthony set down his jacket on the sofa and slipped out of his shoes. Then he sat beside Malcolm on the edge of the bed. "You don't seem surprised," he said.

"Surprised that you love me? Feel this," Malcolm said, seeking out Anthony's hand to press it hard against his chest.

Through the wetness of his T-shirt, Malcolm's heart was beating fast: ba-dumm, ba-ba-dumm, ba-dumm, ba-ba-dumm...

"Is that surprise?"

"It's everything," said Malcolm.

Still against a beating heart - ba-dumm, ba-ba-dumm - Anthony's hand pressed harder, until Malcolm was flat on his back, with his feet still on the floor and Anthony propped up by his side.

"I'll switch it off," Anthony said, when Malcolm winced at the fluorescent.

"It makes me look deathly, I know."

"It's blinding you," Anthony said.

"I turned it on to try and write, and I did, I finished what I'd started earlier on when I got back from Belsize Park. I put my pen down feeling happy, but then I caught sight of myself in the mirror."

"And you smashed it."

Anthony crawled over to the switch beside the bed and turned the main light off, then he turned on the two bedside lamps. The 40W light bulbs were weak, and the red shades let their light through unevenly. Malcolm had thrown off his T-shirt, and still lying on his back he had spread out his arms at precisely right angles to his body. His head was yellow, and his body a deepening red abruptly cut off at the knees. When he lifted up his legs and held them straight, bowing his head as though to investigate himself, he looked like another crucifixion. Then his feet fell to the floor again, and his gaze darted backwards at Anthony.

"See how skinny I've become," he said.

"You've always been skinny, and it suits you."

"Everyone thinks I look sick."

"And everyone thinks I'm to blame. Even *I* think I'm to blame, for this morning *and* for tonight."

Malcolm pressed his hand against Anthony's lips. "Let me see you," he said.

Anthony went up on his knees and pulled off his T-shirt.

Malcolm beckoned him closer. "Your skin has this magnificent glow, it's almost as if it's been polished." With the tips of his fingers he combed through the short curly hairs on Anthony's chest, running over the contours and curves around his nipples, then along the muscles that led down to the top of his jeans. "What did I say to you before, you remember?"

"Young Adonis, eat your heart out."

"And my God, those eyes!"

"My eyes are ordinary," Anthony said. "When you looked in the mirror, how could you not have seen yours? They're like golden-orange fire, they burn you with their brightness."

"Ha! Ginger eyes, how amazing," Malcolm said.

"Now shush," Anthony said, and he felt himself blush as he lowered his body over Malcolm's.

"Mind you don't break me."

"I told you to be quiet," Anthony said, before taking Malcolm's mouth into his.

ELEVEN

Mr Anderson and Mr Evans

For the first half hour of their visit, Mr Anderson and Mr Evans had seemed more interested in the monkeys than in Mr Rubens.

"A macaw," said Mr Evans, surveying his cup.

"A *macaque*, Mr Evans. A macaw is a bird, isn't that right, Mr Rubens?"

"Yes, a parrot," said Mr Rubens.

Mr Anderson and Mr Evans had arrived punctually at 10 am and had made a good first impression by ringing the bell, which they had each followed up with an excellent handshake. Mr Rubens had reciprocated with a pleasantry or two about the weather.

"Whereas a macaque is a monkey," said Mr Anderson.

"They're *all* monkeys, aren't they?" said Mr Evans.

"Meissen if I'm not mistaken," said Mr Anderson.

"That's right," said Mr Rubens.

All the necessary preparations had already been made before their arrival. On this special occasion, Mr Rubens had decided to forego his mid-morning coffee and serve tea and cake instead. After showing them through to the sitting room, he had left the two men side by side on the sofa next to the *Amoeba*, and five minutes later had returned from the kitchen with the entire collection of monkeys. It was the first public appearance of the platter's enormous gorilla since the afternoon of Joe Devin's purge.

"The orangutan's my absolute favourite," said Mr Anderson.

"Mine too, I think," said Mr Rubens.

"And is that a gorilla under that delicious-looking Battenberg cake?" Mr Anderson asked.

"How rude of me, would you both like a slice?"

"That's *most* kind," said Mr Anderson, "but really we shouldn't."

"Really we shouldn't," said Mr Evans.

Mr Rubens used the side of the cake knife to push the Battenberg cake to one side, revealing the rest of the gorilla.

"How splendid!" Mr Anderson exclaimed enthusiastically.

"I prefer the chimpanzees," said Mr Evans.

"Apparently they're rather partial to eating other monkeys," said Mr Anderson.

"Only occasionally," said Mr Rubens. "They mostly eat fruit."

"Dog-eat-dog," said Mr Evans. "That's the kind of world we used to live in."

Both young men somewhere in their early thirties and dressed smartly in almost identical suits, Mr Anderson and Mr Evans were otherwise remarkably different. Mr Anderson was tall and very thin, with sharp birdlike features. His shiny jet-black hair was violently divided into two by a parting so straight and precise that the bare scalp it exposed looked like a scar. Short and rather plump, Mr Evans had a face as ill-defined as an out-of-focus blur. His hair was the palest shade of blond and very fine, making hardly any contrast with the colour of his skin. It had taken Mr Rubens some time to notice the angular arch of his eyebrows, or indeed that Mr Evans had eyebrows at all.

"Did your sister have a favourite?" asked Mr Anderson, sharpening his voice while fixing Mr Rubens with a smile.

The air had turned rank, and as he stopped himself from retching Mr Rubens nearly choked on his second sip of tea.

"Eunice?"

"Eunice Guernica," said Mr Evans.

"We're both very sorry for your loss," said Mr Anderson.

They really are sinister, probably more sinister than either Eunice or I had ever imagined, thought Mr Rubens.

"Eunice died two years ago," he said.

"All the same, you must still miss her terribly," said Mr Anderson.

"Yes, we were very close," said Mr Rubens.

"Eunice Guernica and Anthony Pablo," said Mr Evans. "Unusual names for children."

Watch it now, Pablo, you better keep your cool or these monsters will have you for breakfast, that's what my sister would have said if she were here, and that's what I must do.

"Unusual names for anyone," said Mr Anderson.

"Our grandmother was Spanish," said Mr Rubens.

"Ah, yes, the Spanish connection," said Mr Anderson.

"Marta Beatriz and the May Day demonstration in Paris," said Mr Evans. "Then a wedding and a visit to see *Guernica* at the Paris Exposition."

"It was a long time ago," said Mr Rubens.

"1937," said Mr Evans.

"A *very* long time ago," said Mr Anderson.

"Only seven years shy of a century," said Mr Evans.

"You seem very well informed," said Mr Rubens.

"We are," said Mr Evans.

"It's a very important part of our job," said Mr Anderson. "And fortunately, our French and Spanish friends are as meticulous as we are at keeping public records."

"Exceptionally *detailed* public records," said Mr Evans.

"Mr Evans speaks excellent Spanish," said Mr Anderson.

"I hardly speak any," said Mr Rubens. "Neither did my sister. Come to think of it, nor did our father."

"That *is* unusual," said Mr Anderson.

"Considering his interest in Spain," said Mr Evans.

"As well as his mixed heritage," said Mr Anderson.

"After everything that happened, my grandmother thought it was best to move on," said Mr Rubens.

"And who could have blamed her?" said Mr Anderson.

"Your father should have listened to her more," said Mr Evans.

Do they know about Joe Devin? Mr Rubens wondered. *Is that why they sent round a postman with a pencil moustache? But what has any of this to do with Museum Service? Perhaps they've come to tell me that my day has been cancelled, that my family history makes me unworthy of a day at the National People's Museum...*

"He married very young, I believe," said Mr Anderson, looking at the inside of his cup as though it might reveal another monkey.

"My mother too," said Mr Rubens. "They were both very young,"

"Eighteen, as I recall. And only nineteen when your sister was born." Mr Anderson let out a big sigh. "Your poor mother must have been so unprepared."

"Are you sure you wouldn't like a slice?" asked Mr Rubens.

"A slice?" said Mr Anderson.

Of my life, thought Mr Rubens.

"Of cake," he said.

"Thank you, not for me," said Mr Anderson, letting go of his teaspoon to give his open palm a little wave.

"Nor for me," said Mr Evans, badly mimicking the gesture with a wiggle of inelegant fat fingers.

"Eunice liked the gorilla," said Mr Rubens.

"And the painting you *all* liked so much has been safely stored away," said Mr Anderson.

"Wars get people killed," said Mr Evans.

"But paintings about war don't get wars started," said Mr Rubens.

"It's actually in New York now," said Mr Evans.

Probably sold off to the New CIA, thought Mr Rubens.

"Then I'm even more grateful that we had the opportunity to see it," he said.

"Mr Rubens," Mr Anderson began forebodingly, pausing as he shifted himself forward on the sofa, putting down his cup and saucer with barely a clink. "It would be wonderful to have the Meissen monkeys on display on your day at the National People's Museum, do you think that might be possible?"

Mr Rubens could have sworn that Mr Evans pulled a face.

"Our technical team will take good care of them, I give you my word," Mr Anderson went on.

When Mr Rubens lifted his cup to his mouth as a pretext for gulping down a large amount of air, he was not at all surprised that in spite of these dangerous, menacing men, no great burst of menace was filling his lungs, or his nostrils any odour of danger. And the reason he was not at all surprised was simply that the rankness he had previously discerned, although it had not disappeared, had now become pervaded with the absence of his fear.

"Mr Rubens?" said the voice of Mr Anderson.

"He's fallen asleep with the cup in his hand," said the voice of Mr Evans.

What a pair of morons, thought Mr Rubens. "And the *Amoeba*, of course," he said, snapping open his eyes to peer at the two men with fresh determination.

"The amoeba?" For the first time Mr Anderson's voice betrayed a hint of irritation.

It was Mr Rubens' turn to fix him with a smile. "This rather unique piece of 60s design," he said, swivelling a little to the right and then a little to the left.

"I think he means the chair," said Mr Evans.

"How very perceptive of you, Mr Evans. Indeed I *do* mean the chair. And yes, I'd also be happy for the Meissen to go on display."

"It *is* your day, Mr Rubens. The technical team will do their utmost to accommodate *all* your requests. Working with enthusiasm and dedication, they really are quite exceptional at what they do. They're a credit to the Ministry, aren't they, Mr Evans?"

"They are," said Mr Evans.

"All the more so, I think, as they aim to be as invisible as possible. Their work will be unobtrusive, allowing the creation of a space as authentically *you* as this room, capturing not just its appearance but also its *soul*."

"I wasn't aware that this room had a soul," said Mr Rubens.

"Oh, but you underestimate yourself, Mr Rubens."

"I do?"

"The aura is of restraint and good taste, wouldn't you agree, Mr Evans?"

"Restraint and good taste, Mr Anderson, yes," said Mr Evans.

"With a note or two of flamboyance, perhaps. Which only serves to underscore the restraint."

"Well, thank you, I'm flattered," said Mr Rubens. *Not quite as flattered as you'd like me to be.* "But now I wonder if you might allow me to ask you some questions."

"Please, go ahead," said Mr Anderson.

"Ever since receiving my summons, I've been curious to find out by what process the Ministry makes its selection for service. I'd really like to know on what grounds I was chosen, for what I assume must be an honour – to be shown at the National People's Museum. I did try to ask the lady who called me to make this appointment–"

"That would have been Dorothy," said Mr Anderson.

"Dorothy had no information to give you," said Mr Evans.

"Yes, that's what she said," said Mr Rubens. "And then she told me I should wait until today and put all my questions to you."

"Well, we are the Evaluation Panel assigned to your case," said Mr Anderson.

"She said that too," said Mr Rubens. "And I wondered what that meant – my 'case'."

"You didn't like the ring of it," said Mr Evans.

"No, I didn't," said Mr Rubens. "It made me feel like I'd done something wrong."

"And have you?"

"No, Mr Evans, I certainly haven't. I'm sure you'd know if I had, you seem to know everything else."

"It is a rare honour indeed, Mr Rubens, to be summoned to serve at the National People's Museum," said Mr Anderson.

"But to what do I owe this rare honour? Why was I selected in the first place?"

"Ours is not to reason why, I'm afraid. The important thing is that you were," said Mr Anderson.

"And what exactly are you here to evaluate?" Mr Rubens insisted. "You seem to have gone to an awful lot of trouble to find out things that happened to my family even before I was born, so someone must think they're important, only I can't for the life of me think why. What's it matter that my grandfather wanted to fight against Franco, or that my father called his children Pablo and Guernica, or that years ago he took us to a museum in Madrid to look at a painting?"

"Now he wants to do our job for us," said Mr Evans.

"So your job is to investigate my past?"

"Our job is to understand who you are, to put you into context, as it were, and make as full a picture in our minds as we can," said Mr Anderson. "So, Mr Rubens, let me try and help you understand who *we* are. As a general rule, the Selection Panel select according to certain criteria, and then we evaluate according to ours. Once we have evaluated, the case goes back to the Selection Panel, who will then either confirm or cancel their selection."

"So there are two panels assigned to my case."

"As there are to *every* case," said Mr Anderson. "And in the event of confirmation after an evaluation, a technical team is also assigned to the case, and finally a date is set for service. That is the procedure. It's really very simple."

"Wouldn't it make more sense to do the evaluation first, before the selection?"

Mr Anderson shrugged his shoulders and gave another wave with his hand.

"I see," said Mr Rubens.

"As I said before, ours is not to reason why," Mr Anderson said. "Our job is to offer the Selection Panel an opportunity of cross-checking, we have no involvement in making the selections."

"And that's all there is to it," said Mr Evans. "The Selection Panel do their job and we do ours."

"To safeguard the integrity of the process, the selection and evaluation criteria are naturally confidential, and in any event are rather fluid," Mr Anderson said. "No two cases are ever the same, are they, Mr Evans?"

"They're not," said Mr Evans.

"Which does make our job that much more interesting," said Mr Anderson.

"Then I have another question," said Mr Rubens. "What will your recommendation be, to cancel or to confirm?"

"Oh, but we don't make recommendations," said Mr Anderson.

"There's another panel for that," said Mr Evans.

"Now now, Mr Evans, tut-tut," said Mr Anderson.

"It was just a joke," said Mr Evans.

"No, we just give the Selection Panel our appraisal of the facts *as we see them*, in other words not barely but as coloured by these very important face-to-face meetings. Important but occasionally also very pleasant, I must say. Today really *has* been a pleasure, Mr Rubens, thank you!"

"The lady I spoke to said there might need to be more visits," said Mr Rubens.

"I don't think more visits will be necessary, do you, Mr Evans?"

"I don't think so, no," said Mr Evans.

"And if after your appraisal the Selection Panel come to the conclusion that they shouldn't confirm?"

"That wouldn't be good news," said Mr Evans.

"But you really shouldn't worry too much, cancellations are rare, very exceptional indeed, wouldn't you say so, Mr Evans?"

"*Very* exceptional," said Mr Evans.

"In fact," Mr Anderson continued, "I'm almost certain you'll be hearing from the technical team very shortly." And giving both his thighs a loud slap, "Mr Rubens, I think we've taken up quite enough of your time, so unless there's something else, Mr Evans and I should be making our excuses."

When the two men rose to their feet, so did Mr Rubens.

"There's one last thing I think I should mention," he said, as he led the way through to the hallway. "Just in case it's something the Selection Panel might expect you to appraise."

Mr Evans had already opened the front door and was holding it ajar.

"Go on, Mr Rubens, don't keep us in suspense," said Mr Anderson.

Be careful now, thought Mr Rubens. *It's a fine line between being courageous and being stupid.*

"I've never visited the National People's Museum," he said.

"Well, you wouldn't have, would you," said Mr Evans. "You're not a Party member."

"Only Party members are permitted to visit the National People's Museum," said Mr Anderson.

"I'm not allowed to visit it, but I'm going to be shown there," said Mr Rubens.

"That's about the size of it," said Mr Evans.

"You are, however, free to visit any of the local People's Museums," said Mr Anderson.

"Do you think that might be useful?"

Mr Anderson gave his shoulders one more shrug. "For the exhibits at the National there's always an accompanying pamphlet, which in my opinion makes all the difference."

"An accompanying pamphlet?"

"Compiled by the Selection Panel," said Mr Evans.

"Based on our appraisal of the facts," said Mr Anderson.

"Of the facts *as you see them*," said Mr Rubens.

"Of the facts as we see them, that's right," said Mr Evans.

"And will I ever set eyes on this accompanying pamphlet?"

"Normally they're also reserved for Party members," said Mr Anderson, "but I promise to try and make sure you are handed a copy at the end of your day."

It's also a fine line between being courageous and finding excuses, and this is your last chance to show them you're not frightened by any of their nonsense. There's probably nothing they don't know already, so you've nothing to lose, except your self-respect if you keep quiet.

"I suppose in your appraisal there'll be a mention of my acquaintance with Minister Devin." In the freeze-frame silence that followed, Mr Rubens rolled his eyes. "Obviously I meant *ex* Minister Devin," he said. "And when I knew him we were both still in our twenties. Surely you must know he was gay."

Mr Anderson at last sprang to action, shooting a glance at Mr Evans as he pushed his arm out of the way to slam the door shut.

"Perhaps we'll have that slice of Battenberg cake after all," he said, fixing Mr Rubens with another of his smiles.

TWELVE

Madeleine

"You can say it now, and this time it will actually be true."

"Say what?"

"That it smells of sex in here," said Malcolm.

It did, and it didn't. The predominant smell was of something much bigger than sex, as though the act that had surged over the words *I'm in love* and *I love you*, not erasing them but rather making them pathetically incomplete, had itself been encompassed by a single yet infinite moment of climax. This circular description fell short, as it had to. Anthony was now more than one. In a mutual yielding up, he and Malcolm had ceded to each other a small but indivisible part of their essence.

He ran his nose around Malcolm's torso, across the ridges of his ribs down to his navel and beyond, filling his lungs with what suddenly felt irretrievably his. And it didn't surprise him that they each no longer had their own smell, that their smell was now the same. Their union was already complete, and they would never again feel entirely apart.

But apartness preyed on Anthony's mind all the same.

"Tell me about what happened tonight at *The Bell*," he said.

In the air of Malcolm's room, the dull tang of historical sadness persisted, but within it floated particles of sadness that belonged to the present, cutting through the elation like grains of burning sand. If enough of them managed to settle, Anthony decided that together they would constitute fear, of dependence and ultimately of loss, either his or Malcolm's. But fear was the last thing he wanted to feel, and he buried his face under Malcolm's arm, to breathe in with its wetness the will to be strong.

"Tonight at *The Bell*, you were snogging the hideous Joe Devin."

With the beat of Malcolm's heart in one ear - ba-dumm, ba-ba-dumm, ba-dumm, ba-ba-dumm – and in the other the sound of playful scolding, Anthony felt torn between the two sides of an evening divided by the uttering of words that were quickly superseded by gasps.

Had Malcolm wheezed while the two of them made love? He was not wheezing now.

"That's not what I meant."

"You're mumbling," said Malcolm.

Anthony sighed deeply, taking in more strength. And after putting on a smile he raised his head.

Malcolm laughed. "Your nose is drenched. Here, let me dry it." When he had wiped it with his hand, he stretched out his arms, and then he turned onto his side. "Hold me," he said.

With barely a movement, Anthony's body wriggled until it had filled every gap, and his nakedness had joined with Malcolm's completely.

"That's so nice," Malcolm said.

"Jesus, you're burning," Anthony said.

"Of course I'm burning! It's humid and hot and we've been having incredible sex."

"This morning you looked like you'd been punched by the sun, then in the evening on the way to *The Bell* you were wheezing, and two hours later you collapsed."

"I did *not* collapse; I just felt a bit dizzy. And people were fussing, so I told them I'd forgotten my inhaler."

"You don't have an inhaler." Anthony stretched his mouth wide open until he had a third of Malcolm's neck between his teeth.

"I don't *need* an inhaler. And don't you dare bite me!"

Anthony pulled back so he could speak. "So tell me what's wrong with your breathing."

"We're going around in circles." Slipping out of Anthony's embrace, Malcolm sat up on the edge of the bed, facing the empty wall where the mirror had been.

"You've never, ever lied to me," Anthony said.

"Are you saying that I'm lying to you now?"

In Malcolm's heavy whisper, so plainly empty of admonition, Anthony could read only hurt - either the hurt of being accused unjustly or the hurt of being found out.

"Wait," Malcolm said, balancing his elbows on his knees and leaning forward to deliver his head to his hands. "Do you think it's possible to ever really know another person? I mean to *really* know them?" Already his body had collapsed itself and snaked its way back into Anthony's embrace.

Anthony had held his breath while he shrugged, once and then a second time. And after taking in more air through his nose, he blew it out over the area of Malcolm's neck he had held in his mouth.

Malcolm's shoulder rose and fell. "You could probably make love with your breath," he said.

"I don't suppose it is, not completely," Anthony said. "But I think I know you well enough to know I can trust you."

"Trust me not to lie, or trust me not to keep anything from you?"

"I don't trust you not to not want to worry me," Anthony said.

"You don't trust me not to not want to worry you..." Malcolm repeated the words very slowly. "That's a really ugly sentence," he said, and as he broke into quiet fits of laughter, Anthony could feel his body convulse. "There's *so* much you keep to yourself," Malcolm went on. "I've always told you everything."

"What would you like to know that you think I haven't told you?"

"Your mother's name," Malcolm said.

"You haven't asked Eunice?"

Malcolm shook his head. "I wanted to hear it from you."

"My mother's name was Madeleine," Anthony said.

"Madeleine," said Malcolm. "It's a beautiful name." And turning around with another writhing movement, he rubbed his nose gently against Anthony's chin. "I'm not keeping anything from you, I promise. My chest's been a little bit heavy, that's all."

"Heavy?"

"It's probably all that smoke we breathe in at *The Bell*. And the acrobatic sex was all in my head, so I'm not exactly fit. But hey, I'll be fine now I've got you, we can exercise together in bed. Yep, more sex with Anthony, just what the doctor ordered!"

"Well, if it's what the doctor ordered..."

"I can show you the prescription if you like."

"Mmm, don't stop," said Anthony.

Shadow

It was dawn. The cooing of plaintive pigeons came from everywhere at once, as though a grievance had been wired into the building. More melodious warblers, scarce in this part of the city, still managed intermittently to make themselves heard.

Even though it was open, the single window in Malcolm's room let in hardly any light. The air outside was still, and the burgundy curtains were lined and efficient.

Only around the edges was there evidence of daylight, a narrow band of brightness that constantly flickered. When Underground trains were running, their rumble made the whole building shake. But even when they weren't, Malcolm's room had a permanent shiver, as though at night all the years of vibration were distilled into a gentle massage.

The sounds of sex had shut out the sounds of the rest of the world – Anthony had not even heard any sirens; nowhere else could the night have been more self-contained than it had been within these walls. Like a musical accompaniment to his and Malcolm's noises, within the night's shiver there had been only the jingle of cheap cutlery and the quaver of the few plates Malcolm kept in a stack. Cars may have gasped their way along Gray's Inn Road, nearby scavengers foraged the areas around public houses for leftover booze, other lovers made loud noises of their own in their bedrooms, but this one night had belonged to Malcolm's room.

The night, however, had passed, and Monday was beginning in earnest. The first train rattled past, its boom boring through the skin of the earth and into the bone of the structures above it, shaking people awake and slapping the weekend out of any lingering reluctance to end. By seven o'clock, Malcolm's room was a nauseating hubbub, an invasion of noises and smells from the street. Efficient as they were at keeping out the light, the lined Burgundy curtains seemed if anything to magnify everything else.

The temperature outside was rising, and to keep out the heat and the noise Anthony got up and pulled the window shut through the curtains. Then he walked to the taps and drank a glass of water before tiptoeing back to the bed.

Behind his eyelids, Malcolm's eyes seemed to be moving. *He must be dreaming*, Anthony thought, but then he wondered if he mightn't have been fooled by the illusions of the room's constant shiver, which by now had nearly reached its daytime peak. When he breathed in hurried mouthfuls of air, the smell of their two bodies, so entirely united earlier on, had again become distinctly divided. There was now an unfamiliar remoteness in Malcolm's that cut its way through Anthony's sense of foreboding and filled him with imminent dread.

"Malcolm?"

The movement behind Malcolm's eyelids had stopped. The sweat on his forehead was cold. His chest was still.

"Malcolm? Wake up!" Anthony was on his knees, his hands cupped around Malcolm's shoulders.

Malcolm's eyes snapped open, staring straight into Anthony's, curious but peaceful.

"Mm-hm."

"You're awake," Anthony said, taking off his weight from Malcolm's shoulders.

"Mm-hmmm." As though trying to make sense of the strange scene he was somehow at the centre of, Malcolm was squinting, and the deep frown that had formed on his forehead made Anthony smile.

"I didn't mean to startle you," he said.

"You didn't?" Malcolm's voice was hoarse.

"We should start getting ready for work."

Malcolm narrowed his squint. His frown pinched on his mouth and twisted his lips.

"You're pulling faces at me," Anthony said.

"Did you think I was dead? Oh fuck, you did, you thought I was dead!"

And what was Anthony supposed to say? That in the middle of sex their smells had become indistinguishable;

that in the morning their original smells had returned; that Malcolm's face had looked too placid while he slept; that his chest had been too still and the sweat on his forehead too cold; that, yes, as a cumulative consequence of all these absurd observations, Anthony had feared he might be dead?

"I thought you might have fainted again."

"You're such a bad liar." When Malcolm laughed, his laughter was more hoarse than his voice.

"Let me get you a glass of water," Anthony said.

Propped up against his pillow, Malcolm drank the water while holding onto Anthony's hand. "You thought I was dead but you're too scared to admit it in case I freak out, and then I might not tell you things, because I'd know you'd be too worried." He put down the empty glass and tightened his grip of Anthony's hand. "But I know you're too worried already, and even though I'm sure it crossed your mind that I was dead, I'm not freaking out. Actually, I think it's very sweet."

"You do?"

After shutting the window, Anthony had left a small dividing line between the curtains, and the bright beam of light that fell through it was now unevenly dividing Malcolm's body into two. One side was golden, steeped in life's translucence, the other a shadowy crimson, dull like a fragment of badly carved stone.

"It's sweet but it's also very funny, in a morbid sort of way." The two entangled hands moved together from the shadow to the light. "I mean, imagine if I *was* dead, on our first night together." Now they swung into the shadow. "It would be worse luck for you than for me." With a sweeping gesture they returned to the light.

"Because you'd be dead," Anthony said.

"Whereas you wouldn't be."

"Unless I jumped out of the window."

"It's not high enough," said Malcolm. "You'd have to hang yourself instead."

When he tried to laugh again, he nearly choked. His cough was dry and coarse, like gravel that was churning in a drum, and Anthony was now behind him, patting his back. Then at last the coughing stopped, but Malcolm still struggled to breathe. He was wheezing again, gasping for breath while his shoulders rose and fell, his chest refusing to swell. The light had left him completely; it had shifted onto Anthony, as though all of it were needed to illuminate the cavernous depth of his fear.

THIRTEEN

Expedited Status

While Mr Rubens idled in the *Amoeba* pretending to enjoy his mid-morning coffee the Wednesday after Mr Anderson and Mr Evans had paid him a visit, the telephone rang. Gloria had already been and gone. Her new husband, or boyfriend, or whatever he was, had apparently been stricken with an outbreak of shingles, and she had asked to leave early. Mr Rubens had been only too happy to oblige. *I hope she's not calling to say she's coming back,* he thought, as he lazily dislodged himself from the *Amoeba*.

"Is that Mr Rubens? Mr Anthony Pablo Rubens?"

Mr Rubens recognised the voice immediately. It belonged to the same drab official who had refused to answer any of his questions.

"Speaking," he said. "Am I correct that you are the lady I've spoken with already about my summons?" Mr Anderson and Mr Evans had mentioned her name, but it had completely slipped his mind. It was something like Doris, or maybe Dolores. But no, it was neither. Could it be Deborah, perhaps? Or Deirdre?

"This is Miss Palmerstone, from the Museums Ministry Information Desk," answered the voice in its familiar drone.

"The lady who called to arrange the Evaluation Panel's visit," said Mr Rubens.

"That is correct," said Miss Palmerstone.

"Dorothy!" said Mr Rubens, suddenly remembering her name.

"As I was saying, Mr Rubens, this is Miss Palmerstone, from the Museums Ministry Information Desk."

"Good morning, Miss Palmerstone, what can I do for you?"

"Nothing at all, Mr Rubens, today the purpose of my call is to inform you of certain developments pertaining to your case, it does not require your assistance."

"I see," said Mr Rubens.

The telephone was on a small bureau set against the wall to the left of the door to the kitchen. Dating from the art deco period, it had been an impulsive buy, like so many of his possessions. Every so often, whenever memories of loved ones gathered in crowds so thick that they threatened him with darkness, Mr Rubens would embark on another spending spree. The reprieve was always temporary, but formed part of a routine that helped him to continue to function. This particular piece of furniture, in figured walnut and leather inset top, had a special significance, and Mr Rubens had deliberately placed the black old-fashioned telephone on it. At the end of almost every conversation, he would remain standing over it and spend a few extra moments reminiscing. Over the years he had discovered the palliative quality at the heart of even the most potent reminders of grief.

"Following their visit, Mr Anderson and Mr Evans have completed their evaluation of the facts–"

"You mean of the facts *as they saw them*," said Mr Rubens, twisting the telephone's cord as he leaned against the side of the bureau. It was not yet the time for reminiscing.

"And in view of their appraisal, the Selection Panel have decided to confirm your selection for service."

"Really?"

After his last-minute disclosure, Mr Rubens had not known what to expect. Mr Anderson and Mr Evans had been shocked, not so much, they had seemed very keen to explain, by the fact of Mr Rubens' acquaintance with the former Minister of Information, and even less by the hardly very exciting revelation that this acquaintance had consisted of no more than a moment of regretted intimacy almost half a century ago, as by their own unforgivable incompetence at having missed any facts that even in some trivial way might have pertained to their appraisal. No sooner had they used these very words to make their unprompted admission than they had countered it by asserting that *none* of the new facts disclosed by Mr Rubens pertained to their appraisal, even in the most trivial way. Cloaking sly reassurance in blatant propaganda, they had gone on to argue that the Government Party had never been a moral crusader, and individual freedoms around such intimately personal matters as sexuality, far from being curtailed, were in fact being actively promoted. The Ministry for Public Health and Wellbeing had even introduced pioneering legislation that decriminalised moderate sex-party drug use, while regulating every stage of distribution - a measure that had proved "particularly popular among gays of all ages, as you probably know," Mr Evans had declared to Mr Rubens. And the draconian legislation controlling access to and exchange of information may not have at the outset proved universally welcome, but it was now one of the government's most popular reforms. The lives of its citizens were no longer subject to the whims of manipulative algorithms. The indiscriminate accumulation of personal data had been brought to an end. At long last the State had taken back control of information on behalf of the people.

"In addition, your case has been upgraded," said Miss Palmerstone.

"*Upgraded*?"

"It has now been granted Expedited Status, and must proceed accordingly. The Selection Panel's decision is final, with no right of appeal, subject always to the exemptions as specified already in your summons."

"Under 16, over 80, gravely ill, or suffering from a mental disorder," said Mr Rubens.

"A *serious* mental disorder," said Miss Palmerstone.

"My mistake, I do beg your pardon," said Mr Rubens.

"Expedited Status means that your service at the National People's Museum will take place within twenty-eight days from today, the precise date depending on the technical team's assessment of your needs. They will be contacting you later on this morning to arrange an appointment for any day before the end of this week."

"I understand that it's compulsory, and I also understand what it means," said Mr Rubens, "but what I'm not so sure about is whether or not I should feel pleased."

"Pleased, Mr Rubens?"

"Are you able to tell me if Expedited Status is supposed to be a good thing?"

"It is certainly regarded as an upgrade."

"An upgrade to my case."

"Precisely."

"But is it supposed to be a good thing *for me personally*?"

"A good thing for you personally in what way?"

"Let me ask you the question in a different way," said Mr Rubens. "*Why* did the Selection Panel deem it necessary or appropriate for my case to be granted Expedited Status? Might it have been something Mr Anderson and Mr Evans recommended, following their appraisal of the facts?"

"I'm afraid I don't have that information."

"And there's no one I can speak to who has."

"You're quite right, sir, there is no such procedure in place."

"Of course there isn't," said Mr Rubens.

"You are naturally at liberty to make your own conjectures and ultimately form your own opinion on the matter, always taking into account all the relevant facts, including the discussions you had with Mr Anderson and Mr Evans. But I will say this. Museum Service is a duty and a privilege, and both aspects of it are enshrined in legislation, as I'm sure every citizen appreciates."

The steadfast cadence of Miss Palmerstone's voice had finally cracked. Mr Rubens had caused her to lose her temper, and she had retaliated by resorting to veiled threats. This did not necessarily mean that she was actually in possession of even a single piece of useful information, but if she was, then this might at last be an opportunity to extract it from her.

"Well, you *say* that both aspects of it are enshrined in legislation," said Mr Rubens, "but everything I've read in the 'Explanatory Notes', or indeed heard from you, Miss Palmerstone, has made no mention of it as a privilege, or made the least attempt to explain *in what way* it is regarded as a privilege. Even though you assured me Mr Anderson and Mr Evans would be able to answer all my questions, I'm not sure that they have. They confirmed that the selection wasn't random, and that it was an honour to be shown at the National People's Museum, but how can anything compulsory be an honour unless it has a worthwhile purpose?"

"And are you suggesting, Mr Rubens, that Museum Service has no such worthwhile purpose?"

"No, Miss Palmerstone, I'm not suggesting that at all, you've misunderstood me."

"In what way have I misunderstood you?"

"You see? 'In what way?' you ask. Because it's clearly not enough for you that I've stated you've misunderstood me, I also need to *justify* my statement. And *that's* what I'm suggesting, that it's simply not enough to be told that something that's being forced on you is an honour and a privilege, unless it's also explained to you *in what way* it is supposed to be an honour and a privilege. No doubt Museum Service has a *very* worthwhile purpose, which I'm afraid makes the Ministry's refusal to communicate that purpose all the more unfortunate."

"Mr Rubens, you have been selected for Museum Service at the National People's Museum. Following a visit by the Evaluation Panel assigned to your case, the Selection Panel have decided to confirm your selection for service, which has now been granted Expedited Status—"

"And the technical team will be contacting me later this morning to arrange an appointment."

"To take place by the end of this week at the latest. As regards your claim that the Ministry refuses to communicate, I can see that Mr Anderson has made quite an exceptional written request to the effect that at the end of your day at the National People's Museum, you should, if possible, receive a copy of the accompanying pamphlet normally reserved for Party members."

"That's very kind of Mr Anderson."

"It is," Miss Palmerstone agreed, having grasped none of the irony Mr Rubens had not made any attempt to conceal. "And I hope it might provide you with some answers."

"I hope so too."

There was a brief silence, then the sound of Miss Palmerstone clearing her throat. And when she spoke again, the monotony of her voice had succumbed to the outpouring zeal of a fanatic.

"Although I have to say that in my personal opinion as a citizen," she began with enthusiasm, possibly as tears were welling up in her eyes, "a day at the National People's Museum is so self-evidently an honour that any attempt at explanation could only ever fail to do it justice. There is such a thing as too much information, Mr Rubens, and the government's policy, as you know, has always been to do away with as much of it as possible."

Albeit without emotion, Mr Anderson and Mr Evans had gone to great lengths to make an almost identical point, probably in the hope it might have justified how some purely inconsequential facts had escaped them. But escaped them they had, and since they were inconsequential, while Mr Anderson nodded Mr Evans had suggested it was best they were consigned to the oblivion they deserved, completely forgotten, *for everyone's sake*. "*For everyone's sake*," Mr Anderson had made a point of repeating emphatically.

"All Departments are subject to strict guidelines as set out by the Ministry of Information," Miss Palmerstone concluded.

"Perhaps the Ministry of Information should rename itself the Ministry of *Less* Information," Mr Rubens retorted before hanging up.

It was still not the time for reminiscing. This was one conversation that had not made him want to retreat to the past, because suddenly the present seemed more pressing. With the telephone back in its cradle, Mr Rubens made his way back to the *Amoeba*, almost tripping over a corner of one of the rare Persian pieces Eunice had accused of being rugs. If he fell over now and broke a leg, would that entitle him to claim the exemption of being 'gravely ill', or would he still have to serve? With one leg rigid in a plaster cast, the *Amoeba* would be impossible to sit in, spoiling the entire composition he had painted in his mind.

She might have been unfair to his Persian carpets, but Eunice had been right about everything else. Mr Rubens suddenly felt terribly alone, living unloved and unnoticed in a nightmare worse than *1984*, a hideous world that took itself for granted. He had gone out of his way to be difficult and rude, first with Mr Anderson and Mr Evans, and then with Miss Palmerstone, and although he may have ruffled some feathers, really he had had no more effect than an irritating child throwing tantrums. No one had taken much notice; there had been no midnight knocks on his door.

But he was glad that they were expediting his selection. The sooner this unpleasant experience was over, the better. And it struck Mr Rubens that what made it unpleasant was not that it was probably just frippery and fluff, or the danger it was something much more sinister than that, but the fact that he had no one he could laugh at it with, or be afraid of it with, or enjoy it with if it happened to be fun. Everyone who had belonged to his world at one time or another was gone. Mr Rubens would make a very lonely exhibit indeed.

Kevin

It couldn't have been more than five minutes since his conversation with Miss Palmerstone had ended, and the telephone was ringing again.

Busy morning, thought Mr Rubens, as once again he had to crawl out of the *Amoeba* to answer it. *Let's see what idiot I can irritate next.*

"Yes?" he answered bad-temperedly.

"Is that Mr Rubens? Mr Anthony Pablo Rubens?" The words were the same, but the voice was a man's, and it was cheerful.

"Speaking." Immediately his tone had mellowed, to reciprocate the voice's good humour.

"And a very good morning to you, Mr Rubens, how are you today?"

"Very well," said Mr Rubens, "and you?"

"Well, I say morning, but actually I see that it's already afternoon - it's already afternoon and I'm babbling... Oh, dearie me, I've not even introduced myself yet. This is Kevin from your allocated technical team, and I'm very well too. Right then, Mr Rubens, I believe you were expecting my call?"

"I was, yes," said Mr Rubens.

"Of course you were, of course you were," said Kevin, "and I know because Dorothy told me you were, and if there's one thing about Dorothy you can always rely on, it's that she never gets appointments mixed up. I have yours right in front of me in black and white: Mr Anthony Pablo Rubens, NPM with Expedited Status, a call this morning, a visit by the end of the week. And I know that it's already afternoon, but when I called your number earlier, maybe a quarter of an hour before noon, I swear to you it was busy. It was busy, Mr Rubens, I swear."

Babbling by his own admission, and rather prone to repeating himself, Kevin was a breath of fresh air all the same. *He's definitely not a robot*, thought Mr Rubens.

"Yes, Dorothy and I were on the phone for some time."

"Yes, yes, so she told me. When I couldn't get through, I thought your line might be down, so I called her to ask if she'd had better luck. And she confirmed that you'd spoken, but otherwise she didn't sound happy *at all*. The two of you had an argument, she said."

"I wouldn't go that far," said Mr Rubens. "Possibly I asked too many questions."

"Well, you were perfectly within your rights to ask as many questions as you liked. Problem is, it's not Dorothy's job to answer questions, and probably you asked questions she didn't know the answers to, so I imagine that you got her all flustered, she was flustered when I talked to her, she was really quite upset, which for Dorothy is unusual."

"It wasn't my intention to upset her," said Mr Rubens.

"Just frustrated you weren't getting any answers, am I right? And I told her so. 'Can't blame a man for wanting to *understand* things,' I said, being inquisitive is in our genes, part of human DNA. 'And to be honest with you, Dorothy,' I said, 'I'm an inquisitive man myself.' But no, she wasn't having any of it. It's her dream, you see, getting a summons and having her day at the National, so it's beyond her why anyone who's had the privilege should be anything other than over the moon."

"She did get a little defensive."

"Sounds to me, Mr Rubens, and please don't quote me on this or I'll get into trouble, sounds to me like those clowns who came to see you didn't do a very good job, they're the ones who should've answered all your questions."

Clowns? As though electrified by the description, Mr Rubens felt unstable on his feet. And not quite knowing how it had happened, for the first time since acquiring it he found himself sitting on the art deco bureau.

"They seemed more interested in my crockery," he said, merrily dangling his legs.

"And believe it or not, that's nearly all they've given us instructions about – take good care of the monkeys, they wrote, they're antique. Oh, and there was something about an amoeba."

"That's my chair," said Mr Rubens.

"If I've told them once, I've told them a thousand times – don't embarrass me, please, give me instructions *I can understand*. Ha! See what I mean? I tell you, Mr Rubens, it's in our DNA. Funny name for a chair, though, must be quite special in some way."

"It's a very important piece of 1960s design," said Mr Rubens. "And it's incredibly comfortable."

"Not a problem, Mr Rubens, not a problem. In *my* book, there *are* no problems, only solutions. I've thought that ever since I was a lad, it's been what you might call my philosophy, right up until they cheapened it by making it a Government Party slogan. And that's another thing I've always thought: that you can't trust politicians."

Mr Rubens kept quiet. *I don't know this man from Adam*, he thought. *He sounds genuine enough on the phone, but it's probably best not to take any chances.*

"Mr Rubens?"

"Still here," said Mr Rubens.

"I've a big mouth, I know, and you're worrying it might get me into trouble, but I'm lucky, Mr Rubens. I'm lucky that I really like my job, and I'm lucky that the people at the Ministry know how bloody good at it I am. So whatever this Museum Service malarkey is all about, I promise you we'll make the best of it. That's actually our last bit of instruction from the Ministry, to give it all we've got and make sure that we conjure up something quite spectacular for you. You must've made quite an impression, Mr Rubens, if you don't mind me saying so. NPM with Expedited Status, a great space to work with and a dedicated four-member technical team, you're going to have quite a day, you can at least be sure of that."

"Have you ever visited the National People's Museum, to see any of the exhibitions that you've helped to set up?"

"I'm not a Party member, so I couldn't, but I don't think I'd have wanted to even if I could. Please don't get me wrong, I may just be the head of one of the Ministry's technical teams but I think of myself as an artist, and when people like yourself who've an eye for design tell me that they're happy with the outcome, it's a gratifying feeling. But really that's as far it goes, I've no interest in gawping at people I've worked with while they're sat behind glass. When I first took the job, I did go and see one or two exhibitions I helped to put up at a local, and it's putting it mildly to say that I didn't enjoy the experience at all."

Mr Rubens stopped dangling his legs. "I'm surprised at your candour," he said.

"I've been speaking with you freely, Mr Rubens, because from everything I've heard, I think I can trust you."

"From everything you've heard?"

"Just snippets, really, mostly things I've heard from Dorothy. Now *there's* a blabbermouth if ever there was one."

"And what's Dorothy been saying?" After switching the receiver from his left ear to his right, with a single leap Mr Rubens left his perch on the bureau.

"Mostly what I've told you already. Basically, they hate it when anybody asks too many questions - you know why?"

"Because they don't know the answers," said Mr Rubens.

"And those people they send round, they don't know jack shit either. They've *none* of them been taught how to think. All they're good at is parroting nonsense."

"So they think I'm a troublemaker," said Mr Rubens.

"I'd be lying if I said otherwise," said Kevin. "You're what's known in the Ministry as a 'ped'."

"A *'ped'*?" Mr Rubens was horrified.

"Short for 'pedant'," said Kevin. "And it isn't by chance that it sounds like something else. God forbid that anyone should blame the system, so what they like to do instead is try and vilify whoever dares to call it into question."

"Why, then? Why the National People's Museum and the Expedited Status, why the great space to work with and the four-member technical team? Why all this for a *'ped'*? Why you, of all people?"

"'Why', Mr Rubens? I don't think that's a question that's even *supposed* to have an answer. 'Ours is not to reason why,' you must have heard that one before."

"I have, more than once."

"I'll let you in on a little secret, Mr Rubens. There isn't a 'why', or everyone would know what it was. They've done all what they've done, and now they're trying to get us to believe we've each one of us become more important – they *need* us to believe we've become more important and they need us to believe there's a link, that they've *made* us more important, or what's it all been for, all the horrible things that they've done?"

"Perhaps you're being more candid than you should," said Mr Rubens, but his words had drifted back and forth through the wires unheeded.

"They're forever playing with words, with words and with our heads. Museum Service is actually a very good example. We're told it's so important that it has to be compulsory, and it *sounds* important, doesn't it? If we're told something's important, not knowing *why* it's important gives it a sort of mystique, and that *proves* it's important. It's all smoke and mirrors, of course, but you see what I mean. There's a handful of people at the top who're really quite clever, you have to give them that."

"But still you say you enjoy what you do."

"I'll let you in on another little secret, Mr Rubens. There aren't any truths any more, only illusions. We're all in the gutter, I'm afraid, but every now and again it's good to shut our eyes to the rest of the world, take a big breath and just gaze at the stars."

"I'm reminded more of Kafka than of Oscar Wilde."

"I hear you, Mr Rubens, I do. My advice, for what it's worth? Never think in black and white, nothing's *ever* either or. Try and imagine just a little Murakami in between, and I promise you an experience you'll enjoy. Now then, which day suits you best for the appointment? It's Wednesday today, so it'll have to be either Friday or tomorrow."

Murakami? Never think in black and white, nothing's *ever* either or? This man was so unlikely that he almost rang true. Self-proclaimed dissident, artist, philosopher, he was undoubtedly bright, but was he brave or was he brazen? What would Eunice have thought? Mr Rubens *wanted* to trust him, but at the same time he was glad he had kept his reserve. He had listened to Kevin politely but had not said very much - little more than what he had already said to Dorothy and the clowns.

"Let's say Friday," he said.

"Friday it is, we'll be with you at nine o'clock on the dot. Thank you, Mr Rubens, I've enjoyed our little chat, and I'm really looking forward to the monkeys!"

There was a reason Mr Rubens had asked for an appointment on Friday. His nose had told him that tomorrow would be dry, whereas Friday would be a washout. He had already decided to pay a visit to one of the local People's Museums, and since it would be dry and also relatively warm, tomorrow seemed the perfect opportunity. Although he had a few things in mind for his expedited day, a visit to a local People's Museum would hopefully provide him with fresh insights that might lead to new ideas, which he would then be able to discuss during his appointment with Kevin and the technical team. For once the weather was proving propitious.

I wish I could have smelled the man's breath, thought Mr Rubens.

FOURTEEN

Slogans

After six hours' solid sleep, undisturbed by uneasy dreams, Mr Rubens awoke on Thursday morning with a hot, dull pain in his knees.

That'll teach you a lesson for leaping off the art deco bureau, he thought, *and for sitting on it in the first place.*

He did some gentle stretching exercises that, really, he should do every day, and also took a couple of pills after breakfast. Within half an hour the pain was almost gone, and only now, when they had already settled back to their usual unattractive shape, did Mr Rubens realise that earlier his knees had been badly swollen.

I don't know my own body any more.

He looked at himself in the mirror, which he rarely did, for good reason.

In the first place, mirrors always tended to remind him of Malcolm. And his own appearance reminded him of how quickly and yet how slowly time had passed. Time was a conundrum, its vagaries the stuff of paradox and contradiction. Its slippery nature was hateful. It was inexorably real, and at the same time as illusory as any of Kevin's truths. While too readily it seemed to bend at different moments, there was *always* too little of it, even as one wished it away.

I can guess, more or less, what Eunice would have made of all this, but if Malcolm were here, we would have revelled in each other's curiosity, like we used to in the short time I knew him.

Abstract thoughts of time and its slippery nature had tired him, and Mr Rubens had deliberately turned to the mirror again. Looking his reflection up and down, he wished for memories of Malcolm to crowd him.

But when they did, they jarred with the sight of his body, naked except for a white pair of Y-fronts. Thoughts of time were intruding again, now not abstract but concrete and brutal. If Malcolm were here, he would be the same young Malcolm that Anthony had never been without. Memories did not become old unless they were shared. What confronted Mr Rubens as he examined his reflection were the consequences of a life cut short by grief and then restarted - of holding on to people he had loved and then letting go, while at the same time *refusing* to let go, holding on to memories that never grew old.

But I've always been with you. I've looked at your body every day. Mr Rubens' voice belonged to Malcolm too. Enduring at the heart of their inseparableness, a part of him had always remained.

Mr Rubens took his time getting dressed. He had riffled through his wardrobe, wondering what people wore when they visited a People's Museum. For some reason that he couldn't quite articulate, he imagined an implied obligation to be smart. It had probably something to do with the days when trials were still being held in open court, and the association he had made in his mind between Museum and Jury service. The last time he had worn a suit was for his leaving party at work, but since he had already decided that he would wear a suit on his day at the National, he would also wear a suit today, as a mark of respect for his fellow unfortunates. But once again he was prejudging, when he had promised himself that he would keep an open mind until after his visit, when his opinion would at least be based on fact.

For God's sake, pick a suit, assuming there's one that still fits you.

In fact, they would all still fit him, in the same way all his trousers and jackets and shirts did. The years had made his body decrepit without changing its shape. If one didn't look too closely (and why would anyone want to?), he looked remarkably good for his age, and as long as he avoided leaping off art deco bureaus, he was also quite fit. He had never been a narcissist, and was not even particularly vain, but age had not made him indifferent. He was proud of his appearance; it vindicated his resilience and austere way of life.

As he contemplated his array of suits, it struck Mr Rubens that he couldn't remember the last time he had bought himself anything new. Eunice had insisted on knitting a jumper for him every Christmas, going through too much effort to produce something both of them knew he would wear only once, for the Christmas lunch they shared the following year. And here, at the top of the pile on the left side of the wardrobe, was the one he had *never* worn, because since the intervening September of 2028, there had been no Eunice to share Christmas lunch with.

These festive jumpers had not been ridiculous. The reason Mr Rubens had worn them only once, indoors and only in the presence of his sister, was not that they depicted Santa Claus or reindeers. Each one of them had been emblazoned with a slogan that could have landed both of them in jail. The earliest had harped back to the Spanish connection. NO PASARAN, and LOOR A LOS HÉROES - THEY SHALL NOT PASS, and HAIL TO THE HEROES. He remembered Eunice lamenting how few had been the heroes in the fight against the Government Party's atrocities — there had been no violent uprisings, no groundswell of protests or fireball of riots. There had been hardly any fight, and hardly any heroes to hail.

Then the slogans had become more explicit. I HATE THE NEW LEADER; DOWN WITH THE GOVERNMENT PARTY. They might have been explicit, but they had not been especially imaginative, although the colour combinations had always been beautiful. But what had been the slogan on the jumper he had never worn? Mr Rubens had forgotten. As he began to unfold its greys and reds, the smell of lavender was overwhelming. With his arms extended either side of him, the tip of each sleeve between his fingers, he spread out in front of him his sister's last present. The obscenity of the words made him laugh, but when he dug his face into the wool, all he could smell was his loneliness. He refolded the jumper and returned it to its place at the top of the pile, but then he changed his mind and took it out again.

You wouldn't dare! Oh yes I would. Oh no you wouldn't.

Would he? It was not particularly thick; he could easily wear it under a jacket, and then he wouldn't need to take a coat with him. With a wry smile he laid it out flat on the bed.

Laughter

The sky was pale, as though its blue had been unevenly whitewashed. Overnight, its coating of amorphous cloud would break up into segments of blackness that tomorrow would start to dissolve into rain. Mr Rubens had always been fond of the sky, and not only because he had the gift of foretelling its secrets. In spite of that there was a mystery in its vastness, which no amount of science could dispel. It may have been proved to be finite, but all the same it belonged to an immensity whose purpose was to put man in his place.

The bare trees and colours of his street, whose smells he breathed in with the chill that was already full of vapour, filled him with a sense of wellbeing. One consequence of the upheaval that had turned the whole world upside down was a later coalescing around unthinkable discoveries that had rapidly stemmed global warming. The earth was breathing again. The achievement had been claimed by the Government Party and by all its international equivalents as theirs, when in fact it was the consequence of breakthroughs that offered cheap solutions. As the world sighed with relief, welcoming an age of new prosperity, in their majority the citizens of every country had all but forgotten their governments' crimes. Old freedoms corresponded to old values, and in this unbrave new world the heroes to hail had become even fewer.

At least the air is fresh again, thought Mr Rubens. And at least there would be a future in which things had the chance to be different. It *was* a silver lining, which his sister had refused to acknowledge sufficiently.

Since the terrible night of the election, when his well-to-do neighbours had all stayed barricaded in their homes, Mr Rubens had only ever seen them fleetingly, never hesitating on their doorsteps as they rushed to come or go. They were keeping to themselves as they had in the years of the pandemic, perhaps hoping to shut out the miasma of the new world in the same way they had shut out the virus. *I have no more right to judge them than they have to judge me*, thought Mr Rubens, almost slipping as he trampled on the freshly fallen leaves, taking ever faster strides along the curve of the long cul-de-sac, suddenly as eager in his hurry as his neighbours.

On the main road at last, outwardly still as bijou as it had been when Mr Rubens moved to Highgate, bioelectric cars whizzed past with hardly a sound, at set speeds that could not be exceeded. Cyclists only cycled in the designated lanes. Smart phones weren't so smart any more, but threatened to be smart enough to spy, and as far as Mr Rubens could see, the few people who had them only used them for emergencies. In these respects, at least, London gave the impression of a much better place, but in so many others it felt like a graveyard.

Like the rest of the country, it had undergone a deep clean-and-polish in which the outward signs of its old threats had been removed. All of Mr Rubens' former haunts had been transformed. Camden was no longer multi-coloured, its anarchy of oddballs and misfits and freaks giving way to a dull uniformity that had neither buzz nor vibe; King's Cross had become a disinfected transport hub, its corners free of litter and its decadent vitality extinguished. The government's narrative was a simple one of cause and effect: as a consequence of 'difficult decisions', the streets were now virtually crimeless, trains and buses were running on time, housing was adequate, health and education were decent, and *everything* was clean. These were the people's new 'freedoms', and they were possible only because they had taken the place of the old ones. But the consequence, as far as Mr Rubens was concerned, of constricting it within this clinical façade was that the city's very soul had been wrung out. Ironing out its shambles had only made it bland.

Mr Rubens took the bus to central London, on his way to the local People's Museum at Somerset House in the Strand, where the Courtauld Institute of Art used to be housed before it was closed down. The spotless single decker was empty, save for two teenage boys. Dapper in their crew cuts and matching blue blazers, their voices insolently loud, they evidently wanted to be heard as they vied with each other in extolling the New Leader. *Little that they know that Big Brother isn't bothering to watch them,* thought Mr Rubens, gulping down a good-natured laugh. At the stop on Charing Cross Road just after Leicester Square, he disembarked behind them, and watched them strolling off holding hands, heading north towards Soho. *Hmm,* Mr Rubens thought to himself. He remembered that the last time he had travelled to the centre of town was for the Almodóvar season at the Curzon. That, too, had been an occasion for raising an eyebrow. As he turned to walk in the opposite direction, he suspected that these small incongruities were not accidental.

Architecturally, at least, Trafalgar Square had been preserved, but even though it had remained intact it did not feel familiar. As he walked around its lions stretching his legs, it struck Mr Rubens how different it was without crowds of either people or pigeons. An over-polished Nelson gleamed into the sky as though he had been dipped into bleach, and the other heroes' statues shimmered on their plinths even in the absence of sunlight. It was as if the whole square had had its patina scrubbed out, erasing with the accumulated dirt any meaningful sense of its history. Unnerved by this sensation, Mr Rubens stood still for a moment by the fountain, to enjoy the constant gurgle of the water with his eyes shut.

Nothing had changed and yet *everything* had changed, and it was this invisibility that he found most disturbing, for it depicted by omission all the old freedoms. The vitality hidden in things that may have once got on his nerves had been snuffed out: there were no groups of tourists taking selfies; no men of God yelling fire and brimstone; no demonstrators marching or chaining themselves onto railings; no feverish sounds, or smells of sugared almonds and poisonous hot dogs – unbelievably no smells *at all.* The loudness of these absences was unendurable; it was all Mr

Rubens could do to click his eyes wide open, and cast around for memories that might oppose the deadly dearth.

The old National Gallery, where he had fallen in love with Caravaggio, was now home to the officialdom of the Museums Ministry; gazing at the building's colonnaded entrance from beside Nelson's column, Mr Rubens wondered what the odds were that Dorothy's desk faced the wall where *Boy Bitten by a Lizard* had once hung – in Room 31, if he wasn't mistaken.

The bitten boy's pained expression, the raising of his fragile shoulder, the sensuality of his mouth, had all reminded him of Malcolm, and the cracks in the paint of his freckles. In those early days, almost everything reminded him of Malcolm.

Along the Strand, in whose doorways and side streets so many homeless people had at one time or another sought refuge, the day seemed to have brightened; momentarily the sun had broken through, lighting up the shiny drabness of this opulent part of the city. Traffic was light, mostly cyclists and buses, and the few smartly dressed pedestrians had a brisk, purposeful spring in their step. If one had drawn a half-mile circle around Mr Rubens, it would have encompassed most of government. He was right at the centre of power, witnessing its paper-shuffling cogs as they moved from one Department to another. Idle hands were the devil's tools, and an effective bureaucracy could never be too convoluted.

Mr Rubens observed these men and women – in the most glaring, despicable absence of all, every one of them depressingly white - as they either overtook or walked past him, some of them alone but most of them in pairs, talking to each other even faster than they walked. And in the ten or fifteen minutes it had taken him to walk to Somerset House from Trafalgar Square, he had not heard even one of them laugh. When had he heard *anyone* laugh? Contentment without laughter was not true contentment. In its widespread lack, Mr Rubens saw hope. The natural need for it might someday be the catalyst for change.

If the Government Party were so clever, they would make it compulsory, mused Mr Rubens, and tickled by the irony he laughed, but his laughter failed to spark a revolution. Every busy passer-by briefly looked at him askance, before quickly moving on.

Perspective

A uniformed guard stood at the entrance to the People's Museum.

"Do I need a ticket?" Mr Rubens asked him.

"Are you visiting someone in particular?"

These people are really quite incapable of giving a straight answer. Well, two can play at that game!

"Is there someone in particular I need a ticket for?"

The guard's eyes narrowed suspiciously. "Are you trying to be clever?"

"No, I'm not trying to be clever," said Mr Rubens.

"Then let me ask you again. Are you in any way acquainted with one of the exhibits?"

"But I don't know who the exhibits are," said Mr Rubens.

"There's no ticket," said the guard. "Admission is free." And making way for Mr Rubens to get past, "Up the stairs and follow the signs. No talking, no photography, no food."

"And no accompanying pamphlet, I suppose," said Mr Rubens.

"There's water fountains if you need them," said the guard.

The interior had been redesigned, consisting now of six uniform cubicles on the second storey, all behind glass and separated from each other by narrow corridors that zigzagged into one another so that no two exhibits could be seen simultaneously. It reminded Mr Rubens of a Museum of Horrors. There was a guard at every second corner, which made the place feel too much like a prison. If there were any other visitors in front of him, Mr Rubens never came across them. The atmosphere did not encourage lingering, with large red arrows on the walls that seemed to instruct moving on. And it was very hot; if he could take his jacket off, he would.

"Can the exhibits see us looking at them?" Mr Rubens dared to ask the second guard he came across.

"Course not, and neither can they hear us," the man answered gruffly.

"So there's never really any interaction with the public," said Mr Rubens.

"None whatsoever," said the guard.

Mr Rubens sighed. "Poor buggers," he heard himself saying.

The guard gave a noncommittal nod, but then his tone mellowed as he bent his head conspiratorially to whisper in Mr Rubens' ear: "A lot of the time they forget they're being watched, it's like they're in a world of their own, the heat in there must drive them cuckoo. Some people find it funny. Personally, I think it's creepy. We even had this guy once— Let me put it this way: you *don't* want to know. But if you're asking my opinion, it's far too many hours they've got them cooped up for. And we've hardly any visitors most of the time, so it's also tough for us. There are times when all we're here for is to escort them to the toilet. Might as well be at home watching paint dry."

"And you're right, it's hot," said Mr Rubens.

"Not half as hot as in those cubicles."

"I've been called to serve at the National," said Mr Rubens. "That's why I'm here, this is actually my first time at a People's Museum."

"You've come to test the waters, I suppose - see what you're in for."

"Something like that," said Mr Rubens.

"Well, I can't say I've set foot in the National – you wouldn't, would you, after spending half your life in *this* dump – but if it's any consolation, they say there's no comparison. Spacious, well-curated, fully air-conditioned–"

"You know someone who's been?"

"Liam has, that's the guard you met downstairs at the door. He can't have enough of the place."

"So he must be a party member."

"To be honest with you, I think that's the reason he joined. One of the guards there convinced him, and now he claims it's the best thing he's done in his life."

"Has he told you why he likes it so much?"

The guard gave a shrug. "Can't say I've ever asked. Seems like a fetish to me, watching people being caged up. Only God knows what he likes to get up to with his missus."

"His missus must know too," said Mr Rubens, and they both broke into a titter.

"Shh!" said the guard, struggling to compose himself. Then waving Mr Rubens on with a pat on the back, "Good luck with your day at the National. But if you're thinking of wearing that jumper, make sure you have it on the right way round, not back to front."

"Thank you, I'll do that," said Mr Rubens.

"And thank you for making me laugh," said the guard.

"It's me who should be thanking you," said Mr Rubens. "I was beginning to think no one laughed any more."

And certainly none of the exhibits today showed the least inclination to laugh. As he entered the building, Mr Rubens had wondered if a theme of some kind ran through every exhibition, unmentioned but somehow implicit in the grouping together of each day's exhibits. Visitors who derived instruction – or warning – from one exhibition might feel buoyed or inspired by another, and be no more than amused by a third. But instead there had been nothing. Despite his endeavours, Mr Rubens had failed to discern any plausible thread that, even in some strange way, could have served to connect these seemingly dissonant people. If his experience was typical, it was hardly surprising there had been no other visitors, or that most of the exhibits, probably as uncertain as he was of why they were there, had appeared to him so utterly glum and pathetic.

In the first cubicle, bare but for a three-piece-suite that had seen better days, a fat middle-aged man snoozed in one of the armchairs, apparently oblivious to the world. Looking more closely, Mr Rubens noticed an old, much-thumbed *Playboy* magazine on the floor by the sofa; then his gaze fell on a book that lay next to the man on its side. Either it had accidentally slipped from his lap or an effort had been made to convey that impression. Had it not been for its skewed position, its title would have been impossible to read: *The Interpretation of Dreams*, by Sigmund Freud. Mr Rubens walked away scratching his head.

In the second cubicle, a woman far too heavily made up stood behind an imitation bar pretending to be pulling pints. The glitzy décor of plush velvet furnishings and a tacky chandelier was redolent of a bordello. Mr Rubens stood closer to the glass and pushed the frame of his glasses more firmly over the frown above his nose. No single object stood out; if there was any hint of mystery, it was contained in the expression of the woman. She was smiling, but her smile seemed somehow unnatural. And on one side of her face, her mascara had run down her cheek as though following the trail of a tear.

The third exhibit dissipated in an instant the gladdening effect of Mr Rubens' repartee with the guard. Every available wall space had been covered with pre-election posters proclaiming the Government Party's violent intentions, and a perspiring young man stood stridently at the centre of the cubicle resembling a Nazi, as indeed must have been his intention. Mr Rubens didn't linger; he felt no urge to look for hidden clues.

The next cubicle provided some welcome light relief. A busy professional gentleman, who clearly must have thought the experience beneath him, had not so much recreated as brought his office with him, and was rather self-importantly immersed in his work. Wearing half-moon glasses and surrounded by untidy piles of paper, he was bent over his desk poring over a document to which occasionally he would pause to make additions, pulling back from it every so often to suck on his pen.

In the fifth, a man as old as Mr Rubens looked bemused at the early arrival of Christmas. Fairy lights blinked on and off on the fake Christmas tree he stood next to, turning him blue, then yellow, then red, while he leaned on his stick looking colourful but vacant.

In the last cubicle, the tableau was of mourning. Facing away from the glass, as though turning her back on the world she was sharing her grief with, a woman clad in black sat motionlessly in a stiff wooden chair, staring at the picture of a handsome young man hanging on the opposite wall. Aside from the revulsion he had felt for the Nazi, of all the days' exhibits the woman in mourning had made on Mr Rubens the strongest impression.

If the purpose of Museum Service was to afford the State an opportunity to celebrate its citizens, today's exhibits at the local People's Museum in the Strand had evidently failed to grasp it. In the midst of dreary objects, tawdry propaganda and glitz, they had all seemed intent either on making a statement or on demonstrating their indifference. A show of drudgery, tragedy, or rage hardly constituted celebration in *anyone's* mind. Perhaps the exhibition had been badly conceived. How many exhibitions had Mr Rubens seen in his lifetime where an artist, or more likely an over-ambitious curator, had glaringly failed to convey their purported intention? Unless of course the intention of today's exhibition had been to show that there *was* no connection, nor any unifying link binding the disparate bunch of exhibits together, because even in New Britain everyone was different. Or it might be that by giving them a space to perform, the people who had locked away the nation's art had wished to make artists of its citizens in order to make art more democratic.

Unlikely, thought Mr Rubens.

The Government Party knew better than to encourage such dangerous notions of democracy and difference. Unlikely, too, that the National People's Museum would live up to its grander pretences.

On the other hand, was it not entirely possible, even likely, that in his search for a rational explanation for this bizarre and bewildering enterprise, Mr Rubens had naively ascribed to the State more than the State may have wished to ascribe to itself? He recalled the day of the Evaluation Panel's visit. "Every citizen," Mr Evans had remarked, "has the freedom to make as much, or as little, of their day as they wish to."

The true purpose of Museum Service was control, *not* celebration. But couldn't tables be turned and alternative mirrors put up in the smoke? *Perspective*, that's all it came down to. Even if Museum Service was not, after all, a celebration by the State of its citizens, did it still not afford one the very unique and public opportunity to celebrate oneself? One merely had to have faith that there was something worth celebrating. If his day at the National People's Museum would be what *he* wished to make of it, then he, Anthony Pablo Rubens, resolved absolutely that he would make nothing less than the most of it. Yes, he was proud to be shown.

FIFTEEN

Cobwebs

After leaving Somerset House, to clear his head of cobwebs
Mr Rubens decided on a stroll along the embankment. The
view towards the west was still impressive; the sharply
angled concrete buildings of the Southbank had the cold
economy of nuclear reactors, and shared the desolation of
the first play he had seen at the National Theatre: Pinter's
No Man's Land, with John Gielgud and Ralph Richardson.
Marta Beatriz had taken him and Eunice to see it, and even
though at the time he was only fifteen, its mysterious,
alienating quality had made a strong impression on him. In
2025, one after the other the buildings of the concrete
complex had been requisitioned by the government, their
proposed new function shrouded in mystery. Eunice had
visited Highgate with rumours of surveillance hubs and
torture chambers, until one day they reopened their doors
as ordinary bars, cafés and restaurants.

The skyline looked different without the London Eye,
more different than I ever imagined it would. Mr Rubens
may never have especially admired it, but nonetheless its
absence now filled him with rage. Within months of its
victory at the polls, against public opinion the Government
Party had dared to declare it an eyesore, and the entire art
establishment had championed and then cheered its
dismantling. Little had they known that they had fallen into
a trap: the London Eye had served as the proverbial
sacrificial lamb. If a popular landmark could be torn out of
the sky without the slightest protest from the art world's
elite, then the art world's elite could hardly have expected

the public's support when the Government Party sought a mandate to dismantle the art world itself.

But that had been the least of their crimes, all of which Eunice had catalogued with a precision that at the time Mr Rubens had only understood mathematically: hundreds steadily progressing to thousands and then tens and hundreds of thousands. While Eunice counted human tragedy, Mr Rubens heard only numbers. Looking back, by far their worst atrocity had been the brutalising of the people, whose animal rage he had personally witnessed on the night of the election. Mr Rubens may have kept his eyes shut, but the reek of that night's heinous acts was still in his nostrils.

All through the Government Party's unforgivable cruelties, only the Anglican Church had put up any resistance (the new Pope had instructed acquiescence), which the mass disappearance of its Bishops had scotched. According to a Government Party spokesman, they had all decided to immigrate to Australia, a claim that, as far Mr Rubens knew, the new Australian government had neither confirmed nor denied. With the armed forces firmly in the New Leader's pocket, the few murmurs from the Palace had also soon gone silent, and after the King's abdication the entire Windsor family had sought refuge in Greece, where recently the monarchy had been restored. There had been speculation that Buckingham Palace was to share the same fate as the London Eye. In the end it had become the Ministry of Information.

With his pencil moustache and all his airs and graces, Joe Devin must have made quite a Queen, thought Mr Rubens, and when a grisly vision of the arrogant boy he had snogged in *The Bell* being beheaded at the Tower made him laugh, he did not feel remotely self-conscious.

No laughter and no dogs.

Mr Rubens wondered if the two might be connected. He had been even less enamoured of dogs than he had ever been a fan of the London Eye, but banning them from almost all public spaces had brought to London's streets an even greater sense of separation: the absence of social interchange between dogs had led to a greater lack of social interchange between people. In effect, public places had become less public.

Likely breeding grounds for social deviation, the designated parks where dogs and their owners are still allowed to frolic freely must be heavily policed, thought Mr Rubens.

But the truth was that policing seemed to need no police any more. Could he even remember the last time he had come across a uniformed policeman? Apparently, contentment without laughter or dogs was making almost everyone law-abiding.

It was not that people were discouraged from enjoying themselves, but it was as if they had been trained to enjoy themselves like robots, in bars and nightclubs that Mr Rubens imagined were not unlike the designated parks for dogs. Or as Eunice had described it, as always so much more picturesquely: "Sex, drugs and rock and roll on prescription." Mr Rubens now realised just how much he had relied on his sister for political gossip and news.

Instead of clearing all the cobwebs, his stroll seemed to be causing them to multiply. It was time to cut it short and catch the bus home. Mr Rubens was about to start heading back towards Trafalgar Square, when something made him stop with a start.

Someone was whistling, not the radio of a passing car but a real human being, brave enough to break up the monotony of absences with an old forgotten sound. Mr Rubens recognized the tune straight away: John Lennon's

152

Imagine. Was the whistler's choice accidental? No, Mr Rubens refused to believe so.

You may say I'm a dreamer
But I'm not the only one

Mr Rubens cast around for the unafraid whistler who had sliced through all the cobwebs like a knife, but as suddenly as it had started, the whistling had stopped, and without it to orient him Mr Rubens was lost. While walking around in a circle he looked left and right, no longer even certain if the whistling had actually happened.

"In any case, I'm *not* the only one," he thought, hearing the words as he spoke them out loud without thinking. And as the whistling started again, the slender upper body of a young man leaned forward from behind an even younger linden tree. After cocking his panama hat and widening his lips to acknowledge Mr Rubens with a smile, the man became invisible again, and the whistling resumed one more time before fading away.

The time for reminiscing

Later on that evening, after finishing his dinner and doing the washing up, as he contemplated the arrival of the technical team the following morning Mr Rubens decided that whatever lay in store on his day at the National People's Museum, he had already earned the right to a small celebration of his own. He had not touched alcohol since losing his sister, but tonight he felt like getting drunk.

His feelings as he left Somerset House had been mixed and contradictory, as mixed and contradictory as the hodgepodge of exhibits, but somehow untouched by their sadness. No, 'untouched' was not the right word. And taking their sadness for granted might also be wrong. These were not normal times, or rather the Government Party had superimposed on the times another veneer of 'new normal' – one that Eunice had been right to denounce.

The people he had visited today were ordinary 'new normal' people living 'new normal' lives. In all likelihood they would have been as alien to him even if they hadn't been on show at a People's Museum. Mr Rubens had not so much adjusted as turned a blind eye to a world in which suddenly *everything* felt alien to him. But now in his attempt not to judge the exhibits, he was judging them differently. Was it best not to judge them at all, not even the Nazi?

What was best was to concentrate his mind on himself. Until a few weeks ago, when a postman with a pencil moustache had knocked on his door to deliver a summons, Mr Rubens had lived a monotonous life. For years he had clung to the minutiae of his daily routine, shutting himself off from the rest of the world by shrinking his existence to the ripples of punctuality and idle repetition, quite content in the pretence that they constituted purpose and meaning.

Eunice was right. I've become a prisoner of habit – a boring old fart hiding behind meaningless distinctions. "A matter of ritual, my arse," Mr Rubens almost yelled, his voice too high-pitched in a bad imitation of his sister's. *I miss her so much, I miss her so much, I miss all of them so much,* he then yelled inside his head.

He put his nose to the cork of the excellent claret Eunice had brought with her the day she rewired his doorbell. Had she not fallen asleep on the *Amoeba*, they would have drunk it that evening together. It had seemed to Mr Rubens too exorbitant a gift for such a commonplace occasion, but although it was true that his sister had always been fond of exorbitant gestures, he had often wondered, and was wondering now as he inhaled the deep aroma of the wine, if perhaps the occasion had been less commonplace than he had imagined at the time. Looking back, like Marta Beatriz's and his father's the significance of Eunice's scent had in adulthood always eluded him, whereas his own denial had covered up the critical significance of Malcolm's.

While waiting for the claret to breathe, he gave his nose a scratch. It had barely told him anything today. Everything he might have needed it for had either been dazzlingly obvious, or would have been inscrutable even to his nose. But that was his conclusion now, in retrospect. In the morning, when he buried his face in the jumper he had later put on back to front, he had felt overwhelmed by the smell of his loneliness. That was the moment Mr Rubens could now put his finger on as the moment he had made the decision that life was too short for his nose to be constantly attempting to sniff out its dangers. There was something to be said for the unknown.

And so from that moment on, Mr Rubens had been happy to experience only everyday smells – in spite of all the absences, many still remained: the smell of lavender that kept away moths, the smell of trees and fresher air outside, the smell of the wind by the river, the smell of the claret he wished he had shared with his sister. Each in its own way, all of them contained a small part of the essence of life.

"Cheers!" said Mr Rubens, and as he drank his first glass of wine in small gulps, he recalled one by one the events that had culminated in this small but symbolic celebration. He had not had so much fun, and had not felt so alive, since… But no, he could not make the choice between Eunice and Malcolm – his childhood, and his mother, had been too long ago.

Uncertainty, fear, amusement, contempt, then surprise and bemusement, then the vertigo of a game of Russian roulette, and finally the joy of liberation. All these emotions before even reaching the climax!

"Cheers!" Mr Rubens said again, after refilling his glass. Cheers to the postman, cheers to Dorothy whose dream was to serve at the National People's Museum, cheers to Mr Anderson and Mr Evans, cheers to Kevin who had dared to call them clowns, cheers to the 'new normal' people he had met in the street, cheers to the dogs and the robots, cheers to the guard who had lifted his spirits by laughing, cheers to the dreamer in the panama hat, cheers to all the exhibits, excluding… no, *including* the Nazi, who might not have been a Nazi after all. Mr Rubens remembered what Kevin had said on the phone: there weren't any truths any more, only illusions.

Buoyed by his conversation with the guard and his feeling of communion with the whistler, Mr Rubens now felt a new affinity with Kevin. After Dorothy and the clowns, he had sounded a little too good to be true. It was not what he had said that had made Mr Rubens suspicious; it was the fact that he had said it, so much of it too, and apparently without a second thought! Yes, it was still possible that it had all been a duplicitous attempt to gain his confidence, and that from the outset Kevin's real intention had been to frighten Mr Rubens by letting him know that already he had been blacklisted as a 'ped'. But no, Mr Rubens refused to believe that.

No one had known he had made a decision to visit the People's Museum in the Strand. No one could have planted the guard who had spoken as plainly, or almost as plainly, as Kevin. And certainly no one would have thought to imagine the whistler. Perhaps there were many people like them, who were no longer afraid to speak, or whistle, their mind.

The world may be changing, thought Mr Rubens. And in this new world, where he felt he belonged, it was not an illusion that he wasn't afraid.

"Cheers!" he said, and with his third glass of wine he was cheering himself.

The three glasses of wine had filled him with that pleasant melancholia of nostalgia, and with the fourth now already in his hand, he stumbled his way to the art deco bureau. Would it fit with the *Amoeba* and the curved wood Scandinavian sideboard in his cubicle at the National People's Museum? He liked to think it might. Resting his glass on the leather inset top, he opened a drawer and took out a small wooden box, which he clutched against his chest with both hands for some time, hunching over the bureau as though frozen in mid-gesture. But his stillness quickly turned to a shiver, and the shiver to a tremble so severe that he almost lost his balance. The box rose with his chest as he filled his lungs with air and held his breath, and through the wood he felt the beat of his heart, and the beat of the hearts of all the people he had loved in his life, whose photographs he kept in that small wooden box.

The box had not been opened since Eunice's photograph, the most recent Mr Rubens had been able to find, had been added to the photographs, all of them like Eunice's face down, of Ernest at the bottom, then of Malcolm, and then of Marta Beatriz, for whom it had been opened in 1985. After Eunice had joined them, Mr Rubens hoped that he would never have to open it again. He would not open it now, and he would not look at those photographs unless he had to. They were no more than moments in time, and for as long as he was able to remember the people whose photographs they were, the mere fact of their physical presence in the room where he spent most of his time meant that none of them had ever really left him. He still bore their wholeness inside him. "Here," said Mr Rubens, with a gesture he remembered from the past. But then, as though to quibble with the questionable meaning of words, the small pile of photographs, all still upside down, were suddenly in the palm of his hand, and Mr Rubens was giddy with a rush of unforgettable smells, inseparably joyful and sad. "Here," he said again, and after he had held and then exhaled an even deeper breath, when he returned the wooden box to its place in the bureau, in their undisturbed order the photographs were once more inside it.

It was different with the black and white photograph he always carried with him in its tiny silver frame, which he did often look at. It was not a reminder, because he had entirely forgotten his mother's appearance and all of her smells, but rather it was proof she had existed, and at one time must have loved him. In that respect her black and white smile acted as an affirmation of a wishfulness that would have otherwise lacked any substance. Perhaps that explained why every other photograph needed to stay hidden. On his day at the National, the small wooden box would remain inside the drawer of the art deco bureau, and the image of his mother in his pocket.

Having somehow managed to get back to the *Amoeba*, Mr Rubens thought of the woman in black who by staring at it so intently had drawn his attention to the photograph on the opposite wall. He had assumed that the person in the photograph was someone she was mourning the loss of, probably her son, and had marvelled not only at her courage but also at how intelligently she had wrested control of her day at the People's Museum. But now he couldn't get it out of his mind that her display had been a fraud, protesting by means of a theatrical statement against the voyeurism to which she was being forcibly subjected.

Mr Rubens was losing the thread of his thoughts. Why had he suddenly thought of that woman again? The wine had had the effect of stretching time, so that his memory of his visit to Somerset House appeared to be more distant than it was.

"I was there this morning." He spoke the words out loud, as though hearing them would give them additional weight. But no, they still seemed not to have any bearing on why at this particular moment his mind had left the present to drift back to his visit at the People's Museum.

It was the photographs, I thought of her because of the photographs.

Slicing through the alcoholic mist that at once made him confused and egged him on, Mr Rubens' jagged dilemma came so sharply into focus that he experienced it as physical pain. If he kept those precious photographs hidden, his mother's in his pocket and those of Ernest, Malcolm, Marta Beatriz and his sister in the small wooden box locked away in the art deco bureau, then what on earth was left to show except his own pathetic self and the monkeys?

His own pathetic self and the monkeys would do.

A celebration, Mr Rubens reminded himself. "A celebration with the people I love."

And it was then, as he spoke out those few words, that he realised an omission was the reason he had suddenly thought of that woman again.

More steadily now, he walked again to the art deco bureau, and from a different drawer took out a photograph of Harry.

"I took this myself, the day before he left for Spain. It belonged to your father, but now it belongs to you," Marta Beatriz had told young Anthony on the day she had buried her son.

And that was what had made him think of the woman in black - the forgotten photograph that he had always kept apart, which probably he wouldn't have remembered had it not been for that stirring of emotion outside Cubicle 6 of the People's Museum in the Strand.

Through his thick varifocals, Mr Rubens looked at the young man he had borne a grudge against all his life. How could he have ever doubted his devotion to Marta Beatriz?

"Loor a los Héroes," he said in broken Spanish, but as he turned his grandfather's photograph face down and opened the drawer with the small wooden box, no sooner had he felt the last burden of history lifting away from his shoulders than he suddenly remembered another.

'The family's unsung hero', that was how Marta Beatriz had described the man whom they all owed so much to and whom everyone else had forgotten. Throughout his life, Ernest had longed to know everything about his father, but it was almost as if Ernest Sr. had never existed. *And Eunice and I were no better.* Their great-grandfather had lost his wife shortly after she had borne him the son they had all lost to Spain, but although he had doted on his grandson and had been like a father to Marta Beatriz, who had honoured him by giving his name to her son, it was too late to include him in the box. Any photographs of him that had survived would have all gone up in flames.

Mr Rubens raised his almost empty glass one last time.

"Cheers, Ernest Sr.," he said.

SIXTEEN

Stranger than a dream

The quality of Eunice's claret had not been a bar to Mr Rubens getting terribly drunk. After finishing the bottle, he had not so much slept as passed out, and in the morning he was late getting up. A little queasy already after eating his cereal too quickly, with every minute that passed he was feeling more nervous. The technical team were due to arrive in half an hour, and for all his bonhomie Kevin had not been particularly enlightening about precisely what their visit would entail. Since his second cup of coffee, and as nine o'clock approached, Mr Rubens' suspicions had begun to resurface.

By blathering on about how well he understood Mr Rubens' frustration with various officials refusing to answer his questions, Kevin had cleverly avoided being asked any questions himself, which he might then have been accused of refusing to answer. His metaphors, literary allusions and borderline seditious outspokenness had all the hallmarks of typical diversionary tactics: he had silenced Mr Rubens by dumbfounding him.

Really, I should stop being so paranoid. It's not good to be suspicious of everyone, that's exactly what those bastards want. I should take a paracetamol and stick to my original gut feeling. And if Kevin turns out to be one of the bastards, so be it! What exactly am I afraid of?

The mere fact that Mr Rubens was spending so much time wondering if he should trust the head of the Ministry's technical team was proof that the bastards had got to him already. What possible questions would he have wanted to ask Kevin that Kevin would have gone to such elaborate lengths to prevent him from asking? He couldn't think of any, except perhaps if there was anything he should have done to prepare for the visit, and that was hardly a question Kevin would have wanted to avoid.

Without such specific instructions, Mr Rubens had made what preparations he could. In the two hours she had been there on Wednesday, Gloria had worked like a typhoon, so the house was clean, and Mr Rubens had made a very nice display of the monkeys on the curved wood Scandinavian sideboard. He had bought two types of biscuits – gingersnaps and Bourbons - and would serve tea and coffee in his set of plain white mugs. If necessary, he also had the ingredients to make sandwiches for lunch.

Sitting at the kitchen table, where his hung-over wandering mind had kept him after he had finished his breakfast, Mr Rubens was drawn once again into the psychedelic maze of the wallpaper's op-art design. Momentarily lost in its disorienting spatial confusion, he felt strangely disembodied, tranquil as he allowed its mesmeric effect to transport him to a familiar but unknown destination somewhere far, from where he could observe himself as though in a dream.

Anthony Pablo Rubens
1960 - 2030

Mr Rubens was reading his obituary in *The Times*. The heading made it clear that he was dead, but the words in the text below it made no sense, he could read them but he couldn't understand what he was reading, either because what he was reading was a meaningless obituary or because he had lived a meaningless life.

The roar of Eunice's favourite symphony made the illegible words disappear. Mr Rubens woke up with a start, almost falling over as he jumped out of his chair.

I really shouldn't do that at my age, he thought, and for a second he wondered if he mightn't still be asleep.

A second wave of tinny music made him look at his watch. It was three minutes past nine, and his mind was still hazy but he wasn't asleep.

Stupid dream, Mr Rubens was thinking, as he made his way through to the hall. *The Times hasn't been published in years! It abdicated with The Guardian and the King, as Eunice used to say.*

When he opened the door, a young man almost fell into his arms.

"My dear Mr Rubens!"

Right now, reality was stranger than a dream, and it was all Mr Rubens could do to gasp out the sound of the name:

"Kevin?"

The voice was the same, but if this was Kevin, he was nothing like the Kevin Mr Rubens had imagined while they spoke on the phone – the picture that had stuck in his mind was of someone middle-aged, non-descript and rather plump, whereas *this* Kevin was young, fit and extremely handsome, with gorgeously thick eyebrows and a full head of spiky black hair.

I wish I'd made more effort when deciding what to wear, thought Mr Rubens. In his double-breasted cardigan, corduroy slacks, and pair of moccasins that looked like slippers, he felt old and self-conscious.

"The very same Kevin you spoke to on the phone!" Kevin's lips had broken into a smile, adding bright white teeth to the list.

Unable to smile back, Mr Rubens was now also lost for words. As dumbfounding in real life as he had been on the phone, it was as if Kevin had stolen his tongue. He was about to at least offer his hand, but somehow Kevin had already grabbed it and was squashing it between both of his. Time seemed to be moving too fast.

"It's a real pleasure, Mr Rubens, and believe me it's not often that I mean it when I say that. As a matter of fact, it's not often that I say it at all, one thing I've never been good at is being insincere." To whisper that last sentence, Kevin's mouth had come so close that it tickled Mr Rubens' parted lips with its breath.

In a deep inhalation that he couldn't have helped, Mr Rubens had taken in air filled with everything good he had known in the past and had almost forgotten. He knew he was not being seduced, and that Kevin was not being flirtatious, but otherwise the present was as though in abeyance, suspended by the blow of Kevin's breath that for one priceless moment had returned an enchanted Mr Rubens to his youth. And he did not feel retrospective regret at the thought that he had wasted any part of it; rather what he felt was the coming back to life of all its joys.

"Kev?"

At the sound of the voice that had come from behind him, Kevin turned around to stand beside Mr Rubens without letting go of his hand.

Three strapping young men with rucksacks on their backs, dressed like Kevin in dark green dungarees over grey turtleneck sweaters, had formed themselves into a line just inside of the door, and were all of them brimming with Kevin's good nature.

"And these are the lads who'll be helping us today," Kevin said, as he delivered Mr Rubens to each one of them in turn. "Jack, Martin, and last but not least this is Jamie."

Time had fast-forwarded and then it had rewound, before fast-forwarding again with the same breakneck speed, catching up with Mr Rubens as he briefly shook hands with all three young men. The door had already been closed, and he was about to lead everyone through to the sitting room, when Kevin put a hand on his shoulder and another on Jamie's.

"We don't make a habit of mixing up work with our personal lives, but today I think we'll make an exception," he said. "I know I keep saying the same thing, that it's not often this, it's not often that, and we don't make a habit of the other, but it's true, Mr Rubens, Jamie here will tell you that since our conversation on Wednesday I've been feeling so excited that I've talked of little else."

"It's true," said Jamie, nodding vigorously. "He's *never* been so excited before, not about a job - you haven't, Kev, have you?"

"I haven't, Mr Rubens, Jamie's telling it just how it is, and he's my other half, he should know."

"Your other half?" When Mr Rubens took a tiny step backwards, he felt the hand on his shoulder tightening gently and holding him still.

"Been together five years and married for two," Kevin said. And pointing at Martin and Jack with the side of his face, "As have those two, haven't you, lads?"

"Been together *six* years and married for two, isn't that right, Jack?" said Martin.

"Congratulations," said Mr Rubens, with a short bow of his head, first to Kevin and Jamie and then quickly to Martin and Jack.

"I suppose we were lucky," said Kevin. "We were shitting ourselves when that Devin guy got purged, but it turns out the New Leader has *a lot* of gay friends. Ours is not to reason why, eh, Mr Rubens?"

"Six and a half," said Jack.

"Jack's a stickler for detail," said Kevin. "Comes in very handy in this job, he's a good man to have on the team, and there's no team that's better than ours."

"There isn't, Mr Rubens, everyone says so," said Jamie.

"Because we all know how to work well *together*," said Kevin.

"People call us the four musketeers," said Jack.

"But fortunately not because we're French," said Martin.

"And after your experience with the clowns, I'm sure you'll be relieved you're in good hands. Jack, Martin, Jamie, they're all best at something, and while they're getting on with it, *my* job, in a nutshell, is *you*. It's your day, after all, and I think it should reflect who you are – the *real* Mr Rubens. The idea is to make sure you have fun."

"I don't think they want me to have fun," said Mr Rubens.

"But *we* do, don't we, lads?"

"Or what would be the point?" said Jack.

"Smoke and mirrors, Mr Rubens, smoke and mirrors," said Kevin. "Let's play them at their own game, I say. They're expecting black and white, so we'll try and give them colour instead."

"With a little Murakami thrown in."

"That's the spirit, Mr Rubens," said Kevin, "now we're getting somewhere!"

'Playing them at their own game' sounded easier than it was. Mr Rubens had tried it with the guard at the entrance to the People's Museum in the Strand, and where had it got him? Nowhere. And the guard's game had been simple – asking stupid questions. But *this* game was a mind game of an altogether different order, intelligent in its malevolence precisely *because* it was stupid.

His day should reflect who he was; the idea was to have fun; they'd try and give them colour instead of black and white. His own second-hand 'Murakami' contribution had been in the same incomprehensible vein. *None* of it made sense. But if it all made sense to Kevin, that was good enough for Mr Rubens. He had nothing to lose. Already he had come to terms with the future by deciding in what way it would *not* be unknown.

The arrival of the four men had dazed him, and he had concentrated so intensely on Kevin's words that his mind had been able to record hardly any of their movements or gestures, only four fixed smiles and the weight of a hand on his shoulder. Now at last Mr Rubens was emerging from the mist. His memory of his youth had already receded, and with it all its smells. There were no truths, only illusions, Kevin had told him. But whether it was genuine or fake, in this special camaraderie he felt completely fearless, or rather had his fearlessness confirmed.

With a twitch of his shoulder and a more determined step to the left, he broke free from Kevin's hand.

"If I were to ask you a very direct question…" His gaze was sharp as it flitted from Kevin to Jamie to Martin to Jack, from the teeth of one fixed smile to the next.

So many bright white teeth, thought Mr Rubens.

"Don't be coy, Mr Rubens, ask away," Kevin said.

"Are you all in the resistance?"

"Pfft, the resistance!" Kevin broke the split-second hush without breaking his smile. "Artists, Mr Rubens, that's what we are. Those criminals have stolen all our art, so we try and put art in its place, even if it's just for one day. And we do it for ourselves, not for anyone else."

"We don't do it for Party members, that's for sure," said Jack.

"Only in this case, by letting you in on our secret, our job is to help *you* be the artist, and that's a whole new ball game for us," said Kevin. And to gurgles of agreement from Jamie and Martin and Jack, "What makes this job so special – and makes *you* so special, too – is that this would be our first collaboration."

"I see," said Mr Rubens. "But I still don't understand what made you so sure you could trust me."

"I read your file, Mr Rubens, yours and your sister's. And you're right, I could never be sure, there was always a chance I was wrong. But then on paper you're a 'ped' and I'm part of the system, so..." Widening his eyes, Kevin shrugged his shoulders. Then broadening a smile Mr Rubens was no longer sure he could trust, "Shall we all go take a look at the monkeys?"

Less is more

Mr Rubens' display on the curved wood Scandinavian sideboard had drawn hoots of admiration (this time the side plates' baboons had beaten the sugar bowl's orangutan hands down), as indeed had the *Amoeba* and the art deco bureau.

"Do you think there'll be space for all three?" asked Mr Rubens, ready to forego the sideboard and the monkeys for the sake of the bureau.

"Oh, I should think so!" Kevin reassured him with a pat on the back, before making an expansive gesture that suggested there'd be space to fit the whole room. "What we have here is a lifetime's collection of beautiful things, but let's not forget where you're being shown - it's the National we're talking about, not some second rate local in the Strand, and the cubicle you've been allotted is enormous. It's *too* big, if you ask me, you'll see for yourself when we show you the plans in a minute, but that's definitely better than too small. We like to think of what we do as akin to three-dimensional painting, and size gives us scope for a good composition, which I'm sure you'll agree is really quite impossible without empty space – space for the monkeys to breathe, if you like."

"And for Mr Rubens," said Jamie.

"*Especially* for Mr Rubens," said Kevin.

"For Mr Rubens in a minimalist composition," said Martin.

"Less is more," said Jack.

"Speaking of less, I see you've got no art on your walls," Kevin said.

"That's because I've never thought of art as decoration," said Mr Rubens. "I've always thought its place was in museums, not on people's walls."

Kevin sighed while he nodded. "Except that now its place is to be hidden," he said.

"Ours is not to reason why," said Mr Rubens with a shrug.

"And as they've stripped it all away from our museums," Kevin said, "it's a pleasure when we see it in people's homes. But no one *ever* likes to show it. The irony is too loaded in choosing to hang art on the walls of a cubicle in a museum from which the government has taken out the art. Have you ever read *Hamlet*, Mr Rubens?"

"I've not read it but I've seen it performed, in the days we still had theatre," said Mr Rubens.

"Then I'm sure you must remember the 'play within a play'," Kevin said. "We'd *love* to be as clever and put some art back in the People's Museums by having it on show in people's cubicles, but it would hardly catch the conscience of the Government Party, and I can't honestly say that people are wrong to be afraid, so it goes without saying that we never insist."

"I should hope not," said Mr Rubens, "considering how badly it ended for Hamlet."

"And we'd hate to try and be clever at people's expense. Well, there's no art on *your* walls, so that's one less dilemma for you, but *our* job is only just beginning. Hmm." Kevin's face was pursed in concentration. "You've given us the basics already, so this is what I'm thinking – the sideboard with the monkeys in the foreground on the left, the bureau at an angle further back to the right, and at the centre of the cubicle the swivelling *Amoeba* with yourself in different poses through the day." While his body spun round, his left index finger had zigzagged as though drawing mental pictures in the air, reminding Mr Rubens of Eunice's gesticulated calculations for his doorbell. Then he brought himself to a standstill with a handclap. "We're all *raring* to go, so we better get started," he said. "But first I'm going to need you to sign a Letter of Authority for me, a declaration basically confirming that you've given us permission to be here. Less may be more, but with my babbling I've already kept you standing for too long, is there anywhere the two of us can sit quietly while the boys are unpacking their equipment?" Jamie, Martin and Jack were standing to one side with their rucksacks at their feet.

"The kitchen," said Mr Rubens.

"Jamie?"

Jamie unzipped a pocket on the side of his rucksack, and handed Kevin a folded piece of paper.

"This way," said Mr Rubens

Let's make some children cry

They *had* kept him standing for too long, so long that his knees had gone stiff, and shifting his weight from one leg to another was painful, but pain at his age was a daily affliction, and gritting his teeth as he walked in front of Kevin to the kitchen, Mr Rubens took great care not to limp. He would take some more painkillers later.

"Mr Rubens, this house really is full of treasures!"

Mr Rubens imagined that Kevin's enthusiasm was directed at his fabulous collection of decorative English pottery and ceramics. Dating mostly from the 1930s, the few choice pieces that comprised it were neatly arranged on the shelves of a steel and glass vitrine that stood in one corner of the kitchen, to the right of the door from the sitting room.

"I can honestly say that I've never seen anything like it! It's art, Mr Rubens, not just a piece of design. It's art and it's *alive*!" Kevin wasn't looking at the pottery; he was staring at the walls. "Op art, right? Maybe Bridget Riley?"

"It's from that period," said Mr Rubens, "but it's not by Bridget Riley, at least as far as I know. This particular design was discontinued after too many complaints that it was making children cry."

Kevin roared with laughter. "I should think that it did!"

More laughter, things are definitely looking up, thought Mr Rubens. Pulling out a chair for Kevin, he sat down at the opposite side of the table.

But Kevin hadn't finished with the wallpaper yet. He was staring into it as though it might be hypnotised by him, rather than the other way around.

"Hmm, I think so," he said, mumbling to himself. Then he snatched his stare away from the wallpaper and slapped it instead on Mr Rubens. "Shall we, Mr Rubens? Shall we have it in your cubicle?"

"In my cubicle?"

"We can replicate it almost exactly."

"You can?"

"It's actually a very simple process. We'll take some 3D photographs, and then we'll get it printed to scale. Imagine, Mr Rubens, the three walls and the ceiling of your cubicle all papered over with this maelstrom of spirals, it'll be like you're floating, the ultimate artwork suspended in the transience of life. I wonder if... but no, I think papering the floor as well would actually detract from the illusion. Hmm..."

"How did you know I visited the People's Museum in the Strand?"

"Pardon, Mr Rubens? I'm not sure what you mean." Kevin had sat down, and was facing Mr Rubens directly. He wore his mask of confused sincerity convincingly, showing no sign of being unsettled by either the suddenness or the implication of Mr Rubens' question.

"Why else would you have mentioned it?"

"Mentioned what?"

"A second-rate local, that's what you called it. Someone must have told you that I visited it yesterday. Or maybe it's already been recorded in my file."

"I'm very, very sorry, Mr Rubens. I should never have alluded to your file, or to your sister's. But what I read in them is partly why I've never for a moment suspected there's the slightest chance you might betray my trust. And now with my stupidity I've caused *you* to mistrust *me*. I had no idea that you had visited the local Museum in the Strand. I picked it quite by chance, probably because my mother used to take me to the Courtauld. I still remember many of the paintings – Van Gogh's self-portrait with the bandaged ear, Gauguin's *Nevermore,* the sixteenth century *Adam and Eve.* It really was quite a collection."

Mr Rubens also remembered these paintings. A smile had returned to his gaze, which he didn't want to hide. "You're just too unlikely," he said. "I mean, what were the chances? Not one but *two* gay revolutionary couples in my technical team! In every way you're too good to be true. But it doesn't really matter whether I can trust you or not."

"It matters to *me*, Mr Rubens. You may choose not to believe it, but it matters to me very much." After unfolding and placing the unsigned piece of paper in front of Mr Rubens, Kevin fell back in his chair, holding on to the edge of the table with both hands. He took in air and held his breath, which he slowly blew out in a sigh, as though to goad Mr Rubens into taking a sniff.

But Mr Rubens would not be goaded. Outside it was raining torrentially, just as his nose had predicted. The rain had started to beat against the windows almost as soon as the men had arrived. It would continue raining on and off throughout the day, until late into the night. And tomorrow the sky would be black, but its threat would not come to pass. It was undoubtedly a reliable barometer, but in every other way his 'gift' had been a fallacy. The air contained neither a part of the future nor any trace of the past. In its smells Mr Rubens had only ever discerned his own emotions, which so often he had hidden from himself. It was his jealousy of her swollen lips, and before that the contours of her smile at the obscenely good-looking George Harrison's wink that had given his sister away, not her breath; secret longings he had not been aware of had translated into an old smell of sex in Malcolm's room; on a train, suppressed private sorrows had found expression in a deeper understanding of the world.

Mr Rubens gave his nose a little twitch. "Let's make some children cry," he said. And picking up the piece of paper from the table, "Do you need me to read this, or shall I just sign it?"

Kevin's smile returned. "Does that mean that you've decided to trust me?"

I can't help liking him, thought Mr Rubens. *If this is part of the charade, at least it's the most pleasant part so far. And it's true that it doesn't really matter whether I can trust him or not. Everything's already been decided. The one thing they can't do is read my mind.*

"I like you," he said, leaning forward towards Kevin. "And I believe you when you say that you'd like me to trust you."

"Hmm…" Kevin was sucking on the pen he had suddenly produced from one of his pockets.

"But let's not forget that we're all playing a part," said Mr Rubens. "Or many parts," he quickly added as an afterthought. *I'm in the middle of playing one right now,* he thought, as he held the piece of paper at arm's length.

"Yes," Kevin said simply, pointing with his eyes at the pen.

From the pen, Mr Rubens' gaze darted back to the unfolded piece of paper. He scrunched up his face, as though taken aback.

"This gives your men permission to go through my belongings," he said.

"For the purposes of making your day a success. And only if you sign it," said Kevin.

Mr Rubens took the pen. "I don't have anything to hide," he said, flattening the piece of paper on the table before signing it above his name.

"You certainly have nothing to hide from any of us," Kevin said.

I may like him, thought Mr Rubens, *but I'm still glad that I've hidden all the jumpers with the slogans.* Less was more, and in this case it was safer as well.

"'The secret of being boring is to say everything,'" he said.

"Oscar Wilde?"

"Voltaire," said Mr Rubens.

Kevin rolled his eyes. "The secret of being boring is to write everything down. And believe me I should know; it's my job to read it. But eventually it'll bring about their downfall. 'Too much information,' as people used to say."

"They still say it," said Mr Rubens. "Your friend Dorothy said it to me the other day, when she wouldn't answer any of my questions. 'There's such a thing as too much information, Mr Rubens,' she said. To which I answered by suggesting that the Ministry of Information should rename itself the Ministry of *Less* Information."

"The policy is to gather it but not to give it out, so really it's the Ministry of Too Much *and* Too Little Information."

"Obviously there's too much information in my file," said Mr Rubens.

"Too much for those clowns to have known what to do with."

"Except to add that I'm a 'ped'." Even knowing that it stood for 'pedant', the thought of being described as a 'ped' made Mr Rubens feel nauseous.

"That was Dorothy's doing," said Kevin.

"But they didn't know about Joe Devin," said Mr Rubens.

Kevin's eyes seemed to water as he tightened his brow. "Joe Devin? Know what about Joe Devin?"

"I suppose it was a long time ago."

"A long time ago?" He had echoed Mr Rubens in a muffled whisper, unclearly, as though through a gag, and now Kevin was rubbing his chin with the side of a finger, while his eyes remained liquid and fixed.

"Our lustful but very brief encounter in *The Bell* in the early 1980s, on the night I fell in love with someone else. Or maybe I was already in love."

"There's not a lot about Joe Devin in anybody's file, he saw to that himself." Kevin's voice had recovered, and his gaze broke with his lips into a smile. "We used to call him Minister of Everybody Else's Information." He lowered his eyes for a moment, before returning them again to Mr Rubens. "The 1980s," he said, as though suddenly overcome with nostalgia for a time long before he was born. And then, after another of his sighs, he spoke in a deliberate way, much more sombrely now. "Please believe me, Mr Rubens, when I say you had a very lucky escape."

I had more, much more than just a very lucky escape, thought Mr Rubens. *But not all of it was lucky.*

"So you didn't know either," he said, forcing a smile. "Which I suppose means that Mr Anderson and Mr Evans kept their mouths shut and it's still not in my file."

"First I heard you knew Joe Devin was just now. It's not even in your file that you're gay."

Unbelievable.

"But I'd be lying if I said I hadn't guessed."

"Guessed?"

"The moment you opened the door. And you're absolutely right, what were the chances? Not one but *two* gay revolutionary couples in your technical team! Mr Rubens, we're *all of us* too good to be true!"

SEVENTEEN

The real world is hardly ideal

"Oh my God, Kev, oh my God!" Both hands over his mouth, Jamie stood still in the doorway, staring at the wall with a look half of awe and half of fright. A heavy-looking camera hung over his shoulder, as though ready to take snaps of a ghost.

"Jamie!" Kevin snapped at him.

But Jamie seemed lost in a world of his own.

"Jamie!" Now Kevin had got up and was furiously waving a hand an inch in front of Jamie's eyes. It forced Jamie to take a step back.

"Fuuuck!" he said in a prolonged exhalation, almost losing his balance before steadying himself against the doorframe.

"Jamie!" Kevin snapped at him a third time. "You're a guest in someone else's home, for Christ's sake!"

"Oh my God, Kev, I'm sorry," Jamie said faintly, goggle-eyed as he pressed his hands together and covered his mouth.

"It's not me you should be apologising to," said Kevin.

Jamie turned to Mr Rubens with a jerk.

"I'm so sorry, Mr Rubens," he said. "I came in just to check if you'd signed the declaration, and imagine how I felt when I saw *that*!" With another jerk he pointed at the wall. "Oh my God, oh my God, Kev, I've never seen anything like it, it's *amazing*! I've not had an experience like this since that time in Amsterdam, when we tried those magic mushrooms, remember?"

"Some things *never* change," said Mr Rubens.

"Jamie, that's enough now!"

"I'm so sorry, Mr Rubens," Jamie said again. "There's so many things I like in your house, but this wallpaper... it's... it's–"

"It's better than drugs, my sister used to say."

Jamie's face lit up. "It's *fantastic*, Mr Rubens, and it's really blown my mind, but I'm not sure I'd go *that* far," he said, breaking into a naughty schoolboy giggle.

Suddenly everyone's laughing, thought Mr Rubens.

"When he saw it, Kevin had a similar reaction to yours," he said.

"It's not for nothing that they call us two peas in a pod, is it, Kev?"

"And we've agreed we're going to use it in my cubicle," said Mr Rubens.

"We're going to paper all three walls *and* the ceiling," said Kevin.

"Wow, *and* the ceiling," Jamie said. "That'll definitely pull things together, it's a brilliant idea."

Mr Rubens motioned them both to sit down, and when they had, "I think we should forget about the monkeys," he said.

With his hands and forearms flat on the table, Kevin leaned forward. "Forget about the monkeys? Hmm, I'm not sure we can do that."

"I don't want my cubicle to look like an antique shop."

"Maybe Mr Rubens is right," Jamie said. "The monkeys are nice, but I think they're too old-fashioned. Whereas this wallpaper... I mean, look at it, Kev, it screams *modern* at you."

"It was modern in the 60s," said Mr Rubens.

"The *60s*? Oh my God," Jamie said, "how long ago was *that*? To me it looks so modern that it's almost like it's not even been made yet, like somehow it belongs to the future."

"So modern that it's almost like it's not even been made yet... I suppose that would make it postmodern," said Mr Rubens with a good-natured chuckle, but his wit was more old-fashioned than the monkeys, and it didn't make anyone laugh.

Kevin looked down at his spread-out fingers, raising them slightly to give them a wiggle. Then tightening them into fists, he used them to rap on the table in slow motion.

"The clowns were very insistent that the monkeys should be included," he said in a very low voice, without looking up.

"Everyone keeps saying that it's *my* day, so it should be up to me," said Mr Rubens.

"In an *ideal* world it would be," Kevin went on in the same muffled tone.

"In an *ideal* world the galleries would still be full of art, and *I*'d be left in peace," said Mr Rubens.

"Yes!" Kevin said emphatically, as at last he raised his eyes to meet Mr Rubens'. "But unfortunately, this is the *real* world, and the real world is hardly ideal."

"We could say I changed my mind at the last minute."

"Let me explain procedure to you, Mr Rubens," said Kevin. "By the end of today, we'll have the hologram of a maquette that shows in great detail what your cubicle will look like, complete with its wallpapered ceiling and walls, the sideboard with the monkeys, the desk, and an image of yourself reclining in the *Amoeba*. Then we'll all need to sign another piece of paper, confirming that the image is a faithful reproduction of what's been agreed for your day. And once the Exhibitions Committee have approved it, even the most minor alterations are strictly forbidden."

Mr Rubens shook his head in bemused disbelief.

"Another committee," he said.

"Of which at least one of the clowns will be a member," Kevin said.

"All this pointless bureaucracy," said Mr Rubens.

"Only for the National," said Kevin. "We could have got away with murder if your day was at a local."

"Party members, you see," Jamie said.

"And it doesn't help that they've decided you're a 'ped'."

"Thank you for reminding me," said Mr Rubens.

"It's my duty to apprise you of all the facts," Kevin murmured dully.

"Now you're sounding like the clowns." Mr Rubens took his heavy glasses off and rubbed his eyes. In the blurred outlines of the two young men, he saw memories of Malcolm and himself. He rubbed his eyes again and put his glasses back on. Although it was a safe and simple procedure, he had never been tempted to have his eyesight corrected. Wearing glasses gave him an additional layer of distance, and he also liked being able to see things unclearly by taking them off. "So let's just leave the monkeys out of the maquette," he said.

Kevin raised his hands, as though in surrender.

"If only it were that simple," he said.

"I don't understand why it's not," said Mr Rubens impatiently. "There's nothing in the summons about monkeys."

"It's your decision, of course," Kevin said.

Resting both his elbows on the table, Mr Rubens made a cradle with his hands for his chin. Once it had settled onto its perch, his head began to rock from side to side very slowly. And when it stopped, as suddenly as it had started, "You're scared of them, aren't you?" he said.

"Kev's not scared of anybody, are you, Kev?"

"Not for *myself*," Kevin answered portentously.

Mr Rubens gave a snort. "I'm not scared of anybody either," he said. "I mean, what's the worst they can do to me, cancel my day?"

"That's the *last* thing they'll do," Kevin said.

"I wish you'd stop speaking in riddles!" Bringing forefinger and thumb almost together, Mr Rubens dangled them in front of Kevin's face. "I'm *this* close to resolving this once and for all," he said without raising his voice. "You know how? By going to the other room and smashing *all* the bloody monkeys to pieces! Then you can tell your friends it was an accident. And why shouldn't they believe you? I *am* a doddery old fool, after all."

No body

For a while, neither Jamie nor Kevin said anything. Jamie looked startled, Kevin deep in thought - rather gloomy, judging by his face.

There's something he's not telling me, thought Mr Rubens. *He's not just scared, he's terrified – but why?*

"There isn't a 'why', or everyone would know what it was," Kevin had told him. And the reason there wasn't a 'why'? Because 'why' was a dilution of power. Under the surface *nothing* made sense, and the most dangerous thing was a 'ped'.

Smoke and mirrors worked both ways. "Artists, Mr Rubens, that's what we are." That was all very well for juggling with their consciences, but still they had a job to do. 'Playing them at their own game' required a degree of complicity; it was certainly not revolution.

Mr Rubens should have been more sympathetic. Instead he had behaved like a child, forcing Kevin into a corner. It didn't matter why the monkeys were so important. What mattered was that Kevin was afraid of what might happen if he failed to persuade Mr Rubens to show them.

Of course we'll show the monkeys, Mr Rubens decided, and the words had formed already on the tip of his tongue.

But they remained unspoken.

"Some things are best left unsaid," Kevin said. In the long pause that followed, while the room was still filled with the ominous sound of his voice, his gaze had transfixed Mr Rubens. "I'm sorry, Mr Rubens, but now I need to say them, I don't have a choice."

More threats?

Mr Rubens felt pervaded with sadness, as though an invisible line was about to be crossed. Kevin's many faces were competing, and if the Kevin who was part of the system prevailed, Mr Rubens would be forced to dislike him.

"Jamie, do you mind? You can photograph the wallpaper later." Kevin had briefly averted his eyes, returning them to Mr Rubens while Jamie was still in his chair.

"Kev?" Jamie was now hesitating at the door. When Kevin raised his hand, he disappeared.

"Alone at last," quipped Mr Rubens.

Kevin looked too lost in concentration to have heard him.

"Two years ago, you lost your sister," he said. His eyes had suddenly become opaque.

"My sister?"

"There's no easy way of saying this, so I'll just say it," said Kevin. "Eunice – may I call her Eunice?"

Mr Rubens must have nodded.

"Eunice was a very brave woman," Kevin said.

Mr Rubens felt sick. *Now he's going to tell me that Eunice was murdered.*

"I believe you didn't know she had been summoned."

"Summoned?"

"Museum Service," Kevin said simply.

"Museum Service? Eunice?"

"Summoned to be shown at the National People's Museum."

A thousand different thoughts were assaulting Mr Rubens at once.

"Why would they have wanted to show Eunice?"

"Because they thought it would break her," said Kevin.

"And did it?"

"*They* might think it did."

"You're still speaking in riddles," said Mr Rubens, but his mind had now flitted somewhere else. "How did you know she hadn't told me?"

"That she'd been summoned? I know because she said she wasn't going to."

"When?"

"Not long before the day of the fire."

"So a few weeks earlier, when she was rewiring my doorbell—"

"She already knew. She was trying to protect you, Mr Rubens. She was trying to protect you and so am I."

"But I don't understand what you've actually told me," said Mr Rubens. "Is Eunice the reason I was summoned?"

"It's possible," said Kevin. "It's also possible, perhaps even more likely, that *I'm* the reason you were summoned. The number of coincidences makes me feel uneasy, although it's not out of the question that they are all just coincidences."

Through the side of the long narrow window that measured the whole length of one wall, a single ray of sunshine shot into the kitchen like a searchlight, blinding Mr Rubens and causing him to jolt out of its way. But in a matter of seconds the sun had been hidden again and the room was a uniform grey. Then the pit-pat patter of the rain gave way to the rhythmical clang of a hailstorm that lasted barely longer than the sun. The rain when it returned seemed more quiet.

"Did my sister agree to be shown?"

"I think in the beginning she was curious."

"And she asked too many questions."

"In the opinion of another pair of clowns."

"So she was classified a 'ped'. And now you're worried that history is repeating itself."

"She was classified a 'sub'," Kevin said.

Mr Rubens almost laughed. If he still harboured any lingering delusion that Museum Service was anything other than an underhanded instrument of torture, it evaporated with the fleeting temptation to laugh. To think he had imagined it an honour!

"Which is short for 'subversive'. But it didn't end there."

"It ended with the fire. You're going to tell me that Eunice was murdered."

"I'm almost certain that the fire was a ruse," Kevin said. "Before that, things had got much worse. When I visited your sister with the technical team I was assigned to at the time, it had already been decided that she couldn't be shown."

"You don't look old enough," said Mr Rubens.

"I'm already twenty-eight," Kevin said with a flutter of his lids – involuntary, Mr Rubens suspected. "I've been working for the Ministry since 2025, the year it was set up."

"Why?"

"Why?" Kevin raised his head and pulled his chin up, whistling as he took a heavy breath through his nose. His Adam's apple shivered and swelled when he swallowed.

"Because it was my dream to be an artist, and I also knew that I was smarter than them. Unfortunately, it hasn't always worked to my advantage. Playing chess with an occasionally very lucky idiot makes it difficult to plan your next move. And I was green, it was a while before I realised the stupidity was planned. That's what I meant when I said there were some very clever people at the top."

"Eunice couldn't be shown but the fire was a ruse?"

"I warned her, you see. I didn't trust the people I was working with back then, so I kept my head down, but it wasn't difficult to read between the lines. Suspended Status for a 'sub' could only mean one of two things - being imprisoned or being 'disappeared'."

"I thought the disappearances had ended."

"Over the years they've become a last resort, but no, they hadn't ended then and they still haven't ended." Kevin's gaze was restless, and he seemed to be blinking more often. "You know what Eunice did when I told her? She laughed. 'So *that's* what this is all about,' she said. 'And there was me thinking they just didn't like art.' On the day of our visit my job was to distract her, and she and I were in her garden at the time, having tea while the others were going through her things. She kissed me on the cheek and told me not to worry, but then she thought of you. She was afraid that she might get you into trouble. I suggested that whatever she was planning, she should talk with you first, but she was adamant that it was safer if she didn't."

"Are you telling me that Eunice is alive?" Behind his varifocals, Mr Rubens' eyes were welling up. His breathing had become uneven, and his heart was beating too fast. The heating wasn't on, and in winter the kitchen was usually cold, but suddenly he felt very hot.

"The following night there was a fire," Kevin said. "When the fire brigade arrived, it was already out of control. It's never been clear how it started. And as far as I know, no body was found. They told you Eunice was killed in the fire because they don't like to admit to loose ends. But I don't know if that means she's alive. The house was gutted, Mr Rubens, completely destroyed."

"It's been two years–" *She would have found a way to contact me by now,* Mr Rubens was about to say, but he didn't. He felt hollow, filling up with anger mixed with sadness and disgust. "I don't understand what you're trying to tell me," he said. "That I'll be a 'sub' unless I agree to show the monkeys? That my case might be 'suspended' and I risk being 'disappeared'? 'There's no easy way of saying this,' you said, but I'm not sure what you've actually said."

Kevin leaned back in his chair. "I'm not sure either," he said. "But I think I'm being tested. And I honestly think that my fate is in your hands."

"In *my* hands or in the monkeys'?"

"The clowns may be stupid, but they like their little games," Kevin said.

"The first time you called me… how could you have been so reckless if you thought you were under suspicion?"

"I'm sorry, Mr Rubens. And there's no easy way of saying this either, but that call was scripted. The words were my own, and most of them I actually meant, but the purpose of the call was to test you, and the clowns listened in. So really I should have said that we're *both* being tested. We're being used to test each other."

There aren't any truths any more, only illusions.

"You really think it's possible that Eunice might be alive?"

"It's possible, yes," Kevin said.

"Then you might have saved her life," said Mr Rubens. And before Kevin could answer, "They're expecting black and white, so we'll try and give them colour instead."

Kevin's face was beautiful again. "With a little Murakami thrown in?"

"*Of course* we'll show the monkeys," said Mr Rubens.

EIGHTEEN

Time was only now

Taking half-empty breaths, Anthony watched Malcolm sleep. The artificial brightness of the room somehow made its peripheral edges less sharp, as though rippling in the haze of a dreamy mirage. It was as if (in this room, in this building, in the world to which this city belonged) nothing else existed except Malcolm.

Malcolm's eyelids seemed too tightly shut, and the redness of his hair brought out vividly the whiteness of the sheets. The fever had taken its toll, painting Malcolm different shades of ash, almost black around his eyes. His breathing was irregular, broken up by the spasms of a gravelly cough that made his body shake. These heart-rending fits came and went at intervals that failed to measure any discernible signs of improvement.

Sunday July 15, 1984: the best day of Anthony's life. Ignoring all its warnings, in the morning he and Malcolm had haggled for the *Amoeba* together, and in the hours after midnight had yielded to each other completely. It was now Tuesday afternoon, one meagre day after Malcolm was admitted. It was possible the two antibiotics being given intravenously needed more time to work. Time had suddenly become an urgency of moments, not an abstract of unknown possibilities that stretched into a flexible future. Time was only now.

Early on Monday morning Malcolm's room near *The Bell* had been flooded with sunshine. Anthony had drawn the curtains hoping that natural daylight might have gradually freshened the air and restored Malcolm's colour to life. Instead it had imbued the familiar human smells, stale with sex and the effort of breathing, with the suffocating reek of despair.

"I'm taking you to hospital right now."

Malcolm had not dared resist.

Since arriving at the Emergency Department, time had collapsed into a sequence of silences followed by more urgent tests. Within hours had come the day's darkest moment.

"A room all of my own, how about that?"

Malcolm's eyes had brimmed with a golden-orange smile whose welling of affection could not have been faked. He had even clapped his hands, and Anthony and the nurses had laughed. Then Anthony had found a place to cry. And after sobbing in a corridor alone, he had worn the disguise of a smile as he gripped Malcolm's hand, while his gaze feigned the sparkle it lacked. Until almost the end, he had not found the heart, or the courage, to unburden them both of their mutual pretence of a brave face.

The doctors, the nurses, how do they manage? Anthony just couldn't understand. There was no doubt in his mind that everyone's fondness for Malcolm was real. They all spoke with kindness while making an effort to smile, and Malcolm had made them all laugh more than once. *Does he make jokes even when I'm not around?* He probably did. Even in sickness, Malcolm wore his big heart lavishly on his sleeve, as though more preoccupied with other people's feelings than his own. What *were* his feelings - right now, in this place? Anthony couldn't imagine. Every time he tried to, the thought of Malcolm's pain invariably returned him to his own, as though Malcolm's feelings were merely an extension of his, constrained by limits it was easier to assume were universal. It struck him that perhaps this was how everyone 'managed'. He was managing too, and although he knew he had to, it made him feel ashamed that he could. *For Malcolm's sake* somehow rang hollow. Within the vastness of his love, Anthony's one wish was to take Malcolm's place.

"My one and only love," was how Malcolm had described him, and they had written down his name on all the forms. He was spoken to with patience and warmth, and outside Malcolm's room there was often a hand on his shoulder. If anything, the attention made Anthony feel more bereft.

"How are *you*?" one of the nurses had asked him, and the question had seemed to him obscene. He had brushed it aside, as though even to consider it could only have intensified his guilt, by making him feel even more like a thief.

In the early hours of Wednesday Eunice picked him up in her van. He needed to rest, someone must have told him – *for Malcolm's sake*. Eunice drove him to his flat, where he picked up some clothes, and then she drove him home, to Marta Beatriz. She was waiting for them to arrive, and Anthony broke down in her arms. Then he had a shower and went to bed. After barely three hours' sleep, he was up. Eunice and Marta Beatriz were already dressed, waiting for him in the kitchen. He had spoken to Eunice from the hospital call box and then in the van, but had left out the details he was filling in now, quickly, so that he could hurry back to be with Malcolm. Yes, Sunday had in spite of its warnings been the happiest day and night of his life, and from shortly after sunrise Monday had conversely been the worst, which did not mean he had *any* regrets. He was glad he could be there for Malcolm...

"They're not sure what's wrong yet, but I think it's something serious. Why else would they have put him in a private room? And no one's reassured me that he's going to get better. We should know more this morning, after the bronchoscopy results." His own voice had sounded stilted to him, recounting facts as though they lacked any emotional meaning.

"Shouldn't someone call his parents?" asked Marta Beatriz.

"He doesn't want anyone there except me."

"Not even his mother?"

Anthony almost snapped. But as the gravity of his grandmother's question sank in, it made him hold back. It was too easy, taking Malcolm's words at face value or being angry on his behalf. *It's too easy taking my own feelings at face value.* He was being too possessive, claiming Malcolm's illness to himself as though that might help to contain it.

"I'll ask him again." His voice had softened. At last he had made peace with his fear – for Malcolm *and* for himself.

Or so he thought. Making peace was easy when a future lay ahead of the peace.

When the bronchoscopy results came through, they confirmed what the doctors had suspected.

Malcolm listened to the diagnosis impassively. He had a fungal infection in the lungs, PCP - pneumocystis pneumonia. He was taking the correct antibiotics. His condition was serious but stable. There had already been *some* improvement.

"How are you feeling?" the more senior of the doctors asked him.

Malcolm didn't answer straight away. For a few moments the room fell silent. Anthony observed the scene as though from a distance, temporarily detached from his body and his emotions as he scrutinised his own expression in detail, before he realised the expression he was studying was Malcolm's.

He reached for Malcolm's hand, and no sooner had Malcolm yielded to his grip than his eyes filled with life and he broke into one of his smiles.

"Much better than yesterday," he said. "And my temperature hasn't been over 100 all day."

"He's not coughing so much, either," said Anthony.

"Good," said the doctor. And after glancing at his colleague, "Good," he said again, gently squeezing Malcolm's shoulder.

"I'd like to go home soon," Malcolm said, but his breathing had suddenly shortened, and he started to cough.

"Let's get you better first, eh?" the same doctor said, after waiting for the cough to subside. "In the meantime, apart from Anthony is there anyone you'd like us to contact?"

"To say what?"

"To say you're here," the doctor answered. "In case they'd like to visit."

"What for?"

"To see you."

"There's no one."

"Malcolm, are you sure?" Anthony said.

"I'm sure." Malcolm's hand left Anthony's grip to make a pointing gesture. "Everyone I love is here already." His voice had eased back to its frailty.

There would have been no time for anyone to visit.

Later in the afternoon, Anthony sought out the two doctors. Without the smiles they had always worn for Malcolm, and without laying a hand on his shoulder, they outlined the bleakness of Malcolm's condition. The pneumonia was the imminent danger, but beyond it was no longer the unknown. An underlying illness, for which there was no treatment, was damaging Malcolm's immune system, and would eventually destroy it completely. Even if he managed to fight off this infection, soon another infection would follow. As he listened to them, Anthony had felt the future slipping away, and then vanishing completely. He could think of no questions to ask except one, and the answer to the question he asked was a short exchange of signals that meant Yes. In the immensity of the one night he had spent with Malcolm, Anthony would soon remain alone - *alone but forever more than one.*

Breaking down, he begged for Malcolm to be spared the desolation, *at least for now*, and the doctors were both easy to persuade. Malcolm didn't need to know. Not until he got better. Not unless he got better.

"How long have you and Malcolm been together?" one of them asked, when Anthony's sobbing had stopped.

But time had lost its meaning, and Anthony did not give an answer. *At least for now*, 'now' was all there was - and 'now' was not for long.

And when the other doctor dared to ask him if he was afraid *for himself*, Anthony's reply was that he only had Malcolm to lose.

Everyone's in love with you

When he opened the door to Malcolm's room, a nurse was adjusting the bed, raising Malcolm to a more upright position.

"There he is," said the nurse.

"Come, sit," Malcolm said, patting the side of the bed.

"In the chair," said the nurse, pushing it closer as she moved around it to the door. She blew Malcolm a kiss before leaving.

"Everyone's in love with you," said Anthony.

Malcolm gave a short, feeble laugh. A sigh caused him to cough. He looked radiant in his paleness, Anthony thought.

"I'm not afraid to die," Malcolm said, almost cheerfully.

"No one's going to die." Anthony winced at the shrill sound of his voice, and he bowed his head a little to kiss Malcolm's hand. "You're not going to die," he said softly.

"Your breath is cold," Malcolm said. "I feel like mine is poison."

"It's probably the drugs," Anthony said.

Malcolm took another shallow breath. "I never suspected," he said, his eyelids almost closing as he lowered his gaze. "If I had, then–"

"Stop," Anthony said.

"If it was possible to go back, to the day before Sunday–"

"Please, Malcolm."

"I wish you'd gone home with Joe Devin."

After making a show of shrugging his shoulders, Anthony raised both of his hands in the air. "I don't suppose it matters that Sunday was the best day of my life."

Malcolm smiled wistfully. "And now this. Probably we'll never even kiss again." His gaze had wandered, and he was crying without making any sound. Anthony could see the wetness streaming down the sides of his face.

It happened almost automatically. In a split second, as though without any necessity for intervening movement, Anthony's mouth was taking in Malcolm's, its coolness prevailing, joining them together in the same indivisible union of one.

In that eternity regrets were laid to rest.

A sudden flash of whiteness

It was as if their kiss, by which their love had at last broken free, had marked the perfect moment for Malcolm's goodbye. Their lips had barely disentangled. Their gazes were still locked. The rapid beating of their hearts danced to an almost identical rhythm. Anthony could feel the double thumping – his own within the hollow of his ribs, and Malcolm's through the thinness of his hospital gown - as his chest tingled over Malcolm's like a gentle caress. Even under his shirt, his skin sizzled with feeling, as though he and Malcolm were still naked in bed.

Everything happened very quickly, in stages that registered with Anthony in slow motion. First the weakening of Malcolm's breath; then the gradual glazing over of his gaze; then the tapering arrhythmia of his heartbeat; and finally the distant gurgling noise in his throat.

In the instant of absolute silence that followed, a sudden flash of whiteness forever reshuffled the world.

NINETEEN

Nothing escapes them

The wooden rectangular surface had been cleared of empty mugs, gingersnaps, Bourbons and crumbs, and after being wiped with a lightly damp cloth was ready for the hologram projection. At its centre stood a small circular machine that resembled a toy flying saucer. Its revolving dome consisted of a multi-faced lens that made a buzzing noise as it filled the air with rays of different colours.

"Lights off," Jamie said, and at the click of a switch all the random rays coalesced into the promised three-dimensional maquette of Mr Rubens' cubicle that flickered almost instantly to life above the kitchen table.

"Now enlarge," Kevin said.

Immaculately scaled, the hologram was barely the size of a shoebox.

"It has to stabilise first," Jamie said.

"If he's told me once, he's told me a thousand times," Kevin said.

"Times four," Jamie said. "Better?"

"Wow, look at that!" Kevin said.

"Fantastic, isn't it, Jack?" said Martin.

"It is, it's fantastic," said Jack.

"What did I tell you, Mr Rubens, when it comes to technology my Jamie's an absolute wizard!"

Mr Rubens had never seen anything like it. In every small detail the projection corresponded with what they had agreed, and surveying it was like gazing into a crystal ball and having a glimpse of the future. One side of the cubicle gave the impression of glass, and its three walls and ceiling were patterned with the spirals of the wallpaper's spatial confusion. Just as Jamie had predicted, the contrast with the whiteness of the floor brought the sparseness of the cubicle together into a unified whole. To the left, in the front behind the glass, the monkeys glistened on the sideboard. To the right, much further back, the art deco bureau had been positioned at a right angle to the sideboard. The box of photographs would stay invisible in one of its drawers.

"I don't think anyone would dare raise an objection," Kevin had said, and likewise with the photograph of Mr Rubens' mother, which *of course* he would be able to carry in his pocket.

And at the centre of the cubicle, there was Mr Rubens himself, or rather his tremulous likeness, swivelling this way and that in the gorgeous *Amoeba*, basking as ever in the affectionate light of the fibreglass lamp that loomed overhead.

It really was amazing. Kevin and his friends had every right to call themselves artists.

"A room all of my own, how exciting!" In a conscious reconstruction, Mr Rubens was clapping his hands. This was exactly what his real room would look like, and what he would look like inside it. *And Malcolm will be there to see it, and to share my fifteen minutes.* "Hmm..."

"What is it, Mr Rubens, have we got something wrong? It's easy enough for us to make adjustments."

"Kev's right, Mr Rubens," said Jamie, "all I have to do is tweak the program."

Mr Rubens was shaking his head, but with the lights off probably no one could see him. "It's perfect, Jamie, well done," he said. "But presumably my cubicle will have a door?"

"Invisible behind the wallpaper's busy design," Kevin said. "The whole of the back wall slides open, so that we can get everything in, and there's also a small door on the wall to the left, for access and in case you need the bathroom. The glass, though, is fixed."

Jamie switched off the flying saucer, and *POOF!* Mr Rubens and his cubicle were gone. Then someone turned the light back on.

"The glass is fixed and I'm not going to be able to see or hear anything through it," said Mr Rubens, pulling out a chair and sitting down. "The guard at the local museum in the Strand explained that to me."

"Take the lads to the other room and start packing up," Kevin said to Jamie.

"Sure," Jamie said.

"Don't forget the flying saucer," said Mr Rubens.

"I'll come back for that later," Jamie said from the door, and then he followed Jack and Martin to the sitting room.

"Yes, he enjoyed your conversation," said Kevin, sitting down beside Mr Rubens.

"You've lost me now," said Mr Rubens. "Which conversation?"

"Your conversation yesterday, with the guard upstairs at the local museum in the Strand. And before you jump to conclusions, I only found out this afternoon, while we've been here. A message came through on my phone."

"A message came through on your phone?"

"While Jamie was in here, taking photographs of your amazing kitchen walls. I went through to the other room for a while, you remember? And I *was* going to mention it when I came back, but then I got thinking – about how things have changed since *The Bell* and being gay in the swinging 1980s - and it completely slipped my mind."

"The 1980s were hardly swinging," said Mr Rubens.

"Oh, I'm sorry, Mr Rubens, have I gone and put my foot in it *again*?"

"It's fine. That's all ancient history now."

"You're too kind," Kevin said.

"But what definitely isn't ancient history," said Mr Rubens, "is my visit to the People's Museum in the Strand, or why anyone should care about my conversation with the guard."

Kevin started tapping his fingers on the table.

"Apparently you made him laugh," he said.

I'm beginning not to like him again, thought Mr Rubens.

"And because I made him laugh, he's now in trouble?"

Kevin gave a frown. "I don't know, Mr Rubens. Should he be?"

"Not if it were up to me."

"But, unfortunately, it's not up to you, and that's the point I'm trying to make. You need to be more careful."

"I hadn't realised it's illegal to make people laugh."

"You're a 'ped', Mr Rubens. You're a 'ped' and Alex is a guard in a People's Museum."

"This conversation is absurd." Mr Rubens brought his hand down on the table with a thump. "The guard had no idea I was a 'ped'."

Kevin's fingers had stopped tapping and his frown had disappeared. "Alex didn't know you were a 'ped', you're absolutely right," he said, and resting his arm on his elbow, he looked at Mr Rubens while holding one side of his face in his hand. "In this terrible world, we've *all* become used to mistrusting each other, it's a matter of self-preservation. I imagine Alex went to bed after work, couldn't get a wink of sleep, and by the morning had decided you were probably a spy. So what's the first thing you think he did when he went back to the Strand? He gave the Party Representative a word for word report of your entire conversation."

"And confessed under torture to the heinous crime of laughing at my joke," said Mr Rubens, but Kevin ignored him.

"Of course, as you correctly pointed out, at that stage no one knew who you were. But as everything's recorded these days, in less than two minutes *everyone* knew who you were."

"He did most of the talking, and neither of us said anything wrong."

"But you were there, Mr Rubens. You were there asking questions again."

"I'm pretty sure I only asked him if the people in the cubicles could see the visitors outside."

"A fair and reasonable question," Kevin said.

"So why on earth are they making a fuss?"

Kevin leaned back in his chair, so far that his weight pushed it up on two legs.

"Because they *like* to make a fuss, it makes them feel important," he said. "They like everyone to know that nothing escapes them."

"You're in terrible trouble if nothing escapes them," said Mr Rubens.

Kevin chuckled mischievously. "Touché, Mr Rubens, touché!"

Well? Do I like him or not? I can't make out if he's torturing me or trying to protect me. Perhaps what he enjoys is doing both. In some strange variation of Munchausen's syndrome by proxy, first he likes to scare me and then he plays the knight in shining armour arriving in a gallop to save me.

"But there was also something else," Kevin went on, more seriously now. "Something else that apparently caught their attention."

"You're going to tell me that the whistler was another of the Ministry's clowns."

"The whistler?"

"Yesterday on the embankment, in the panama hat."

"A panama hat in this weather? Mr Rubens, they don't have the imagination!" Still balancing his chair on two legs, which Mr Rubens thought was too familiar, and not particularly good for the chair, Kevin bent his head to one side. "No, this has nothing to do with any whistler on the embankment. But it does have to do with attire, peculiar or otherwise."

"Attire?"

"Have you decided what you're wearing on your day, or not yet? Most people seem to like buying something new, but then you're not like most people. You're not like most people at all, Mr Rubens, you're really quite exceptional - one might even say unique."

"I'll not be buying anything new," said Mr Rubens, "but I'm not sure if that makes me unique."

"Oh, but you underestimate yourself."

"That's what Mr Anderson said."

"He did?" Kevin brought his chair down at last. "Well, that doesn't surprise me."

"It's called flattery," said Mr Rubens.

Kevin's features tightened. "I'm hurt, Mr Rubens, I thought by now you'd be able to trust me. All the same, I think you're very wise to be sceptical – I'd be sceptical too."

"I need to be more careful, you said."

"I did say that, yes."

"It's a matter of self-preservation."

"It's exactly that for all of us," said Kevin. "Which brings us back to what you're planning to wear on your day."

"Is there a dress code for the National?"

"Not as such," Kevin said.

Mr Rubens took his glasses off and pressed against the bridge of his nose. Suddenly he felt very tired. "You never like to give a straight answer," he said to the blur that he knew must be Kevin.

The blur chuckled mischievously again. "Guilty as charged," Kevin said, coming back into focus when Mr Rubens put his glasses back on. "But that's not actually my intention. I just have a natural dislike for taking anything for granted, so I'm always trying to avoid asking leading questions. That's what lawyers like to do, and I'm not a fan of lawyers, are you?"

"You're doing it again," said Mr Rubens.

"Oh dear, I don't seem to be able to help it, do I? Let me cut right to the chase then, shall I? It's a silly thing, really, but it's been brought to my 'urgent attention', which means I can't just ignore it. Apparently, the guard you were talking to yesterday noticed you were wearing your jumper back to front, is that right?"

"They really do like everyone to know that nothing escapes them."

"Was there a reason you were wearing your jumper back to front?"

Mr Rubens got up and poured himself a glass of water from the tap. He drank it slowly, and then he returned to his chair.

"I'm sure you know the answer already," he said.

"I know *you*, Mr Rubens, and I also know what Martin found upstairs."

"Upstairs?"

"In a case under your bed, I believe."

"But it was locked."

"And Martin unlocked it. You did give your permission, Mr Rubens."

"Apparently so."

"So did you knit all those jumpers yourself, or did someone else knit them for you?"

"Eunice did."

"Eunice, of course. And which one were you wearing yesterday? Presumably the same one you were planning to wear on your day, but naturally not back to front."

"The one that says JOE DEVIN SUCKED MY COCK," said Mr Rubens.

Kevin broke into wild, uncontrollable laughter; he had his arms wrapped around his waist and was stamping his feet on the floor. "Oh, Mr Rubens… you're killing me… Joe Devin sucked my cock… I've never laughed so much in all my life."

"I think I should remind you that you're laughing in the presence of a 'ped'."

"But I'm not, Mr Rubens, I'm laughing in the presence of a friend."

"Anyway, it's not actually true."

"Joe Devin didn't–"

"Joe Devin certainly did not."

"Hmm… Are you sure now, Mr Rubens, or are you just being shy?"

"Quite sure. It was Eunice's idea of a joke."

Kevin took a breath. And after wiping his eyes with the back of his hand, "Well, I think it's priceless," he said. "Martin must have missed it, he probably freaked out when he came across DOWN WITH THE GOVERNMENT PARTY and I HATE THE NEW LEADER. I know *I* did, when he told me. It's easy enough to fob those idiots off, but if you turned up at the National in one of those… But no, *of course* you weren't going to. JOE DEVIN SUCKED MY COCK, that's absolutely brilliant, and *typical* Eunice!"

"It's brilliant but I wouldn't get away with wearing it, would I?"

"Ah, Mr Rubens, how I wish I could tell you that you definitely *would* get away with it, nothing would give me more pleasure."

"But you can't."

"But I can't."

Malcolm wouldn't like it anyway, thought Mr Rubens.

"So, we'll take away the suitcase and I'll fob those idiots off, and no one will be any the wiser."

"You've never asked me about Malcolm," Mr Rubens said suddenly.

Kevin sat up, scrunching up his face as he inflated his chest.

Here's my chance, thought Mr Rubens. *All I need to do is take in a gulp of the air he's about to exhale. That should tell me if I should trust him or not, and if I can't, then it means I'm in danger.*

As though reading his mind, Kevin turned to face him and began to blow the air out of his mouth. "Here, I dare you," he seemed to be saying, in an even more deliberate attempt to goad Mr Rubens into taking a sniff.

Mr Rubens felt a coolness caress him. Its steady stream occupied space like a physical object. But then rather than slowly dispersing, it vanished completely, displaced by the heavier body of air Mr Rubens had breathed out in its place. *A fallacy, remember?* Without outward signs – the smallest change in his expression or the trace of a sound - he gave a little laugh to himself.

At that same moment, as though some part of his breath had caught in his throat Kevin broke into a cough. Its spasms accelerated wildly, and his face became red. Now he was frantically pounding his chest with his fist; he was choking.

"Water," said Mr Rubens, but Kevin said No with his eyes, and he swivelled in his chair to poke the air behind him with a finger.

Mr Rubens stumbled to his feet and repeatedly slapped Kevin's back with the flat of his hand. Eventually the coughing stopped.

"Thank you, Mr Rubens, I'm fine now."

Before returning to his chair, Mr Rubens filled another glass with water from the tap and handed it to Kevin.

"Malcolm," said Kevin, "the boy you used to go to *The Bell* with. I know what you've told me, what else should I have asked?"

"He was more than just the boy I went to *The Bell* with, he was the most important person in my life."

"You were lovers?"

Mr Rubens nodded. "But just for one night. It's not in my file?"

"I told you, Mr Rubens, there's nothing in your file about your love life."

"My love life ended that same night."

"I don't know what to say."

"Malcolm died a few days later. We kissed for one last time and then he died." And once again remembering his grandmother's gesture, "It may sound like a cliché but he's always been *here*," Mr Rubens went on, bringing two hands together to press hard against his breast.

"Alone?"

"No, not alone."

"The box of photographs in the bureau," Kevin said.

"And the photograph I carry in my pocket," said Mr Rubens.

"Thank you," Kevin said.

Mr Rubens gave his shoulders a shrug. "For what?"

"For trusting me with things about your past that only really matter to you."

"Because they are the most important," said Mr Rubens.

TWENTY

The living second-guessing the dead

At that dreadful moment after their kiss, Malcolm's room became a hubbub of movement and voices, and a nurse had led Anthony to a place he could barely remember, where he sat alone for an hour waiting for the news that he already knew. Malcolm McCarthy, aged 24, was pronounced dead at 17.32 on Wednesday July 18, 1984. At that same moment, Anthony's rights became those of a stranger. What had belonged to him so entirely in life now belonged to someone else.

The same two doctors took turns to shake his hand.

"We're really very sorry for your loss," they said, one after the other.

Anthony nodded, once, twice, but couldn't think of anything to say. It was as if he had remained in the same silent film in which he had watched Malcolm die. In the next frame, with no inkling of how he had got there, he found himself in Malcolm's street, staring up at the window with the curtains undrawn, imagining a thousand broken pieces of mirror putting themselves back together. He then retraced the steps of their last journey to *The Bell*, before walking to the station to call Eunice from a phone box. He had done all his weeping before Malcolm died.

Taking with him little more than his aloneness, the next day he moved back to the family home. Vauxhall lacked its warm familiarity, in which his recollections came more easily to life. Reclining in the *Amoeba*, he would recall the sensuality of Malcolm's fragile body, and feel intoxicated by the tingle of its heat. If he closed his eyes while ruffling his hair, the hand that was ruffling his hair would be Malcolm's. It was as though his body had recorded three-dimensionally all the physical moments he and Malcolm had shared and was able to replay them at will.

Anthony's grandmother talked about Malcolm without fussing. Eunice, on the other hand, was fraught. As though reliving Ernest's death, once again she gave vent to her grief by being angry, almost constantly raging against Malcolm's parents.

"They've been acting like thieves. Malcolm's life was here. His work was here, all his friends are here, and so are you. When he was sick, he didn't want them anywhere near him, he chose to be only with *you* when he died. We all have a right to be at his funeral. We have a right to say goodbye."

It was Sunday, just four days after Malcolm had died, and the three of them were in the kitchen having breakfast – a few slices of toast and a large pot of coffee between them.

"Tomorrow you should call the hospital," Eunice insisted.

"What for?"

"To remind them that Malcolm did *not* die alone."

"They know that already," said Marta Beatriz. "And I'm sure Malcolm's parents know it too."

"I doubt it makes things easier for them," Anthony said.

"But it *should* make things easier for them if they knew they were respecting Malcolm's wishes."

"Malcolm's only wish would have been not to be sick."

"So you don't think he'd have wanted you at his funeral?"

"I don't think he'd have cared either way," Anthony said.

"But *we* care," said Eunice.

No one's stopping you from caring, Anthony wanted to say.

"No one's stopping any of us from caring," he said. "I plan to go on caring for the rest of my life."

"But not at the expense of living it, I hope, because I'm sure that's not what Malcolm would have wanted," said Marta Beatriz.

"Malcolm isn't here," Anthony said.

Do they really think they know what Malcolm would have wanted? he wondered. Or was it just wishful thinking, the living second-guessing the dead as a means of more quickly forgetting?

Anthony was not going to forget. His grandmother had not forgotten either, but wishing something different for him than the life she had settled for of caring for others – dead and alive - more than she had cared for herself, she had been able to imagine what Malcolm might have wanted but not that what Anthony wanted might actually be something else.

"Malcolm isn't here but he'll always be here," said Marta Beatriz. When she reached for Anthony's hand, so did Eunice.

When it left the pile of hands, Anthony's gaze fell unfocussed on his sister. "I'm not sure what they'll be able to tell me, but I'll give the hospital a call in the morning," he said.

The coldness of objects

Ten days later he was back at work, serving the machine that served Thatcher. And every Sunday he would put on his panama hat and walk to Camden, for an English breakfast at the Italian café and then a look around the market. The coldness of objects attracted him, more than ever now.

"Aha, one half of the duo of hard-bargaining sophisticated boys of beauty has returned to the scene of their crime! Beware, longsuffering dealers. Hurry up and shut your stable doors, before all your *Amoebas* have bolted!"

"Charles," said Anthony, putting down a clockwork tinplate robot made in Occupied Japan.

He had dreaded this moment, and had been studiously avoiding *20TH CENTURY FURNITURE* and all the stalls around it. But this was now his sixth or seventh visit to the market since the morning of the most momentous day of his life, and hearing Charles's voice hadn't really surprised him.

"But where's your accomplice today? It's a *lovely* day for coming to the market, beautifully cool and overcast, perfect for our young Apollo's complexion, more gorgeously wan than even the most delicate fine china from Japan."

"Malcolm's dead," Anthony said.

Charles's eyes became lifeless. "Dead?" His voice barely rose over the market's customary hullaballoo.

Anthony nodded. "We weren't even together when you met us, but we were by the end of that day, the *best* day of my life. And half a week later I was with him when he died."

"You were with him..." Charles struggled to finish the sentence. His face had reddened, and he seemed about to burst into tears.

"We kissed, then he was gone," Anthony said.

"Well, that's–" Charles cut himself short. "I'm so, so sorry," he said. "If there's anything, anything at all–"

"Thank you," said Anthony. "I think I'm going to buy that robot over there. It works and it's in perfect condition."

"And it has its original box," said Charles. Then putting on his dealer's voice: "Robin, my dear, what's the very best price you can do for my friend on that dreary little robot from Japan?"

No more talk of death

Malcolm's parents gave their son a private funeral. The hospital had been unable to give Anthony any details, and Anthony had not insisted.

He had kept to himself the underlying cause of Malcolm's illness. Increasingly the press carried stories of a growing epidemic, and of the threat from a deadly disease all the more frightening because it was also infectious, mostly affecting men who had sex with other men. Stoked by a largely homophobic press, the climate was one of hysteria. Without judging Malcolm, Eunice and Marta Beatriz would not have been able not to worry constantly for him. One sneeze and they would go into a panic.

Malcolm must have been very unlucky. This recurring thought was absurd, a meaningless and dangerous truism. An unreliable measure of misfortune, statistics insidiously judged a disease in relation to its victims, and therefore also risked judging the victims themselves. Malcolm was unlucky not because of *how* he had died but because he was dead, in the way that millions of people all over the world were unlucky every day. There was no valid distinction that made some either more or less unlucky than others. 'Why Malcolm?' was the same as 'Why me?' – a self-centredness that went against the vagaries of nature, which by their coldness only objects could defy. Malcolm had been lucky that he hadn't suffered more.

Sometime after Christmas and the end of 1984, Anthony decided he was almost ready to move back to his flat, but his plans were about to be thwarted.

On Valentine's Day his grandmother had turned seventy-three. Soon afterwards Anthony began to notice she had lost and was still losing weight. And even though she never complained, by the strain that ever more deeply was marking her face, and an awkward stiffness in her movement that increasingly was hard to disguise, the rapidly progressing symptoms of deterioration betrayed her.

Old age, Anthony thought, at the first suspicion that something more serious might be wrong. *It's just old age,* he told himself again and again, even as the evidence stacked up that on the contrary the problem was probably *not* just old age.

"Grandma's getting old," he said to Eunice, when already it was March. If he had hoped for reassurance, it would not be forthcoming.

Eunice looked at him as though she hadn't understood. She opened her mouth, but then she closed it again. In her blue overalls she looked even more like a boy, handsome but completely at a loss.

"Something's wrong," Anthony said.

He might as well have spoken to a wall. Eunice glared at him without expression, not talking, not moving - barely breathing, as far as Anthony could see, but still the air between them was stifling.

"Something's wrong," he repeated.

Eunice was still frozen. Her eyes seemed focussed on something behind him. Then making a fist of one hand she brought it down hard on her breast. One thud came after another, as though mimicking the beat of her heart.

"What are you doing?" Anthony asked.

"Ach, it may sound like a cliché, but soon she'll be *here*, where Harry and our father and Malcolm are, too."

"You're mocking me," said the steady voice of Marta Beatriz.

When Anthony jolted around, his grandmother was standing right behind him, gaunt but erect.

"I don't understand," he said. His mouth was dry, and his throat felt constricted. He stumbled to the *Amoeba* and sank into it.

"Here!" Eunice yelled, bent over as her fist came down again and again on her breast.

"Stop it!" said the steady voice of Marta Beatriz.

When Eunice started to laugh, Anthony felt part of a bizarre choreography, as though he were a mute painted mouth in a rehearsal for a play by Samuel Beckett.

I must be dreaming that I've lost my voice, he thought. *The light in our sitting room seems as artificial as the light in Malcolm's hospital room. Perhaps we're still together in his room near The Bell, naked side by side in his bed...*

But he was not in a dream, and Eunice was still laughing, laughing and rhythmically hitting her breast, yelling "here, here, here!"

Anthony was back on his feet, holding on to the side of the *Amoeba*. *I don't understand,* he thought, as his gaze darted from one woman to the other. It struck him how majestic his grandmother looked, as utterly majestic as the tall, graceful trees of the gay cruising ground in Hampstead Heath – and suddenly almost as ancient. Without any lipstick or make up, her hair neatly falling in one curve to just above her shoulders, she was dressed in charcoal grey – a tailored two-piece suit over a thin cashmere sweater – and the gleam of her double string of pearls failed completely to contrast with her paleness. Not one of her features had dimmed, but their symmetry now seemed askew, as though knocked out of kilter by the puckering-up of her face. *She looks like she's dressed for her own funeral.*

And I've been so preoccupied with the pretence of carrying on as normal that I've been blind to what's been staring me in the face.

Eunice's laughter had morphed into wailing, which was perhaps what it had always been. The loud guffaws had given way to barely a shiver of sobs; while her fist remained pressed against her breast, her other hand was screening her eyes, her body still stooped while both elbows made angles that jarred with the air. She, too, resembled a tree, not ancient but whose youth had been made crooked by the weight of too much snow. *Too much sudden snow, too much early snow, too much snow...*

Do something, Anthony said to himself, but while he tried to decide which tree he should attend to first, he saw his grandmother's fingers caressing his shoulder as her otherworldly shadow shuffled past him, on its way to envelop his sister.

"I don't understand," he said again, but the two women had locked themselves in an embrace from which he felt excluded, and had either not heard him or not comprehended his need. He felt aggrieved by the multitude of contradictory assumptions that had led to him being kept in the dark, where he had now been abandoned to fend for himself, as though his grandmother could not make up her mind if she thought he was stronger or weaker than Eunice.

"I am neither," he said in a whisper.

His eyes had welled up, his new spectacles were misting and his vision was blurred. As their single mass approached him, in the night sky of Eunice's blue overalls his grandmother's pearls had the sparkle of stars. With a blink there was darkness. Its black contained a silence that joined them together, and they stayed like that for some time, drawing strength from each other while breathing as one. And as they slowly fell apart without being disunited, the time had come for difficult words.

"You were too upset already," said Marta Beatriz. "Eunice was, too, but I needed to tell someone. It was selfish of me."

"No," said Eunice.

"You could never be selfish," said Anthony.

"It's true, Grandma," said Eunice.

"Sometimes I forget that your sister is as sensitive as you are. In so many ways she takes after your father, but there's also a lot of your mother in you both. And I'd like to think you've also taken something from me – something good. But mostly you've grown up to be yourselves, two young people with a mind, and a heart, of their own. It's a relief to me you'll always have each other, even if you eventually also have someone else. You just don't know if it'll happen or not, either of you."

She was wrong. Anthony knew.

This prelude did not augur well. Telltale signs foretold terrible news.

"I have just one wish," Marta Beatriz went on. "To die here at home. When the time comes, we'll get help. And I'm too much of a coward to let myself suffer, so you don't need to worry, I'm already well prepared."

"I don't understand," Anthony said, but this time he knew that he *had* understood, and how selfish it had been of him to cling for so long to denial.

"Ach, my darling," said Marta Beatriz, lowering her tone to pinch his cheek, twisting it the way she used to all the time when he was still a little boy. "There's nothing to understand." And narrowing her eyes as she looked at him sideways, almost with a smile, "But you know that already, I think. There's been *too* much death in our family for us to wonder if there's anything we don't understand."

"If you're sick, it doesn't mean you're not going to get better," Anthony said, as though even now still in thrall to his selfishness.

When his grandmother laughed, her smile was upside down.

"Then let's just say I'm dying," she said. "Good, I've said it. And now that I've said it, let's all agree that it's out of the way. No more talk of death while I'm around!"

TWENTY-ONE

Treasure

The next morning a parcel the size of a shoebox was delivered to Anthony's desk. Wrapped in plain brown paper and tied together with elaborately tangled string, it was addressed to 'Mr Anthony Rubens' and the stamps had a Liverpool postmark.

They've sent me Malcolm's ashes, Anthony thought. He lifted the parcel, but its weight revealed no secrets. *If it is Malcolm's ashes, what should I do with them? What would Malcolm have liked me to do with them?*

Am I seriously debating what Malcolm would have wanted me to do with his ashes? Malcolm wouldn't have cared. He would have been annoyed with his parents for inflicting this ridiculous dilemma on someone else - unless they were fulfilling his instructions.

All of Anthony's muscles had tightened. Once again, he was tying himself in knots, speculating wildly instead of just unwrapping the parcel and looking inside it. In the end he put it down on the floor beside his desk, out of sight.

He was shocked at how little the news about Marta Beatriz had affected him, at least in any palpable sense. It had not stopped him from sleeping, nor had it given him terrible dreams. And in the morning, while Eunice brooded in a corner with her cornflakes, he had slurped his way through his - effortlessly heeding his grandmother's wish of 'no more talk of death'. There had been *too* much death already, she was right, and the cumulative absences were already beginning to feel like a numbness, making Anthony wonder whether 'here' might just be an empty cliché after all. But then no sooner had the parcel arrived at his desk, and the soft, affectionate curves of 'Mr Anthony Rubens' had caused him to look at the postmark, than the warmth of Malcolm's memory was instantly rekindled.

This warmth was a fortress. Surrounded by coldness, it was Anthony's refuge, a place in whose apartness the losses he had suffered were denied. But it was not yet the place for Marta Beatriz; for the moment, *nothing* had changed. His grandmother's warmth was her own, and he would bask in its glow for as long as he could. They would open the parcel together.

At the end of a day that passed slowly, he came in with the unopened parcel to find Marta Beatriz snuggled up in the *Amoeba* with a book. Without closing it she put it upside down on the armrest.

"Don't get up," Anthony said, when already she had staggered to her feet, unstable but beaming, and dressed as elegantly as the day before. *As though every day might be her last,* Anthony thought.

"What's that under your arm?" His grandmother had skewed her neck to one side and was eyeing up the parcel as though it might contain her salvation. "A present, for me?" And straightening to wag a finger at him, "Ach, darling, you shouldn't have!"

"I think it's from Malcolm's parents, it's got a Liverpool postmark," Anthony said.

"Malcolm's *parents*?"

"It arrived this morning at the Ministry."

"This *morning*? And you've managed not to open it yet?"

"It must be his ashes."

"His *ashes*?"

"I can't think what else it could be."

"Then let's open it, for God's sake!"

"In the kitchen," Anthony said. He put one arm around his grandmother and gave her a kiss. Over her shoulder he looked down at the book she had been reading - *Illness as Metaphor*, by Susan Sontag. Without meaning to, he shook his head.

"What is it?" his grandmother asked.

"No more talk of death, you said, and you're reading a book about illness."

"I'm reading a book that's helping me not to feel guilty. Now come on, let's go fix you a drink and then we'll open the parcel together."

"Maybe we should wait for Eunice."

"Talk of the devil," said Marta Beatriz.

Eunice came in looking flushed. "Fucking Tories," she said.

"That's the spirit!" said Marta Beatriz. "But your brother's had a parcel from Liverpool, and we're about to find out what's inside. Will you join us in the kitchen? You look like you could do with a drink."

"The whole country needs a drink with that *bitch* still in charge. She goes to war and gets re-elected, and now it looks like she's finally managed to have her revenge on the miners. How? Divide and rule, how else? Split the workers first, and then fuck them over."

"Anthony thinks that it might be Malcolm's ashes."

"Malcolm's *ashes*?"

"It's from Liverpool," said Anthony.

"From Malcolm's parents?"

"It arrived this morning at the Ministry, and your brother hasn't opened it yet. Now *please* can we go through to the kitchen and find out what's inside it?"

"Why the kitchen?" Eunice asked.

"I need a knife," Anthony said.

"But they wouldn't have cremated him, they're Catholics," said Eunice.

"Oh, for God's sake, my knees are beginning to hurt," said Marta Beatriz.

"And apparently we both need a drink," Anthony said. With his grandmother leaning on his arm, he began to lead the way to the kitchen.

"Who's been reading *Illness as Metaphor*?" asked Eunice, as she followed behind them.

"You should both read it too, when I've finished it," said Marta Beatriz.

While his grandmother prepared two large gin and tonics, Anthony slowly unwrapped the parcel after cutting through the string with a knife. Inside it was a badly battered Doc Marten's shoebox, its corners fortified with tape.

"I remember this," he said. "Malcolm kept it in his room, and before that I was with him when he bought the steel toe cap brogues from Camden Town. They used to *kill* his feet."

When Marta Beatriz had joined him and Eunice at the table, and he and his sister had both had a sip of their drink, Anthony lifted the lid. What looked like a pile of old notebooks almost filled the box up to the rim. At the top lay a white unstamped envelope addressed simply to 'Anthony Pablo Rubens'.

"That's his handwriting," said Anthony.

Eunice seemed enraptured. "Yes, I recognise it too," she said with a gasp, before taking another big gulp of her drink.

Anthony nodded. Carefully he took the envelope out of the box, handling it as though it were a priceless piece of china. From its weight and feel he estimated that it couldn't have contained more than one sheet of paper – two at most.

"Open it!" said Eunice. When she leaned across the table towards him, he recoiled, stretching back into his chair with the envelope held flat against his chest. He couldn't help imagining her snatching it from him.

"Eunice!" Marta Beatriz placed her hands side by side on the table, as though about to lean on them in order to get up. "We should give your brother a moment," she said.

"No, I'd like you both to be here when I read it," Anthony said.

"Aloud?"

"Eunice!"

"Aloud," Anthony said. The knife he had used to cut the string was still on the table. Inserting its point in a small gap at a corner of the flap, he ran it smoothly across the top, cutting through it. Holding it apart with two fingers, he took a peek inside. He then used the tips of the same two fingers to take out the folded piece of paper. Unfolding it confirmed that it was just a single sheet.

His eyes ran to the end, in a heartbeat. *Malcolm* - the letters slimline and compressed. Overcome with emotion that filled his eyes with tears, he started to read, snuffling every so often.

Kings Cross, Sunday June 17, 1984

My dearest Anthony,

You're never going to get this, because nothing's going to happen to me. But you know me - I don't like to take any chances. If you're reading this note, it should have come in a box with my stories. I'm not ready yet for endings, so really they're all still unfinished, although I like to think of them as finished beginnings. The idea was to write the endings later. There isn't something special I expect you to do with them. You were always complaining that I wouldn't let you read them, so I thought you might like to. Time will help you imagine different endings for them. You can also give them all different titles.

By the way, in case you hadn't guessed, I'm in love with you. I've been in love with you almost since the first day we met. I sleep with other men with my eyes closed, to try and pretend I'm with you. It's the truth, and as you're never going to read this, I don't care if it sounds really cheesy. It makes me feel much better that I've got it off my chest.

I should go now. You're coming over soon, so I need to get ready.

Love you always,

Malcolm

P.S. It's now the middle of July, and my favourite of all the stories is the one I wrote today, after our adventure in Camden. It's in notebook No. 6.

When Anthony had finished reading, his voice cracking as he read out Malcolm's name, and again as he read out the postscript, "I need to blow my nose," he said, wiping his face with the back of his hand, but before he had time to get up, his sister was handing him a tissue. He turned the note around, but the other side was blank.

"*Time will help you imagine different endings*," said Marta Beatriz, reaching out to cup his hand with her long fingers, still youthful in spite of her age and her illness. "Will you read his favourite finished beginning to us?" she asked, squeezing his hand with strength that surprised him.

"Now?"

"When you're ready," said Marta Beatriz,

He brought her hand to his mouth and gave his grandmother's youthful long fingers a kiss. Then he reached into the box and took out the notebook at the top, numbered 1 on the cover. Below it, five more were numbered 2 to 6. At the bottom some sheets had been stapled together and folded in two.

"Is there nothing from his parents?" asked Eunice, bending over the table to look inside the box.

"It's enough that they've sent me the parcel," Anthony said.

"Ach, this *treasure*," said Marta Beatriz.

Malcolm's tales about his childhood and his parents' tragic lives, however entertainingly he had told them, had been tinged with a darkness that not even his glistening bare buttocks could have lightened. He had worn a kilt to come out to them; exposing his behind had been his final farewell. And it *had* been final - their next encounter had again been with his nakedness but this time in a morgue. Had Malcolm lived, Anthony would like to think that eventually there might have been a way to make peace. It would have been worthwhile, even if it didn't entirely amount to understanding or even forgiveness. Anthony hoped that by sending the parcel, in some small and perhaps inarticulate way, while fulfilling Malcolm's wishes his parents were also expressing their love.

Picking out the notebook with 6 on the cover, Anthony read out the name below the number. 'Malcolm McCarthy'. Further down, as on all the numbered notebooks, Malcolm had written:

THE EXTRAORDINARY FUTURE ADVENTURES OF MR RUBENS

Anthony turned over to the first page inside.

For Anthony Pablo

He turned another page and continued to read.

AN UNEXPECTED VISITOR

Undaunted by any fear of flatulence or heartburn, Mr Rubens was thoroughly enjoying his mid-morning coffee.

"There is a time and a place for everything," he was fond of saying, and as a matter of ritual, not routine – an obvious distinction – this was certainly true of the orderly way in which he chose to live his life.

Anthony paused for a moment, to blow his nose again before carrying on.

TWENTY-TWO

Charles and Diana

From the pancreas to the liver and then to the lungs, her cancer had spread with the rhythm and speed of a nursery rhyme, and with Anthony and Eunice next to each other beside her, Marta Beatriz had died in her own bed on a bright August morning less than half a year after her birthday. She had opened her eyes one last time, smiled with her gaze as she turned it without vigour in her grandchildren's direction, and had not shut them again.

Anthony had read Malcolm's stories to his grandmother many times over. *The Extraordinary Future Adventures of Mr Rubens*, and in particular the story Malcolm had marked out as his favourite, had made both of them laugh, but really the satirical depictions of Anthony in a future without Malcolm were deeply unsettling to him. They were funny precisely because they were bleak, but the raw reality of a future without Malcolm had made the blackness of their humour too opaque. Their detailed observation of Anthony's traits, and particularly of the way they might evolve, read at times like the predictions of science. *All* of Malcolm's stories were bleak. Anthony would not be reading any of them again. Their lasting effect had been more deeply to imprint his melancholia.

And suddenly eight long years had passed and it was 1993. Thatcher was gone. Communism had collapsed. And Anthony had used his inheritance to buy a house in Highgate. Life had continued very much as a routine, a steady progression towards an unexciting middle age. He and Eunice saw each other often – 'in need of modernisation', as the Estate Agents' blurb had rather euphemistically described it, his two storeys of Victorian semi-decrepitude provided Eunice with a cornucopia of odd jobs requiring her urgent attention.

Anthony had carried on collecting, overfilling his new home with the coldness of more and more beautiful objects – from which he was able to derive ever-diminishing pleasure. This lack of fulfilment was a reminder of his youthful compulsion to have casual sex, as though one more encounter might have made up for the utter desolation of the last. Malcolm had been his salvation, and shortly afterwards his devastation, which the loss of Marta Beatriz had cemented. The orderly way in which he lived his life was *not* a matter of choice. 'Here' had brought about an overwhelming aloneness, increasingly large parts of which he spent in the *Amoeba*.

"I'm in love," were no longer words he ever heard from his sister. Staying put in Belsize Park, she too had contained herself in a routine - while Anthony collected, Eunice protested.

"You should have an HIV test."

It was a Saturday afternoon in March, and she had been in Anthony's house since eight in the morning laying a new bathroom floor. He had practically forced her to join him in the sitting room for coffee. Since being accused by her of being 'a pompous arse' and 'a prematurely old pretentious queen', he usually had coffee and tea with his sister in the mugs he had bought specially from Leicester Square – one bearing the portrait of Charles and the other of Diana. Eunice had refused him the pleasure of batting an eyelash. Anthony suspected that the two of them liked to bicker with such zeal as a means of furtively acknowledging their dread of a day when they mightn't even have one another.

After her third Garibaldi, Eunice set down her Prince Charles on the tallest of the coloured Perspex cubes that separated Anthony's new sofa from the *Amoeba*, puffed up the leather cushion and burped.

"You should have an HIV test." Her tone was flat, almost as though she were dispassionately recommending another type of biscuit.

Taken by surprise, Anthony spat coffee into his mug.

"Serves the bitch right," said Eunice.

"What's suddenly brought that on?"

"I've *never* liked her," said Eunice.

"Now you're being facetious."

Eunice gave the leather cushion one more punch.

"Aren't you worried? I take it you and Malcolm didn't use condoms. No one did in those days."

"No," Anthony said.

"No, you're not worried?"

"No, we didn't use condoms."

"And you've never been tested."

"No."

"But you had sex only once."

"More than once."

"In one night?"

"Yes."

"It would be a weight off your mind. And if the test comes back positive, which is *very* unlikely, then we'll make sure you take good care of yourself."

Anthony laughed. "It's a death sentence, Eunice, not a cold."

With the cushion in her lap, Eunice bent over it to breathe in his face. "Life is a death sentence," she said. "HIV is just a virus."

No, they hadn't used condoms, but was Anthony worried? Was he frightened? He had grown so distant from himself that his feelings were alien to him, with harsh metallic smells that he couldn't decipher.

"How did you know?" he asked Eunice.

"About what caused Malcolm's pneumonia?" And when Anthony nodded, "It wasn't too difficult to guess from what you told us."

"You mean you've known all this time? Did Grandma know as well?"

"I don't think so," said Eunice. "Not from me."

Anthony dipped a Garibaldi into his tea.

"Sure, I'll have the test," he said.

"Good! I've booked you an appointment for Monday. You'll need to see a counsellor first, and we won't know the result for two weeks."

There are people you can talk to

A young woman clutching a file strode to the waiting area and called out Anthony's name. When he got up, she smiled at him sombrely.

"Hi, Anthony, I'm Alison. How are you?"

He followed her to a small consultation room, past the mostly young men whose names had already been called. They had moved to this end to wait for a nurse or a doctor. Anthony had been among them earlier that morning.

She sat behind the desk, and Anthony directly across her. The distance between them was short. A vase of two wilting roses, one red, one pink, seemed to accentuate the grating excess of fluorescence. Nothing could have made the room more cheerful. Anthony made no attempt to read its smells.

Alison opened his file. "You saw Dr Annan this morning," she said, without looking at it.

"Yes," Anthony said.

"You'd like to have an HIV test."

"Yes."

"You're not sexually active at the moment, is that right?"

"Yes."

"But you may have been exposed to the virus."

"Yes."

"I believe you lost your partner to AIDS..." She picked up his file.

"Malcolm," Anthony said.

"Almost nine years ago," said Alison.

"Yes."

"But you don't have any symptoms."

"No."

"Any illnesses since losing your partner?"

"I answered all these questions this morning," Anthony said.

"I know," Alison said, putting down the file again.

"My file is one page long."

"What I'm trying to do is identify your needs," Alison said. "Help you address any issues that may still be outstanding."

"Issues?"

"Grief, primarily. Possibly feelings of guilt."

"Guilt?"

"This would be your first HIV test?"

"Yes. It should say so in my file."

"How would you feel if the test came back positive?"

"The first time I had sex with Malcolm was on the night before I took him to hospital, and he was dead within a week. It's not possible he caught the virus from me. I'm not stupid enough to feel guilty. And if my test came back positive, I wouldn't blame Malcolm."

"'Why him and not me?' Has that thought never occurred to you?"

"It did at the time, yes. But it's irrational."

"Guilt can be irrational, too."

"I don't feel guilty."

"That's good to hear," Alison said. "And how would you feel about the future? If your test came back positive, I mean."

"I should know either way. There may be things I'd do differently."

"And is there someone you can bring along when you come back for your results in two weeks' time?"

"My sister Eunice," Anthony said.

Alison stood up. She picked up some leaflets from a stack on her desk and offered them to Anthony.

"There are people you can talk to," she said. "People who've shared your experience, who've either lost someone to HIV or are living with the virus themselves, quite often both. No, I can't even begin to imagine what it must have been like losing Malcolm when both of you were still so young."

"Thank you," Anthony said.

Alison's smile was less sombre now. "And whatever your result, we're here if you need to talk to us again about your sexual health."

Anthony took the leaflets and followed Alison, to join the queue for blood tests. He shook her hand and took a seat.

Free condoms

"Anthony Rubens?" He had walked down the corridor towards them while flicking through the files in his hand –

two or three, if Anthony had counted them correctly. His expression was blank.

Eunice got up first. "I'm his sister," she said.

When Anthony smiled at the young doctor, the young doctor smiled back. "Hello, Anthony," he said. "My name is Dr White." He made a gesture for Anthony and Eunice to follow, and he led the way back towards the rooms at the end of the corridor.

As he held a door open for them, another door opened. A male nurse had his arm around the waist of a boy in his teens, steering him towards an unknown future while he sobbed. A grim-faced older boy about Anthony's age followed closely behind. *How would we have coped if that had been us?* Anthony wondered. It was an impossible question, and he would rather not have asked it.

"Anthony?" The young doctor's smile was gone.

How do they manage? The question had returned from the past to distract him, and Anthony had stalled at the door.

"Sorry," he said.

All three were sitting down now, the young doctor behind his cheap desk, facing Anthony and his sister. He opened Anthony's file, double-checked the name and date of birth.

"That's me," Anthony said.

The smile returned. "It's good news, your HIV test came back negative," he said.

"Oh, thank God!" Eunice said.

The young doctor got up. "There are people you can talk to," he said.

"Alison gave me some leaflets," Anthony said.

"Good," said the young doctor. "And would you like some free condoms today?"

TWENTY-THREE

Nothing's really ended

"I don't suppose you took any," said Kevin.

"Condoms? No, I didn't."

"That's one hell of a story, Mr Rubens. But have you really never read Malcolm's stories again?"

"I thought I couldn't," said Mr Rubens.

At around nine o'clock, everything that needed to be signed had been signed, and the technical team had taken advantage of a five-minute lull in the rain to load all their equipment and a suitcase full of jumpers in the van they had parked at one of the power points at the end of the road. They had said goodbye to Mr Rubens at the door, but at the last minute Kevin had asked if perhaps he could stay for an extra half hour.

It was now almost eleven, and he and Mr Rubens were still in the kitchen sharing a second bottle of wine.

"The scraps at the bottom of the shoebox were the stories Malcolm had already read out to me, raw, queer, surreal, hard-hitting stories from which I was absent. And the six notebooks were full of my adventures in a future without Malcolm, unfinished playful stories that were probably meant as a humorous warning."

"Time hasn't helped you to imagine happy endings," Kevin said.

Letting air out through his nose, Mr Rubens shook his head. "I've imagined a thousand different endings to each and every one of them, all of them unhappy because Malcolm was gone." From the burgundy colour of the wine in his glass, Mr Rubens turned his gaze to the brown, almost black, of Kevin's eyes. "But then one day, while I was still in

Belsize Park, I picked up Malcolm's favourite again and realised that I'd memorised it almost word for word. Somehow it was different from the rest, and I'm sure that's why Malcolm had singled it out. It was filled with all the warmth of his presence, and he knew I'd be able to feel it. Suddenly it felt so familiar that it made me want to imagine it differently, with a beginning and a middle from which Malcolm didn't need to be absent."

"You made the story yours," Kevin said.

"I made it mine and Malcolm's," said Mr Rubens.

"And do you know how it will end?"

"*Where will it end? Where will it end?*" Mr Rubens could still remember Malcolm mouthing the Joy Division lyrics while they danced next to each other in *The Bell.*

"Moving to this house seemed like the end of a chapter," he said. "I left everything Malcolm had written behind, and the end of the chapter turned out to be the end of the story."

"But it wasn't, Mr Rubens. Nothing's really ended. Would I still be here if it had?"

Mr Rubens now tilted his gaze to one side as he smiled. *So much* had happened in the last fifty years, but *his* world had not changed by one iota. He had lived life under the surface, unnoticed and almost untouched, closer to the dead than to the living, kept afloat by threads that had then snapped completely, until a postman had knocked on his door.

"I know it must sound odd, but apart from that one story everything else in the shoebox was more of a comfort to Eunice than to me."

"Of course it was," said Kevin. "I mean, she was obviously in love with him, wasn't she?"

A flutter went through Mr Rubens.

"What *you* had with Malcolm was real," Kevin went on. "But all your sister had were her feelings, and her own imagined endings to Malcolm's beginnings."

After taking two more sips of his wine, "I don't know," said Mr Rubens. "I can't speak for Eunice, and she can't speak for herself."

"Kevin, Kevin, you *idiot*," said Kevin, rolling his eyes as he made sideways figures of eight with his head. "You've gone and put your foot in it *again*." Plumping up his lips, he raised his open hands and puffed out air. "I'm sorry, Mr Rubens, as per usual I've been talking off the top of my head. It's like I can't keep what I'm thinking to myself, it's a habit that'll get me into *terrible* trouble one day."

He's so full off shit, and I still can't help liking him, thought Mr Rubens.

"You should try not to think it in the first place," he said.

"I should try not to think it in the first place, I see what you mean. Ah, but you're smiling, Mr Rubens, so I take it I'm forgiven?"

Averting his gaze after staring into eyes whose starkness was broken by the swirl of luscious lips, Mr Rubens looked down at Kevin's glass as he refilled it with the rest of the wine.

"Eunice never told you I was gay?"

"She didn't, Mr Rubens. But she did say that you lived alone in a house full of beautiful things."

Mr Rubens gave a deep sigh of nostalgia. His sister's comment made him think of her slogans. It was as typically Eunice as JOE DEVIN SUCKED MY COCK. *I miss her so much, I miss her so much, I miss all of them so much...*

"Mr Rubens? Are you okay?"

Mr Rubens blinked another smile. "I'm fine," he said. "But it's time you called me Anthony, I think."

"Really, Mr Rubens? Are you sure?"

"Anthony," said Anthony.

"I'm sorry, I'm sorry. *Anthony*, yes!" Kevin said.

The postman knocks again

Tap. Tap-tap.

It was already past the middle of a very cold November, and Anthony was sheltering in the *Amoeba*, covered in a blanket and drinking his mid-morning coffee out of a mug. It intrigued him how even though over the years the photograph of Princess Diana had faded, her droopy-eyed stare still managed to give him the creeps.

He had not dared draw the drapes. Kevin had forewarned him that a letter from the Ministry should be arriving very shortly.

Tap. Tap-tap.

Insipid like a limp handshake, Anthony thought to himself, getting up from the *Amoeba* and straightening his back before making his way in small and careful steps to the front door.

"Good morning, Mr Rubens," the same young postman beamed, his smile like a curved, double-sided arrow pointing proudly at the marvellousness of his cheekbones. Gone was the pencil moustache, and with it the impression of being *very* strait-laced. Even as he stood perfectly still, facing Mr Rubens with his back to the rest of the street, every inch of his shortness had perked up and was bursting with life.

"And a very good morning to you," Anthony said with a more modest smile.

"I *was* going to ring the bell, but if I had then you probably wouldn't have known it was me, and I *wanted* you to know it was me." As he cackled like a very handsome imp, his understated features jiggled with the undulating movements of the sea. His boyishness was no longer wooden, and his gaze today was steady, intense, and apparently in perfect focus. "I suppose you must be wondering why – *why* did I want you to know it was me?"

"To surprise me?"

"'Must be that poker-faced toy soldier again, the one who can't even read,' I bet that's what you thought when you heard me knocking just now."

"It never crossed my mind you couldn't read. And the uniform suits you, you look very smart."

"But I don't think you liked my moustache; I could tell by the way you were looking at it."

"You look better without it," Anthony said.

"Glad you think so, Mr Rubens, my mum thinks so too. I'm Jason, by the way." His handshake was firm, neither limp nor insipid. "Now let's see what's in the bag for you today. Here we are, another Special Delivery and a parcel."

"You're welcome to come in for a coffee," Anthony said.

"I could *murder* a coffee, and thank you for asking, but I can't, if anyone found out I'd get the sack." And after looking quickly left and right over his shoulder, "If they saw me coming in, any one of your neighbours could shop me, we're not exactly popular these days."

"Postmen are unpopular?"

Jason used his eyes to point at his holster. "It's this gun they make us carry. It makes some people think we're all Nazis."

Not unreasonable, thought Mr Rubens.

"I do have an important message for you, though."

"A message?"

"From Kevin," said Jason.

"You know Kevin?"

"Keep your voice down, Mr Rubens," Jason said softly. Then raising his voice as he took out from his satchel a clipboard and pen: "Number 8. Print name and sign in the box."

After signing, Anthony exchanged the clipboard and pen for an envelope and a small parcel. Neither of them bore a stamp, as far as he could see.

"Your day will be an Open Day," Jason said, reverting to his monotone to whisper Kevin's message. "That means everyone can visit, not just Party members. Kevin wanted you to know that he'll definitely be there, and he'd have told you all this himself but the phone lines aren't safe. He also wanted you to have what's in the parcel."

"But how did Kevin know you were my postman?" Anthony asked under his breath.

"Kevin knows a lot of things," answered Jason mysteriously.

After clearing his throat, and bowing his head just a trifle to the right, Anthony pointed with a finger at the prominent sign that invited every caller to 'Please ring the bell.'

Like a seasoned co-conspirator performing his part to a tee, Jason nodded vigorously at the sign. He then saluted Anthony unsmilingly by touching the tip of his cap, and disappeared down the grey deserted street with the clank of perfectly regular strides. As if marching to the drumbeat of a military band, on parade after returning from the front, tired but triumphant, he was very much a man, *not* a machine.

As had always been the way of the world, something old was indeed giving way to something new.

The Appendix

In a long Appendix to his summons, the Museums Ministry was writing to inform Mr Anthony Pablo Rubens that the Exhibitions Committee had approved the maquette of his cubicle, as presented to them by the technical team on his behalf. Under threat of unspecified penalties, not even minor changes were allowed: specifically, no additions, omissions or substitutions.

Today was Tuesday, 19 November. On Thursday, 21 November between 9 and 11 am, a Museums Ministry collection van would arrive at his address to collect the following items: a curved wood Scandinavian sideboard, a complete Meissen tea service hand-painted with monkeys (22 pieces, listed individually), an art deco bureau (drawer contents optional), and a 1960s original *Amoeba* chair. Furthermore, pursuant to the Expedited Status of his case, under Section 2 of the Appendix the following Monday, 25 November, had been designated as the day of his service at the National People's Museum. His fifteen minutes of fame would last a frightening ten hours, from 9 am until 7 pm. Section 3 consisted of a map and a list of detailed instructions regarding his arrival for service (time, Entrance number, ID requirements, etc.).

There was no mention in the Appendix of Monday 25 November being an Open Day. The significance of whether it would be an Open Day or not was not immediately obvious, and at first sight did not seem to Anthony to merit the involvement of the postman. Kevin had specifically told him that even if he was allowed to visit the National People's Museum, he would rather give the experience a miss, so why was his intention to be there on Monday suddenly so important that Anthony should know about it in advance? Shut off behind solid, soundproof two-way glass, he would have no way of knowing if Kevin was among his visitors or not.

Well, if his presence was intended as an act of solidarity, then perhaps it was precisely for that reason that Kevin had gone to such lengths - how else would Anthony have known that his day would not be spent entirely without friends? And Kevin being the Kevin who believed there were no problems but only solutions, he might somehow even manage to communicate with Anthony while he was there. He did seem to be very well connected.

But what did it mean, exactly, that the phone lines were unsafe? That Kevin had got into trouble already? No, that was unlikely. Obviously he needed to be cautious, certainly more cautious than he had been until now, or he would have called on Anthony himself, in person if not on the phone. But had he been in serious trouble, then he would hardly have been able to enlist Anthony's postman to his aid, and not only for relaying a message. Back under the blanket in the *Amoeba*, Anthony gave the pages of the Ministry's Appendix one last shuffle, and then he let them drop to the floor.

The last laugh

The parcel had been sitting unopened on the same Perspex cube where so often his sister had set down her Prince Charles, and Anthony had kept one eye on it even while he plodded through his summons's Appendix and speculated over the significance – or not – of an Open Day at the National People's Museum. To say that already this small package had aroused his curiosity would be something of an understatement; now at last it had his full attention.

Many things about it intrigued him. Wrapped in plain brown paper and tied together with elaborately tangled string, it was addressed to 'Anthony Pablo Rubens' in neat upright handwriting that he assumed must be Kevin's. Although it was much smaller (Anthony guessed it must be a book), it was as if Kevin had deliberately wrapped it so that it resembled the parcel Malcolm's parents had sent him all those years before – except that theirs had been addressed to 'Mr Anthony Rubens', and had been posted - rather than delivered by hand, albeit by a postman.

Casting off the blanket, Anthony levered himself out of the *Amoeba*. Casually he picked up the parcel and carried it through to the kitchen. He sat at the table with a knife and cut through the string, feeling sad that no one was watching. But as he tore away the wrapping, his sadness was soon superseded by a flurry of emotions far more tangled than the elaborately tangled string he had just used a knife to cut through.

He let his fingers drift across the letters that made words on the cover of the paperback book he had separated from the wrapping and string, placing it unopened on the table.

THE EXTRAORDINARY FUTURE ADVENTURES OF MR RUBENS

Malcolm McCarthy

Anthony turned over to the first page inside.

For Anthony Pablo

He turned another page. It was blank, without either a copyright or publication details. And on the following page, Malcolm's stories began anti-chronologically, with the one he had marked out as his favourite and written most recently.

AN UNEXPECTED VISITOR

Undaunted by any fear of flatulence or heartburn, Mr Rubens was thoroughly enjoying his mid-morning coffee.

"There is a time and a place for everything," he was fond of saying, and as a matter of ritual, not routine – an obvious distinction – this was certainly true of the orderly way in which he chose to live his life.

Anthony closed the book and turned it around. The title and the author's name reappeared on the spine, but the back cover was bare. And the parcel had arrived without a note, nothing from Kevin to explain where he had come across the paperback, or when. Why hadn't he mentioned it before? Why had he sent it to Anthony now?

It didn't look new. Without lifting it up from the table, Anthony opened it again to a random page. Bending down, he dug his nose inside it. It smelled as old as it looked – from the early 2010s would be his guess. The binding seemed old-fashioned but professional, with pages sewn together and then glued into the spine. The bright purple cover was well worn, but it had kept Malcolm's stories together. The evidence was strong but inconclusive. If it was possible to copy his 1960s wallpaper exactly, then it was equally possible to manufacture a book that looked and smelled old.

The parcel may have intrigued him, but its contents now stung him neither with excitement nor with nostalgia, but rather with a mystified sense of betrayal, a dull outrage that lacked any sense of direction. If he was angry, *who* was he angry with? And why was he angry at all? Because it was impossible to get any answers. If Eunice was responsible for manufacturing the book, Anthony would like to know why she had kept it from him, but Eunice was dead, and he couldn't ask Kevin because Kevin had sent him a warning that the phone lines were unsafe. *And anyway, I don't have his number.* Locked alone with the book in a circular cul-de-sac of unanswered questions, no wonder he was angry!

Unless... Unless the answer he was looking for was to a question that he hadn't even asked. Was the book a reminder that Eunice might still be alive? His mind suddenly darkened.

She would never have picked purple for the cover. It was a colour she had always detested.

Like pieces of a sinister jigsaw puzzle, the reasons for mistrusting Kevin returned one by one, fitting into each other to add up to an irresistible sum. There had been *too many* coincidences, *too many* 'innocent' slips of the tongue, *too many* convoluted explanations, *too many* unlikely heroes. In a world of smoke and mirrors, Anthony had been deceived. He had not been unaware of the risk to himself, but outwitted by his vanity he had never suspected a plot against Eunice.

Like Kevin the book was a fake. Anthony was certain it had never belonged to his sister. Everything that had occurred since the postman first knocked on his door to deliver a summons had been part of the same evolving trap aimed at snaring Eunice. Contrary to Anthony's initial disbelief, she had *not* perished in the fire that had burnt down her house. The people who had given Malcolm's stories to Kevin must have set it alight after Eunice had already disappeared, and after they had stolen Malcolm's stories. It all now seemed blindingly obvious. Both the parcel and the unexpected news of an Open Day, omitted from the Appendix as though the Ministry's official policy was to withhold the information from exhibits, formed part of one last desperate attempt to goad Anthony into giving his sister away. Except that by protecting him, Eunice had also protected herself. That had been the one fatal flaw in their plan. Anthony had been deceived, but the last laugh was his.

"Cheers!" he said, holding up an imaginary glass of gin and tonic.

TWENTY-FOUR

Abba

Still in his pyjamas, Anthony had finished his breakfast and was lolling in the *Amoeba.* From tomorrow he would be deprived of it, *who knows for how long, perhaps forever,* he thought. What if some high-up Party member, maybe even the New Leader himself, took a shining to it either before or during Anthony's day at the National People's Museum? No one had said anything at all about when he might be getting back either his furniture *or* his Meissen monkeys. It was probably an organised racket - stealing the most valuable items people were being duped into showing. Who would dare complain? *Would I dare complain?* Anthony wondered. His only consolation was that the monkeys were more likely to go missing than the *Amoeba*. It was the monkeys the clowns had insisted on and Kevin had so desperately pleaded for. Why else would they have asked for all 22 pieces? *Good riddance, I'll be glad to see the back of them,* Anthony thought. Whereas depriving him of the *Amoeba* would be a blow. He would miss it terribly. As for all the precious photographs in the bureau, the mere thought of losing them sent shivers down his spine.

Over the years, Anthony had spurned repeated offers of free insulation, hating the thought of living in a space that was hermetically sealed. The new bio-boilers did the environment no harm, and he would rather higher bills than less air. The heating had been on for an hour but the whole house was still cold, and the sitting room was practically glacial - the thick velvet drapes that kept out the draught from the hallway ought by now to have been drawn. Instead they had remained wide open since the postman's first knock on the door. Visitors had come and gone, more were expected tomorrow, and unexpected visitors could not be ruled out.

Pulling up the blanket to cover his chest, Anthony couldn't help feeling morose. Eunice must be alive and Kevin had deceived him; he had thought of little else since the postman's second visit. But suddenly the certainties of yesterday seemed very far away. It was possible that he was wrong on both counts. Eunice might have perished in the fire after saving Malcolm's stories by handing them over to Kevin - wishing Eunice to be alive might have caused him to judge Kevin unfairly. As for the paperback, it might have been no more than a well-meaning gesture, Kevin's way of remembering Malcolm on everyone else's behalf. Whether new or old and whatever its colour, it was hardly a smoking gun.

"All the world's a stage." Anthony spoke the words loudly. "And one man in his time plays many parts." Was Kevin an enemy or was he a friend? It was not inconceivable that he was both.

Anthony no longer either trusted or mistrusted him. *Nothing* was certain - it was not even certain there had been a betrayal. The Open Day might or might not be a ploy, and Eunice might or might not still be alive. Was it really possible she would have kept away from him without a sign of life for all this time? *Hmm…* It was doubtful. On the other hand, unless Eunice was the target and Anthony the Trojan horse, why else would they have wasted so much energy and expense?

It was pointless asking 'why' when Museum Service itself was absurd. Trying to solve its riddles with logic was like trying to square a circle. It could never yield reliable proof.

Slightly shivering under the blanket, Anthony felt too lazy to get dressed. He would need to go upstairs, run a bath, have a shave, brush his teeth…

"Mr Rubens, what you doing?"

Leaping out of the *Amoeba* and manoeuvring his way behind it with a scream, Anthony had brought the blanket right up to his eyes, and was staring at the intruder as though begging for his life.

"Now you like to play hide and seek by yourself?" The shrill voice had morphed into something familiar. "You catch your death without your clothes, is so cold in this room."

"Gloria, it's you."

"Who else you thought it was? Is Wednesday, remember? And today I pull the curtains to the hall."

"No, please don't."

"Every week you say no. Is *freezing*, Mr Rubens."

Anthony only knew that it was Wednesday because tomorrow was the Thursday when, between 9 and 11 am, a Museums Ministry collection van would be arriving to steal his possessions. Gloria had completely slipped his mind.

"I didn't hear you come in, you gave me a fright," he said. "You're not normally here before ten."

Gloria glared at him. "You fall asleep on that *Abba* chair again? Is almost eleven."

"It's an *Amoeba*, Gloria, not an *Abba*."

"Is a chair, Mr Rubens."

"Is it really almost eleven?"

"In my country, we don't give name to chairs."

"Anyway, tomorrow they're coming to take it away. With the sideboard and the desk."

"You *sell* the *Abba*?"

"It's going to the National People's Museum. And on Monday so am I."

Gloria brought her hands to her mouth. "Mr Rubens, you have to?"

"It's just for one day," said Anthony. "I've been selected to do Museum Service. And it's compulsory, so yes, unfortunately I have to."

"Like Miss Eunice," said Gloria, her words becoming garbled as they passed through her hands.

"You knew about Eunice?"

With her hands now around her neck, Gloria shook her head. "I know nothing, Mr Rubens, I swear."

"But you just said—"

She let go of her neck just long enough to cross herself twice. "Miss Eunice asked me not to tell and I promise."

"Gloria, it's important."

"Miss Eunice told me is important not to tell, and I promise, Mr Rubens, what can I do?"

"You did the right thing at the time, and please stop calling Eunice Miss Eunice. You were friends, you never used to call her Miss Eunice."

"She insist I call her Eunice, so I do. But now..."

Throwing her arms around him, she collided with Anthony's body head on, convulsing with sobs. All Anthony could do was to collapse with her into the *Amoeba*.

"Let me bring you a glass of water," he said, and wriggling out of the melee he escaped to the kitchen.

If it was cold, Anthony could no longer feel it.

A spy or not a spy

Another coincidence? Anthony couldn't decide. She might have called her a remarkable woman, but how likely was it that Eunice would have ever confided anything important to Gloria? Well, if she had wanted to confide it to someone but not to him, who else had there been for her to confide it to? Kevin. So what was most likely? That she had confided it to Kevin *and* to Gloria, or only to Kevin, or only to Gloria, or to neither? Perhaps she had confided one thing to Kevin and another to Gloria. *Perhaps, perhaps, perhaps... The only thing I know for certain is that she didn't confide anything to me.* The circle that could not be squared was ever increasing.

When Gloria had drunk her glass of water, she was about to get up from the *Amoeba.* Anthony had sat down beside her on the edge of the Bauhaus two-seater, and was motioning her to stay put.

"I have work, Mr Rubens, I think this morning I start in the kitchen, and I wait for you to finish upstairs. Then I cook something nice."

"Please, Gloria, first we need to finish our chat. You need to tell me what happened to Eunice."

He was pressing her too hard. Cocooned in the *Amoeba* she had folded her hands in her lap and was staring at them while she chewed on her lips. *She looks like she's about to confess to a cardinal sin*, Anthony couldn't help thinking. And she was dressed for it, too. The dark colours she always wore really suited her, and today she had arrived all in black. *Not the most practical colour*, but somehow it would be spotless even after hours of hard work. And the same was true of Gloria herself. Still young at nearly forty, an indomitable freshness countered all her imperfections.

At last lifting her gaze in his direction, she spoke haltingly. "One day your sister told me I'm a spy. But is not true Mr Rubens, is just luck I meet a nice man in the Government Party."

"I thought he'd divorced you."

"But before he divorced me, I already meet another nice man."

"Who was also in the Government Party?"

Gloria nodded.

"So I play a trick at Heathrow to, how you say, buy time? But I don't call who they think I call, I call nice man who likes me."

"You mean a *third* nice man?"

"Mr Rubens, what you think I am! I mean second nice man. So I stay, and is just luck, not because I'm a spy." Gloria leaned forward in the *Amoeba*. "The last few years me and Eunice, we become very close, and I promise her I always take good care of you."

The way Gloria had said 'very close' had been so full of warmth that Anthony believed he could trust her.

"So you know where she is?"

"Where she is?"

That wasn't the right question to ask, Anthony thought. *If Eunice is alive and Gloria knows where she is, the last thing I should want her to do is share that information with me. If Eunice doesn't want me to know, then she's probably right that I shouldn't.*

"It doesn't matter where she is, I just want to know if she's okay."

Gloria's eyes became slits. "What you mean, Mr Rubens?"

"Have you never suspected that Eunice might still be alive?"

"No, is not true." Gloria was shaking her head and speaking through her hands again. "I saw the house after the fire, Mr Rubens."

"But it's possible she wasn't in the house."

Gloria shrank into the *Amoeba* in silence. But then she re-emerged, to seek out Anthony's hand. And when she had it in hers, "Your sister, she knew she was in danger, she told me. One month before the fire she had papers about the

Museum. I know because I open the door to the postman.

Museum. I know because I open the door to the postman. Then these men come to the house–"

"And then she told you that she thought she was in danger."

"'Is safer for Pablo to know nothing,' she said, so I promise not to tell. She always call you Pablo, I think because she love you so much."

"I know," said Anthony. "Did Eunice say one of the men was trying to help her?" he wanted to ask, but he didn't. Even if his sister thought that Gloria could be trusted, she would never have risked compromising Kevin. *And I should also be more careful what I say.* Even if they were intended as a trap, the parcel and the message the postman had delivered might not have come from Kevin at all. That would mean that Kevin was in trouble already. *Should I be hoping I've misjudged him, or instead should I be hoping that he's safe?*

"I come here every Wednesday to keep my promise, you and Eunice are more family than man from the Government Party."

"And you've always been like family to us."

"So now you must tell me the truth." Gloria's tone was firm and emphatic. "You in danger, Mr Rubens? Is that why you give them the *Abba*?"

"Don't worry about me, Gloria, I'll be fine, I promise," said Anthony, smiling as he squeezed her hand. "It's good that they're coming tomorrow to take the *Amoeba*, and on Monday I'll be sitting in it at the National People's Museum. Then on Wednesday you'll see for yourself that I'm still in one piece."

When he stood up, Gloria let go of his hand. He walked over to the art deco bureau, then shuffled his way back to the two-seater.

"Have you seen this before?" he asked Gloria.

"Is a book," Gloria said.

"Yes."

"Is purple," Gloria said.

"Yes," said Anthony. "But have you ever seen it before, anywhere in Eunice's house?"

"Miss Eunice's house?"

"Before the fire."

Anthony was holding the book right in front of her, and Gloria leaned over to look at the title.

"Is about you?"

Anthony nodded. "Have you seen it before?"

"Never, Mr Rubens. I never seen that book in my life."

"Will you do me a favour?"

"You want to sit in the *Abba*?"

"No, this morning the *Abba*'s all yours."

"Anything you want, Mr Rubens."

"I've asked you many times before, but this time I'm going to insist."

"Anything you want, as long as is not to go back to Brazil." And lowering her voice again, "I tell Eunice many times, here is not good with Government Party, but in Brazil is even worse, is always much worse when people are poor. Is true the country is rich now, but the poor are still poor and the rich they don't care, because is never enough what they have. Is a very unfair world, Mr Rubens."

"Yes, it is, and I'm not going to ask you to go back to Brazil. But you're not going to call me Mr Rubens any more."

"I call you Anthony?"

"Anthony or Pablo, whichever you prefer."

TWENTY-FIVE

The face of a sinister state

On the south bank overlooking the Thames, the National People's Museum was a tall brutalist structure consisting of four rectangular monoliths built around a square of empty space that served as a natural skylight. Anthony remembered it both as a ruin and then as the city's International Museum of Modern Art. Originally a massive warehouse, it had comprised hundreds of flexible units that were rented out to merchants individually. Half empty and unprofitable for three decades, a mysterious gas explosion in the early 1980s almost caused it to collapse, and for many years its fate had hung in the balance, until saving it became a cause célèbre. Not without controversy it was purchased for the nation in 1991, and after years of restoration was transformed into IMMA, which opened its doors to the public in 2001.

As a ruin it had resembled a fortress of evil, making up for its total lack of elegance or grace with the scale of its chilling otherworldliness. At the time when both buildings had marked London's skyline while being broken and disused, comparing what had then become known as the Purgatory Workhouse to Battersea Power Station, which had worn its dereliction with unwavering aplomb, would have been like comparing a Stalinist eyesore to the Acropolis. After many picnics in the shadow of the tall walls of the Purgatory Warehouse, that was the analogy Malcolm had used, in one of his rare visits to Anthony's flat in Vauxhall. Standing by the window that ran along one wall like one side of a fish tank, he had begun by likening the Power Station's four chimneys to the columns of the

Parthenon, but in the end had incongruously come down on the side of the Stalinist eyesore and its blown-up blocks of brick.

"The contest is between an upside-down table that tickles you gently and an atrocity that slaps you in the face, and for me the atrocity wins it hands down."

Anthony could still remember laughing, tickled by Malcolm's analogies while entirely disagreeing with his choice. Filled with cherished memories, the years of their friendship had been almost as happy as those short but infinite moments they had spent together as lovers.

In the period when it was IMMA, the reconstructed building's severity had been softened by a succession of neon light installations and giant exhibition banners that had swathed its exterior in colour. But as he approached it now, in the grey light of a late November morning, the bare bulk of its current incarnation seemed to embody a crude barbarity that brazenly went far beyond a slap in the face. If it had once had the mystery and charm of a fantasy film set, it had now become the face of a sinister state.

If he were here, Malcolm would be horrified.

Perhaps for the first time since their hospital kiss, Anthony was glad he was alone. Which was not to say that he would not still be making the most of his day; he was as determined as ever that he would. And 'here' he would be sharing it with Malcolm and everyone else.

Anthony's grey fishbone suit and polished black brogues would complement the black of the *Amoeba*'s brushed leather. His white shirt and bright orange tie would give adequate colour and contrast. The dark square frames of his glasses would draw the eye to his dignified expression, not of fear and no longer of awe but rather of unfaltering determination. Today he would be neither Anthony nor Mr Rubens. Today he would be Anthony Pablo.

But he had not got quite everything right. Not wearing a coat had been a mistake. His nose had warned him, but for the sake of vanity he had decided to ignore it, and now he felt cold to the bone. He had not even put on his gloves – without a coat, there would have been no pockets to put them in – and the tips of all his fingers had turned white. He had arrived in a taxi, but with almost thirty minutes to go before it was time to present himself at Entrance 11, it was all he could do to walk briskly around the building rubbing his hands, the thick mist of his breath like a plume of cigarette smoke.

At eight o'clock exactly he walked through the tall double door. The greyness of outside instantly gave way to a painful glut of light, in which the greyness of the building failed to dissipate. Stripped of all ornamentation, in the vastness of its emptiness the interior was forbidding.

The place could do with some art on the walls, thought Anthony Pablo, and amused by the absurdity of his joke he gave one of his invisible laughs.

To the right, a guard was sitting alone behind a small metal table, immersed in a screen. Someone in the Government Party had a penchant for handsome young men.

"Good morning," said Anthony Pablo.

The guard leapt out of his chair and stood to attention. Rather than absorbing it, his face seemed to radiate light, *like an angel's in a medieval painting,* thought Anthony Pablo. But this angel was wearing an extraordinary uniform that might as well have been designed by one of the extravagant twentieth century greats, like Jean Paul Gaultier or Vivienne Westwood. Someone in the Government Party had taste.

"Good morning, Mr Rubens." His jacket, broad at the shoulders, tapered to his waist almost triangularly, and his cap was made of leather, like a biker's from the days before motorbikes were banned. The way he was wearing it was playful, with its tip pointing upwards, showing off his golden curls of hair.

"I see you were expecting me," said Anthony Pablo.

"Beg your pardon?"

"You knew my name before I had a chance to introduce myself."

"Course I did, or I wouldn't have been doing my job," said the guard, nodding vaguely at the screen.

"Yes, I was early," said Anthony Pablo. "But how did you know it was me?"

"Wouldn't have been doing my job if I didn't."

Another one of those, thought Anthony Pablo. *He's probably been told I'm a 'ped'.*

"But you must've been freezing outside, why didn't you come in?"

"I wasn't sure I was allowed to."

"Allowed to? I don't understand. Why wouldn't you be?"

"My mistake," said Anthony Pablo, "I thought I had to be here at eight on the dot."

"Really, Mr Rubens, we're not in the army. And we wouldn't want you catching pneumonia on your big day at the National, would we? You're not even wearing a coat."

"Another mistake," said Anthony Pablo.

"And no umbrella either," said the guard.

"It's not raining," said Anthony Pablo.

"It's not raining *now*," said the guard.

"And it won't be raining later."

"You don't know that for certain."

But my nose does, Anthony Pablo almost said.

"I daresay we'll be able to find one for you somewhere if we need to," said the guard. "But for now, let's get you processed. First you need to empty your pockets for me. We'll keep everything down here until the end of your day, keys, coins, wallet, the lot - everything except..." He bent down over his desk and looked through a bundle of papers. "Everything except a small black and white photograph."

"In its frame," said Mr Rubens.

"In its frame," the guard repeated uncertainly, but after bending down again, "In its frame, that is correct."

"I also brought my passport."

"That stays here."

"Don't you need to see it?"

"I know who you are, Mr Rubens, I don't need to see your passport."

Anthony Pablo emptied all his pockets, and everything, including his passport, which the Appendix had instructed him to bring, went into a square metal box - everything except a black and white photograph in its tiny silver frame. After examining it, the guard gave it back to Anthony Pablo.

"Very pretty," he said. "Your wife?"

"My mother," said Anthony Pablo, half expecting the guard to bury himself in his bundle of papers again.

"Must be a very old photograph," the guard said instead.

"Even older than me," said Anthony Pablo.

"No, that's not possible, you're pulling my leg!"

"It was taken a year before I was born."

"I suppose that makes sense," said the guard with a frown, as though finding it hard to conceive of a time before Anthony Pablo was born.

"I'm sorry, I forgot to take my watch off."

"Would you like to take it off?"

"I'd rather keep it on, if I may." Anthony Pablo pulled up his sleeve to expose an old Omega Automatic.

"Yes, I'm sure that'll be fine," said the guard. "But you haven't brought a book with you, have you?"

"A book?" *If they know about the book, it means Kevin or the postman must have told them.*

"To pass the time with, Mr Rubens."

"No, no I haven't. No one said I was allowed to."

"There we go again."

"I didn't think of asking," said Anthony Pablo.

"That's right, you didn't think of asking, or maybe you were asking the wrong questions."

"I'm generally curious by nature," said Anthony Pablo.

"So I've heard," said the guard.

"And I have to say that everyone's been very understanding."

"I should hope so, we're trained to be as helpful as we can."

"That's certainly been my experience," said Anthony Pablo. "Mr Anderson even promised I could have a copy of today's accompanying pamphlet."

"Which will be waiting for you here at my desk at the end of your wonderful day at the National People's Museum. You look surprised, were you not expecting Mr Anderson to keep his word?"

"I wasn't sure he would be able to."

"Oh, he's very well-regarded in the Ministry, so he shouldn't have found it too hard. But that's enough of singing Mr Anderson's praises or you'll be late and we'll both get into trouble. One last thing and then I'll call someone to take you upstairs. Medications?"

"Medications?"

"Anything you need to take while you're locked inside your cubicle?"

"*Locked*?"

"For your own safety, Mr Rubens, it's standard procedure."

"I see. No, no medications. Only painkillers occasionally, but today I have no pains."

"Fit as a fiddle, eh? Quite remarkable at your age, well done!"

"Thank you," said Anthony Pablo.

The guard was in his bundle of papers again. "Here it is," he said, emerging with a single sheet of paper. "It is *highly* recommended by the Ministry that you agree to take a couple of pills to slow down your bladder. We wouldn't want you popping in and out of the loo every five seconds, would we, Mr Rubens?"

"But I'll be able to if I need to, won't I?"

"Of course you will. The attendant will explain all that when you're upstairs. So I take it you'll be taking the pills, yes?"

"Yes, I suppose so."

Out of somewhere behind him, the guard produced a paper cup of icy water and another paper cup with two pills. Anthony Pablo put both pills in his mouth and washed them down in one gulp with the water.

"The attendant's on his way," said the guard. "Oh, and I've been told that you're in for a treat, apparently your cubicle looks smashing."

"That's good to hear," said Anthony Pablo. "But if you don't mind me asking, where are all the other exhibits?"

"Exhibits?"

"Obviously I didn't mean the art," said Anthony Pablo, pointing with his gaze at the emptiness around them. "No, I meant the other people doing service at the National today."

The guard's eyes widened as he made a sweeping gesture. "This hall is just a small part of the biggest Museum in the world. And you've seen how many entrances there are."

"I couldn't say exactly," said Anthony Pablo.

"I'm surprised. You must've walked around the building I don't know *how* many times, and every entrance is marked with a big enough number, you can't really miss it."

"So everyone comes in through a different entrance?"

"Let's just say that people who are serving never come into contact, they arrive and leave separately. Has no one explained that to you?"

Anthony Pablo shook his head.

"Well, they should have," said the guard.

"I might have come across one by mistake," said Anthony Pablo, thinking out loud.

"By mistake?"

"While I walked around the building."

"But you didn't, did you? Mistakes are very unlikely these days."

"Even though we're not in the army."

"We are, however, good at doing our jobs."

"And a very good morning to you, Mr Rubens," another voice said cheerfully.

Anthony Pablo turned around to face the new arrival. Rapid blinking caused the lenses of his glasses to mist.

"Kevin!"

"I promised you I'd be here."

"Mr Anderson, I wasn't expecting–" The guard's muttered words barely rose over the sound of paper rustling. "I mean, it's not–"

"I know what's in the schedule, Tom, I wrote it."

"Yes, sir. Sorry, sir. I was saying to Mr Rubens–"

"That mistakes are very unlikely these days," said Anthony Pablo.

"And how good we are at doing our jobs," Kevin said.

"He's taken the pills, sir," said the guard.

"I never doubted for a moment that he would," said Kevin with his usual bonhomie. "Now then, Mr Rubens, let's make our way upstairs and get you settled in your cubicle. You'll be *very* pleased, I'm sure. Jamie and the boys have done you proud."

"Yes, Tom was telling me," said Anthony Pablo, but Tom had already returned to his screen.

In his latest incarnation Kevin may have looked completely different, but even with a pencil moustache he had lost none of his dash. Like Mr Evans and the other Mr Anderson, he was dressed in a dark suit and tie very smartly, his spiky black hair gelled firmly into place as though to avoid being windswept by the speed of his pace.

"You've grown a moustache," said Anthony Pablo, almost running as he struggled to keep up.

"I grew it back especially," said Kevin. "Don't you like it?"

"I'd have thought pencil moustaches would have gone out of fashion," said Anthony Pablo.

"Oh, they did," said Kevin. "But now they're in fashion again."

"Then fashion must be as fickle as politics," said Anthony Pablo.

"Fashion *is* politics," said Kevin.

"Ah, so he's back," said Anthony Pablo. *Still with his head on his shoulders, roaming the corridors of Buckingham Place...*

"It was a big surprise for all of us," said Kevin. "I expect there'll be an announcement soon enough."

"Maybe even a party," said Anthony Pablo.

"Mmm," said Kevin with another of his mischievous chuckles.

All the gallery spaces seemed to have vanished with the art, along with all the elevators, and the escalators, too. Apart from the vast empty hall where Anthony Pablo had reported to Tom, every other space he had followed Kevin through had been one narrow corridor leading to another.

The place must have been gutted and deliberately turned into this maze, he thought, beginning to feel faint as he turned a further corner with Kevin. "Could you please slow down?" he said. "I'm running out of breath."

"Nearly there, Mr Rubens, nearly there," Kevin answered, without slowing down.

"I hope so, Mr Anderson," said Anthony Pablo.

"I suppose you must be wondering how many of us there are." Kevin stopped and turned around, almost causing Anthony Pablo to trip. "Mr Rubens… may I still call you Anthony?"

Leaning back against the wall, "Anthony Pablo," said Anthony Pablo.

Now Kevin gave a short, laboured laugh. "Mr Rubens, Pablo, Anthony, and now Anthony Pablo, there are four of you and only two of me. The other Mr Anderson—"

"The clown," said Anthony Pablo.

"His name is Williams, I believe; he was not a Mr Anderson at all. And to be fair, he was only *playing* the clown. Why not play him as himself, you might ask; why not play the clown as Mr Williams?"

"Ours is not to reason why?"

"Oh, *that* nonsense," Kevin said dismissively. "With *this* Mr Anderson, the *real* Mr Anderson, please feel free to reason why all you like. I think it's only fair, don't you?"

"Fair?"

"In the circumstances," Kevin said gravely.

"In the circumstances." Without intonation Anthony Pablo repeated the words.

"Vanity, I suppose," Kevin went on. "I'm responsible for their recruitment and training, and in overall charge of assigning them to individual Panels."

"An army of Mr Andersons," said Anthony Pablo. "And you train them to be clowns?"

"I train them to be clowns *if necessary.*"

"There are some very clever people at the top, and obviously you're one of them, or at least Mr Anderson is," said Anthony Pablo. He felt the coldness of the wall cutting through three layers, chilling the blood that tickled his extremities by curiously making them hot. "And then there's Kevin the artist and his Technicolor technical team, in every way too good to be true."

"But true all the same." Kevin clucked his tongue. "See these walls," he said, pressing the palm of one hand against a brick. "I sometimes wish..." Retrieving his hand, he made a fist with it and took a deep breath, his face suddenly ancient with lines. "If I can't call you Anthony, really I should call you Mr Rubens."

"And really I should call you Mr Anderson."

"Let's walk while we talk," said Mr Anderson.

Anthony Pablo felt flushed, and the coldness of the building made him more aware that he was sweating. As they passed under giant tubes of filaments that stored and then amplified daylight, the taste of bitter chocolate, dark beyond comfort, prickled at the back of his throat. Following Mr Anderson through another narrow space whose walls made him think of a dungeon, he longed for the *Amoeba* and his cubicle's efficient air-conditioning. Time was unlikely to pass quickly, but it would pass, as quickly as it always did.

"One last corner," said Mr Anderson.

"The place seems completely deserted," said Anthony Pablo. "Is there no one else here?"

"This part of the museum is closed to the public in any case, and it's not even half past eight yet, it's still very early. The museum opens at nine, but not many visitors arrive before midday."

"And each entrance has a maze all of its own?"

"Each entrance has *several* mazes all of its own. There are unfortunately not as many entrances as there are cubicles, which makes *this* a logistical nightmare."

"But why is it so important that you keep us all apart?"

"And at last here's our lift."

They came to a stop in front of an enormous service elevator. Anthony Pablo had not seen one like it in decades. *It must have been here since the days before the Purgatory Workhouse,* he thought, which meant it had survived the explosion. The metal grills of its sliding scissor gate opened like a concertina, to an interior that was large enough for anything that might have fitted in a cubicle.

Oozing yellow luminosity, the light inside the elevator sounded almost radioactive. Pouring out of it shapelessly, it made Mr Anderson look like a ghost. Its liquid whir reminded Anthony Pablo of the time he and Malcolm had stupidly subjected themselves to a sunbed. The memory of his body being assaulted by a buzz of UV particles made the few hairs on his arms stand on end.

"Mr Rubens, today I'm here as Kevin, and I'm here for my friend Anthony, not for Mr Rubens," said Mr Anderson.

"You look like a ghost," said Anthony Pablo.

"And you look like you've just seen one," answered Mr Anderson.

As their eyes met, they started to laugh simultaneously.

Yes, Anthony Pablo decided. It was possible for two contradictory truths to exist side by side.

Kevin must have thought the same.

"Anthony?"

"Anthony," said Anthony Pablo.

"And Kevin?"

Anthony Pablo nodded. "All the world's a stage," he said coarsely. "And one man in his time plays many parts."

"And none more honestly than that of being your friend."

"One thing you've never been good at is being insincere."

Narrowing his eyes, Kevin faced Anthony Pablo from a distance of less than one foot. "That's right," he said sharply. "The whole truth was never in my gift, even if I knew what it was. But no, at no point have I been insincere." He used both hands to grip Anthony Pablo by the neck, tighter and tighter as he pulled him away from the criss-crossing metal of the elevator grill, closer to himself, ever closer to the tantalising moisture of his breath that had now become *their* breath, a hot flow of air that almost united their lips.

"Take my hand," said Malcolm, and at last Anthony Pablo broke away from Kevin's grip, causing the elevator gate to rattle as he fell back against it, his hand now forever in Malcolm's.

"Let's go upstairs," Kevin said. "We don't have much time."

"First I want to know the truth about Eunice."

Kevin answered immediately. "I'm sorry," he said, "it was cruel to make you think she might be alive."

"And the book?"

"The book is your story; it's always been yours."

"Whatever that means."

"Whatever that means," Kevin repeated, smiling as he flexed his open palms.

"You still haven't told me what happened to Eunice. Was she killed in the fire?"

Kevin's eyes darkened, and his face became ancient again. "Eunice was here, in Cubicle 12 of Gallery 2, sitting at the table where you all sat to open the shoebox with Malcolm's beginnings. I was with her on the other side until the end."

"And now it's my turn."

"But in case you're still wondering why, you're not here because of your sister."

"Then I suppose I must be here because of Joe."

"Anthony, I'm your friend and I've read Malcolm's stories. I'm the reason you're here."

Yes, that's as good an explanation as any, thought Anthony Pablo. "Thank you," he said. "And now it's time, don't you think?"

"It's time," Malcolm said.

"After you," said Kevin, pushing back the grill. "We're going to Gallery 2, second floor."

When the elevator came to a stop with a jolt, Kevin opened the gate. "And here we are, Cubicle 12, ready for inspection. And it may look like a building site on this side, but today this small, insignificant door opens to the extraordinary world of Mr Rubens."

An excellent job

But how perfectly judged was his cubicle's graceful economy! No sooner had he entered it than its simple magnificence made Anthony Pablo light-headed. In every respect, the technical team had done an excellent job. Three sides of the generous space, including the door through which Anthony Pablo had entered, had been papered with an almost identical replica of the wallpaper he had in his kitchen. The idea of also papering the ceiling had been an inspired one, and Anthony Pablo was delighted that he hadn't objected. And the floor, not painted white but laid with whitened wooden boards, did provide a counterbalance of plainness that prevented a visual pandemonium that would have probably made *everyone* cry.

Very close to the glass in the front on the right, the curved wood Scandinavian sideboard had a sculptural presence even when viewed from behind. Several pieces from the Meissen tea service had been positioned on it with a minimalist flair Mr Rubens' own arrangement had lacked, the side plates' baboons and the cake platter's gorilla on stands and around them the teapot's chimpanzees, the macaques and spider monkeys, and most prominent of all the sugar bowl's exceptional orangutan. As he examined them from different angles and admired their reflection in the double-sided mirror glass, Anthony Pablo couldn't help thinking that Mr Anderson and Mr Evans had been right after all – the monkeys were really quite splendid, and his cubicle would not have been *quite* as spectacular without them. They somehow brought to life its sparse and geometric composition.

Standing at a right angle to the sideboard but on the opposite side and much further back was the walnut art deco bureau, bare but for a tray with a glass and jug of water. Anthony Pablo had walked over from the monkeys and was giving the leather inset top a caress. After hesitating for a moment, feeling slightly faint even though the air conditioning was working, shivery without being cold but at least no longer sweating, he opened the drawer where he kept the wooden box. It was there. Without lifting the lid, he pushed the drawer shut, and after looking at his watch he slowly made his way towards the *Amoeba*. At the centre of the cubicle, his favourite chair glimmered in the flattering light of the fibreglass lamp that loomed overhead; the technical team had suspended it at just the right height.

Performing Mr Anderson's part, Kevin had explained procedure in detail. Museum staff would bring in coffee with biscuits at 11, and tea with finger sandwiches at 5. A light lunch would be served at 1.30. Everything would be brought in on a collapsible tray table, which would be removed as soon as he was finished. For safety reasons, the door to his cubicle would be locked at all other times. If Anthony Pablo urgently needed to use the bathroom, or in case of any other emergency, there was a bell on the floor by the side of the *Amoeba* – one short ring for the bathroom, two for anything else. In addition, and again for safety reasons, cubicles were at all times being monitored by the Museum's control room.

"But you haven't brought a book, and ten hours is a very long time. Would you like to borrow mine?"

"I'll be fine, thank you."

"Are you sure?"

"My eyes get tired," said Anthony Pablo, "and in any case I don't feel like reading."

"Well then, unless there's something else, I should leave you to settle. In about fifteen minutes a loud bell will ring and the National People's Museum will open its doors to the public. Nine o'clock may be early, but by lunchtime we're expecting a crowd, it's not often that we have an Open Day."

"An Open Day?"

"It's always a last-minute decision, not publicised until the day. There'll be an announcement in the papers encouraging people to visit, but unfortunately not with the names of the people being shown. Theoretically speaking, if things had been different, were there people you'd have liked to invite?"

"No, I don't think so," said Anthony Pablo.

Moving one step forward, Kevin spread out his arms. "My dear Anthony, it really has been an absolute pleasure."

Another flash of whiteness

Anthony Pablo had been lying in the *Amoeba* for barely a matter of minutes when he suddenly felt overcome by a burning sensation in his throat. When he forced himself to swallow, he almost screamed. He was parched, but the feeling – in his eyes, in his throat, in his nose and in his chest - was much worse than dehydration. It was as if all the liquid in his body had been scorched. He took a breath and tried to calm himself. The air was clean and already familiar, almost the same as at home – authentic, like the replicated wallpaper.

Climbing out of the *Amoeba*, he managed to stay upright as he took the few steps to the art deco bureau. He was glad there were no carpets or rugs on the floor. He would have hated Eunice's gloomy prediction to come true in the National People's Museum. His hand shook a little as he poured himself half a glass of water from the jug, smiling at the irony of the metaphor the image of a glass half full of water was conveying to him. He drank the water in a rapid succession of gulps and regarded the glass once again. Anthony Pablo laughed loudly at how easily all trace of ambiguity had completely disappeared with the water. Beyond any doubt the glass was now empty.

How he had got back to the *Amoeba*, Anthony Pablo wouldn't have been able to say. And his thirst had not been quenched. The water had provided relief for as long as he was drinking it only. The same burning dryness still tore away at his throat; stung his eyes; constricted his lungs. But he seemed to be becoming accustomed to it. Certainly that momentary feeling of panic had subsided, and in its place that initial light-headedness Anthony Pablo had felt when he entered his cubicle was reasserting itself in an even more physical way, dislocating him from any notion of experiencing pain. It must have also caused the lapse in which time had seemed to skip, shifting him from the bureau to the *Amoeba*. His mind was in an almost liquid state, drifting freely through the spirals of the wallpaper's spatial confusion. "It's better than drugs," Eunice had said. Its hypnotic effect was to give his racing thoughts a sharper focus while making him unable to hold on to any one of them for long.

The 9 o'clock bell rang so loudly that it returned Anthony Pablo to a slower reality. Swivelling back to face the glass, his one and only wish was for the past to shed its sadnesses and fill the present only with its joys.

And then he saw it, a small bright purple rectangle lying on the floor beside the *Amoeba*, where Kevin must have left it on purpose. He swooped down on it without a second thought, and held it open in his lap. Frozen by the coldness of an object that contained only warmth, his fingers began to turn its pages, slowly, methodically, until he reached the end of his and Malcolm's favourite story.

Leaning back in the *Amoeba*, Anthony Pablo shut his eyes while he took a deep breath. The air filled his chest with no impediment, and when he opened his eyes they no longer stung. Finally free from the shackles of questions, and from the petty preoccupations of time, his mind was at one with his body, fully under his control. Holding on to the armrests, he struck a more formal pose, sitting up erect with one leg crossed over the other – he had wisely taken the precaution of wearing black socks. Framed by the solid pane of glass, he revelled in the thought that he was now at once a sitter for a portrait and the portrait itself. Yes, *the real* Anthony Pablo was proud to be shown. Relaxing just a little at the centre of this striking composition, preferring to resemble Leonardo's *Mona Lisa* than a portrait of a pope by Francis Bacon, he yearned for people to begin to file past.

The room became white.

And in that sudden flash of whiteness who else could have been first but his grandmother. Marta Beatriz waved to her grandson and smiled, and then she blew little Anthony Pablo a kiss. Just behind her, Anthony Pablo recognised Harry. It struck him neither as incongruous nor as absurd that nearly one hundred years hadn't aged at all the handsome young man his grandmother had fallen in love with on a May Day demonstration in Paris. Then Ernest appeared. Anthony Pablo's father stopped in front of the glass and regarded his son with solemnity. When Eunice Guernica came to stand by her father's side, resting her hand on his shoulder, at last at the sight of her brother her face gleamed with pride. And behind them at some distance, perhaps too shy to come closer, still wary of this preposterous family, the shadow of a figure Anthony Pablo would have recognised even in darkness. His heart beating two hundred beats to the minute, he raised himself from the *Amoeba*. Wishing the others a little out of the way, he made his way through to the eager embrace of his mother.

And Malcolm? Where was Malcolm?

Malcolm was here. Malcolm had always been here.

By the same author

The Dead of August

"A sophisticated, comic novel that brilliantly captures the triumph and folly of art, media, and publishing."
Kirkus Reviews (starred review)

Named to Kirkus Reviews' Best Books of 2015

Bowl of Fruit (1907)

"BOWL OF FRUIT (1907) is an incredible read, with well-crafted characters and a plot that is refreshingly original."
IndieReader (5 star review)

POLK, HARPER & WHO

"As with other Cacoyannis novels, the language, the cleverness, the juxtaposition of heartbreak and humor and the presence of truly hilariously drawn characters is at least half the pleasure of reading the book."
Casey Dorman - Lost Coast Review

The Madness of Grief

"A well- written, richly complicated, and deeply engaging coming-of-age tale."
Kirkus Reviews (starred review)

Named to Kirkus Reviews' Best Books of 2018

Finger of an Angel

"Cacoyannis is known for his introspective protagonists, but in this exceptional novel he delves even deeper, excavating the darkest corners of the psyche... An erudite, richly layered, and unsettling psychological tale."
Kirkus Reviews

Printed in Great Britain
by Amazon

54953987R00168